MW01109307

THE FOREIGN PAWN

Lee Yagel

Disclaimer

This is a work of fiction. All names, characters, places and incidents are a product of the author's imagination and/or are used fictitiously and any resemblance to actual persons, living or dead, events, establishments or locales is entirely coincidental.

Note for Librarians: A cataloguing record for this book is available from Library and Archives Canada at www.collectionscanada.ca/amicus/index-e.html
ISBN 1-4251-2618-9

Offices in Canada, USA, Ireland and UK

Book sales for North America and international:
Trafford Publishing, 6E–2333 Government St.,
Victoria, BC V8T 4P4 CANADA
phone 250 383 6864 (toll-free 1 888 232 4444)
fax 250 383 6804; email to orders@trafford.com
Book sales in Europe:
Trafford Publishing (UK) Limited, 9 Park End Street, 2nd Floor
Oxford, UK OX1 1HH UNITED KINGDOM
phone +44 (0)1865 722 113 (local rate 0845 230 9601)
facsimile +44 (0)1865 722 868; info.uk@trafford.com
Order online at:
trafford.com/06-1075

10 9 8 7

For all the warriors who courageously
fought ... and may still be out there.

In Matthew 26:34, Jesus said to Peter,

"Assuredly, I say to you this night,
before the rooster crows,
you will deny me three times."

PROLOGUE

The cessation of hostilities in World War Two brought an end to the greatest loss of life mankind has ever known. More than fifty-five million (55,000.000) people, over half of them civilians, died in that horrendous war—and that total does not include the eleven million (11,000,000) or more Jews lost in the Holocaust.

At that historic moment the Cold War and a repetitious denial began. The Soviets divided Germany in half with an Iron Curtain, blockaded Berlin, erected the Berlin Wall and shot those who tried to escape from the East to the West. The United States established the Berlin Airlift, broke the blockade, brought the Berlin Wall down and united a democratic Germany.

The Cold War escalated into a Nuclear Arms Race from which neither side could withdraw. All governments of both the East and West lied, cheated, denied and committed all sort of overt and covert acts against the other. Each violated the other's sovereignty almost daily. The Eastern communist powers, led by Russia, controlled their media and their people and such acts went undetected at home. The Western democratic powers, led principally by the United States and England had no carte blanche control. To keep things from the public eye they simply covered it up and/or classified it.

In the early stages the public never knew about the USAF Cold War aircraft (B-29s, et al) shot down over Russia during the 1950s and 60s and listed as lost due to "mechanical failures;" or of the innumerable US spies, counterspies and service personnel kidnapped, imprisoned and murdered, and just plain lost to the enemy in Europe. It was kept from the public under the guise of national security and classified as secret. Rightfully so perhaps, because the American public would never have stood still for many of the events that occurred if they had known.

All of the Cold War and hot war "performances" have been and still are played out like a game of political and military chess on an international stage—with the savage details and covert actions hidden from the eyes of the public. Each faction continually checked and counter-checked the other in a game of escalating domination. During all of that the most fundamental players—the pawns so to speak—fell by the wayside.

This is the story of one such man.

CHAPTER I

The crack of dawn revealed the eastern mountains as a black silhouette. Ankle deep snow in the flatlands reflected the orange sunrise. The sky was clear, the December morning bitterly cold. The air was sharp to the nostrils and raw in the lungs.

There were three of them in single file. Shackled hand and foot they hobbled through the snow like zombies in green quilted coats, faded and threadbare castoffs. Heads were hatless, nose and ears red. Bare hands were muffed into opposite sleeves. Face and bodies were swollen, eyes bloodshot, minds drained—fates sealed.

The shortest prisoner was in front, the oldest man in the middle followed by the tallest and youngest of the three, Stanislaus Sedecki. Four armed guards, two on each side, accompanied them.

It was the beginning of their fourth day and they had just been fed.

Bent over bowls of mushy rice they had talked quietly as they ate and agreed that one of two things would happen: Today would be another day of the torture and terror their minds and bodies could no longer handle, or they were about to be executed.

Each wore a bandage on one hand. With his good hand, the small man fingered the last morsel from his bowl and their whispering came to an end. "I can't take any more, do you understand me? I *can't*. I don't think you two can either." He raised his swollen eyes and uttered his final words. "If escape is impossible then death will be a blessing." He paused, "I will not be tied to a stake and shot like a dog."

The other two men stared vacantly at their empty bowls in silent acquiescence.

****

Now, as they were being led across an open area of polluted snow, the small man began to cough. There was no activity near them except a lone truck that idled a short distance ahead. White exhaust vapors floated lazily in the air. As they neared the vehicle the small man in the lead coughed more vigorously.

Sedecki clenched his teeth. His eyes became misty. During breakfast his friend had said, *That's what they do with spies you know, they shoot them.* He knew his friend was right. When the three of them had no more to give, when the excruciating torture ended, if it ever did, they would be shot regardless.

Through misty eyes his squalid surroundings seemed to change. These sullied environs now appeared to him most glorious. The bleak mountains seemed striking, majestic. Dirty snow suddenly became pristine. The air smelled cleaner, even invigorating. But then the horrific, unspoken decision they had made overwhelmed him. Freezing tears began to sting his cheeks. Fragments of his young life that flashed through his mind like a surrealistic dream were abruptly replaced by the existing nightmare.

Suddenly the detail stopped. The dream stopped. The small man in front was bent double, coughing profusely. The first guard on his right reached down to jerk him up. Suddenly the little man screamed and lunged straight up at the guard. The middle prisoner leaped on the guard at his left, driving him backwards and down.

In the same instant Sedecki instinctively sprang to his right and threw his manacled hands over the head of the third guard. They went down in a tangle of arms and legs, rolling twice in the snow. He came up straddling the guard's back with the chain of his wrist shackles under the man's neck. With both hands on the back of the soldier's head he applied a death-choke then clamped his teeth together and closed his eyes—waiting for the bullet he knew was coming.

CHAPTER 2

Darkness descended on New Year's Eve. A huge black locomotive pulling an ugly train moved onto an obscure siding. Behind the coal tender were an old empty coach and a mail car, followed by fifty-six freight cars. Hoarfrost and severe winters had colored the wooden boxcars black and long streaks of grime-crusted snow clung to their sides.

The locomotive came to a stop hissing and clanging amid a cordon of soldiers that had secured the region.

A tarpaulin-covered truck entered the area and backed up to the mail car. Soldiers hastily unloaded it. The sliding door of the mail car closed. The truck drove away.

On the opposite side of the train the engineer and fireman were standing by the engine smoking a cigarette as the soldiers watched.

The army officer's radio crackled. He acknowledged then to the engineer said, "You are cleared to go."

The engineer flicked his cigarette and followed by his fireman he climbed into the cab muttering to himself. The track signal turned green and he pulled on the bar. The monstrous steam engine hissed, gave a pronounced cough then a rapid series of chugs. Slowly, the ugly train began to wind its way out of Harbin.

Hours later, punching billows of black smoke into the frigid night air, the locomotive labored up the snow-covered Da Hinggan Ling Mountains of Northwest China.

When it crested the final pass the engine's throaty roar changed to a hiss. Then through high canyon walls of plowed snow it began a long descent down the north side of the mountains towards the wastelands of Mongolia's Gobi desert.

The engineer lifted a watch from his bib overalls—midnight.

The fireman pitched another scoop of coal into the behemoth's belly, and the last seconds of 1950 gave way to the New Year.

The train reached the flat desert floor. It then raced towards Manzhouli, a lonely village in a northern corner of the barren Gobi, where the antagonistic nations of China, Mongolia and Russia share fragile borders.

A vicious wind screamed across the vast expanse of desert. There was nothing to be seen, no crossings, no lights—nothing but the inky black night and a now-and-then ray of icy-blue moonlight. For no apparent reason the engineer reached for the cord and pulled. The whistle moaned into the dark void—the lonesome wail penetrated infinity.

With a jerk, soldiers in the mail car became instantly alert then settled down again.

The train arrived in the sleeping Chinese village of Manzhouli at 3:15 in the morning. It crept along the western side of town and stopped beyond the northern edge—three miles from the Russian border. Except for the locomotive's hissing and clanging, nothing could be heard but the driving wind. Nothing stirred except blowing sand.

Again, a tarpaulin-covered military truck backed up to the train. The ponderous door of the mail car slid open. Less than a minute later it closed.

The truck, driving with black-out lights, traveled north beside the railroad tracks until it reached the Chinese border post, which was fortified with rings of stacked sandbags and armed soldiers. Military Police constantly patrolled both sides of the quiet demarcation zone. The only contact possible between the opposing forces was field phones.

The truck stopped at the gate. A Chinese Army Major jumped from the cab. He peered into the pitch-black night towards the Russian post just three hundred yards north. He saw nothing but was certain the Russians had left the Siberian village of Zabaykalsk, two miles further north and were here, just yards away, prepared and waiting.

The Major spoke to his Sergeant then entered the station already crowded with other soldiers.

Howling winds blew sand and snow across the flat, barren hardpan that separated the Chinese and Russian stations. A seemingly blank nothingness loomed for miles. Russian soldiers called this sector, "The End of the World." The Chinese knew it as, "The Devils Playground."

Suddenly, brilliant floodlights illuminated the desolated area from both directions.

The exchange would soon begin.

With the strap of his service hat tight under his chin the tall and slender Chinese Major, accompanied by his Sergeant, marched into the wind and lights of no mans land.

From the Soviet side a stalwart major and a lieutenant, both wearing the blue epaulets of the NKVD* strode forward.

The two pairs met in the middle of the demarcation zone and exchanged salutes.

The Chinese officer spoke very good Russian, "I am Major Yu."

"Major Petrovich," the Russian replied. "Are we prepared?"

"We are, as our illustrious government confirmed. Are you ready in accordance with the agreement?"

The Russian grimaced, "Of course." He turned slightly alee of the ferocious wind that whipped the lapels of his greatcoat.

* *NKVD – Narodnyi Komissariat Vnutrennikh Del.* Created as a secret political police it had the right to undertake quick non-judicial trials and executions. It was renamed the MVD in 1946 but use of the NKVD acronym continued.

They broke eye contact, faced their respective stations and motioned. The barrier-bars of the border locations raised and from each direction a truck drove forward. When the trucks reached the group they both turned to the right and stopped with tailgates facing each other, ten yards apart.

On command, two armed guards jumped from the Chinese truck. Four NKVD soldiers leaped from the Russian truck. All had their weapons pointing down, but fingers were near the triggers. Tensions always ran high between China and Russia and this contentious area of the border often experienced serious gunfire.

Observers at both stations had a clear view of the proceedings. Senior officers at each location watched intensely.

The colonel inside the Russian outpost adjusted his binoculars and softly murmured, "Here we go...."

The Russian major barked an order.

Twelve Chinese men, shackled hand and foot, exited the Russian truck and formed two rows by the tailgate. Two NKVD soldiers remained on the truck above them.

Then the Chinese Major spoke sharply into the wind, "Bring them out."

Two pale Caucasian prisoners appeared at the tailgate of the Chinese truck. They wore green quilted coats, had bandaged fingers and were shackled.

When they jumped off the truck one man lost his balance and collapsed.

A soldier quickly jerked him up, yelping in Chinese, "Get up fool!"

The two men stood shivering, gazing vacantly at the ground.

Soldiers on the truck slid a stretcher to the tailgate.

The Chinese Sergeant freed the hands of the two prisoners. Then, as directed, they lifted the stretcher from the truck, hobbled forward and set it on the ground between the officers.

The Russian Major bellowed into the driving wind, "What is this?" He looked at the man on the stretcher with a thick bandage around his head. "Nothing was said about this."

He stooped, pressing on his flapping coat lapel, and looked closely at the inert man with the bloody gauze. "Is he alive?"

"Yes, alive," Major Yu replied coolly, "just unconscious, a temporary condition."

The violent wind pounded the canvas tarps against the truck racks in a relentless tattoo. Major Petrovich sensed the frazzled nerves of his men and those of the tense Chinese. Again he turned slightly from the vicious wind and stared keenly at the poker-faced Chinese Major. "The arrangement was three healthy prisoners for twelve of your countrymen. Not two standing and one half dead." His voice rose as he pointed to the stretcher. "I will have to retain two prisoners and give you only ten of your countrymen to compensate for this one."

Major Yu maintained expressionless eye contact, "The agreement was these three prisoners, Major. Nothing was stated about their physical condition. Here they are," his firm monotone insisted, "and we are to receive all twelve men named in the agreement."

"But I cannot accept this," the Russian blurted into the wind. "This is contrary to my government's terms, to my orders."

"I also have my orders," the impassive Chinaman replied. "If you cannot accept these three prisoners I shall put them back in the truck and the exchange will be canceled. *My* government, major, will accept nothing less."

The Russian bristled at Major Yu's contemptuous retort. All eyes were riveted on the two officers and, as if strangely in tune with the proceedings, the fierce wind slowed and suddenly stopped.

No mans land became deathly quiet.

One of the soldiers on the Chinese truck shifted his stance.

Russian soldiers jerked their weapons to the ready—the Chinese followed suit.

Instantly, Major Petrovich raised his arm without breaking eye contact with the Chinese officer.

Every soldier held his breath.

Senior officers at each of the heavily armed outposts stiffened, eyes straining through binoculars. Crisp orders were given. Soldiers silently appeared at the barrier gates and behind the sandbags of both stations. Others scrambled quietly to machineguns on the roof tops.

Time stood still, like a reel of film stuck in a projector. No one dared to move, even breathe. Slowly, the wind began gusting again then it increased with wild abandon, beating the loose tarpaulins against the racks of the trucks. The foreboding tempo was a ticking death clock.

The wind aggravated Major Petrovich. But the Chinaman, *the heathen bastard*, irritated him more and placed him in a precarious quandary. His government had made his orders quite clear. These three prisoners *must* be exchanged. Should he return empty handed…. The veins in his neck throbbed. Sweat oozed from his temples, turning ice-cold as it trickled down his jaw. He had no time to think or even look towards his station, no time to get on the field set, no time to confer with the colonel—no damned time for anything.

His eyes did not waver from those of the Chinaman. With deliberate slowness he lowered his arm and pointed to the stretcher. "What happened to this man?"

Major Yu smiled, "His head came in contact with the butt of a rifle."

"How long has he been this way?"

"Since yesterday."

The Russian Major hesitated, but realized he had no choice. "Very well, we shall make the exchange," he said acidly. "But if he dies before we reach our destination, your government—at the highest level—will hear about it."

He turned, took a cardboard box from his lieutenant and handed it to Yu. "Here is the roster, the dossiers and the personal effects of your twelve men."

Major Yu gave the box to his Sergeant then produced three large manila envelopes. He passed them to Petrovich with a disdaining voice. "Here are the records for these three men."

Major Yu then nodded to his Sergeant who pulled out a roster and began calling the names of the twelve Chinese prisoners, ordering them to line up by his truck's tailgate.

When that was finished the Russian lieutenant stepped forward and bellowed, "When I call your name come forward and stand by this truck."

He called the first name but no one moved. The prisoner did not understand the Russian instructions. With prodding from a Chinese weapon, he hobbled over to the tailgate of the Russian truck.

The second name was called and the other man was prodded forward.

The lieutenant called the third name, "Stanislaus Sedecki."

Major Yu pointed, "He is the one on the stretcher."

The Chinese Sergeant removed the manacles from his three prisoners and tossed them noisily onto the bed of his truck. The edgy Russian soldiers flinched.

An NKVD soldier handcuffed the lifeless Sedecki to his stretcher. He then shackled the other two prisoners.

In turn, two Russian soldiers removed the restraints from the twelve oriental prisoners. The Chinese Sergeant ordered his countrymen into his truck—without any shackles.

The Russian truck, with an angry Major Petrovich and his three prisoners, left the demarcation zone and drove north beside the tracks for two miles. The truck stopped next to a bizarre looking car connected behind the coal tender of a Soviet steam engine.

The black locomotive and the Russian *Stolypin*, a gloomy-gray metal prison car, were waiting in the heavily guarded customs area. At the *Stolypin's* entryway was an area for guards. The remainder of the car had a narrow passageway and numerous barren cells.

The guards placed the two ambulatory prisoners in separate cells.

Major Petrovich watched the soldiers bring the stretcher on board. "Hold it," he said. "Put him right here where it is warm. I want to make sure this one stays alive until I have him delivered."

They placed the stretcher beside one wall. The unconscious Sedecki did not stir.

The Chinese train, waiting at the northern edge of Manzhouli, was ready to proceed across the border into Russia. There the engine would disconnect then accept and bring back a returning train loaded with Russian goods.

The engineer and his fireman disconnected the locomotive and tender from the train, switched to a siding turn-around and reentered the main track at the rear of the train. They backed the engine and connected to the last car. The engineer and his fireman then stepped down and grumpily greeted last week's waiting stage crew.

The relieving engineer and fireman took command of the train. The new engineer gave a short whistle blast and proceeded to slowly back the train across no mans land to a point on the Russian side where he was told to stop. He disconnected his engine and coal tender and shunted his unit to a siding. There he connected to last week's returning train and pulled it over the border into the Mongolian customs area.

It was a normal matter of commerce between China and Russia frequently conducted at this sensitive border crossing. Only the surreptitious prisoner exchange marked this trade highly unusual.

On the Soviet side of the border the Russian engineer moved his smoke belching locomotive and *Stolpin* car onto the main track then reversed and connected to the Chinese train that had just been delivered. With its string of ugly cars and ill-fated prisoners the Russian eased his train past the sleeping town of Zabaykalsk, Russia.

Beyond town the train gained momentum and snaked its way into the dawn. It headed north towards the Yablonovy Mountains and the main track of the longest rail line in the world—the Trans-Siberian Railroad—and to one of the most feared prisons in Russia.

CHAPTER 3

In the late morning of 3 January 1951 the mercury struggled to reach zero. It never did. A habitual gray overcast pressed low on the town of Tayshet and the NKVD's regional administration center and transit prison, the largest in Russia. The town is also home to one of the Gulag's larger work camps.

The train stopped on a siding. The three prisoners in the *Stolpin* were transferred to a military truck. Not wanting to feel the butt of a rifle the two ambulatory prisoners kept their heads down towards their unresponsive comrade on the stretcher. Occasionally they shifted their eyes past the tailgate. Small drab houses and buildings were covered with snow. Wind sculptured drifts swirled around them. Large concrete buildings came into view. All vehicles traveled single file in deep frozen ruts.

Everything was depressing: Small dark, weather beaten houses, gray ice, gray snow and gray concrete buildings, all enveloped in the gloom of a dreary overcast.

The truck moved through huge prison gates, drove a short distance and stopped.

Stanislaus Sedecki, still unconscious and handcuffed to the stretcher was transported to a one-story hospital.

The other two prisoners were escorted to a processing building, stripped and thoroughly searched. They stood nervously while a heavy-set woman shaved the hair from their heads, armpits, and pubic areas—with a straight razor. They were shoved into cold showers. De-lousing powder was splattered on them. Ragged remnants of clothing were thrown at them. They were given dark bread and a tin of weak soup.

"*Skorei, skorei*—quickly now," the guards demanded. They gobbled the bread then were placed in dank individual cells with no bedding, just a smelly *Parasha*—slop pot.

Interrogation of the two ambulatory prisoners was continuous for two days and nights. Their replies compared to the Chinese reports. They were repeatedly pressed to sign confessions. When they refused they were quite surprised not to be tortured.

Perhaps death could wait, the smaller man thought, *there may yet be a way out.*

On January 5th both men were tried by a *Troika*—NKVD three-officer panel, convicted of espionage and sentenced to death. At the same time the sentence was commuted to twenty-five years of *Katorga*—hard labor, penal servitude in the Soviet Gulags.

With a shipment of other prisoners they were crammed into a boxcar destined for the northwestern tip of Russia and the Siberian Gulags.

In the austere one-story hospital Doctor Ackerman watched the NKVD men transfer the unconscious prisoner from the stretcher to a metal cot. A Colonel also watched.

"His name is Stanislaus Sedecki," the colonel said, then sternly added, "I urgently need to talk to this man. Take good care of him and call me the very moment he regains consciousness." Then he turned and left.

Bernard Ackerman, a dark-haired Austrian Jew, had been a doctor at the University of Vienna. He escaped the Nazi purge in the 1930s and fled to Romania. When Germany invaded Poland in 1939 and World War Two began, he was falsely accused, handed over to the NKVD and sentenced to twenty years. Doctors were in very short supply in the Russian Gulags.

Ackerman removed Sedecki's filthy bandage. Inspected and cleaned the young man's head wound and applied a smaller dressing. He removed the bandages from three fingers of the man's left hand and examined the mangled tips and nails. His nurse helped him strip and wash the patient. Just looking at the young man's physical build it was obvious this was not a long time *Zet*—Gulag prisoner.

He connected an intravenous tube to the man's right arm and covered him with two blankets. His little hospital was not the warmest place in the prison.

Doctor Ackerman began his examination. He measured the patient's height at seventy-one inches. Weight: approximately 195 pounds. Hair: light brown. Eyes: blue. Torso: muscular. Skin tone: very good. Age: he wrote 24 and a question mark.

Blood pressure, temperature, pulse—Ackerman made a thorough examination, ending with: Wound, left posterior of the head. Laceration, three and one-quarter inches, begins exactly one eighth inch above the top center of the left ear and proceeds horizontally towards the posterior of the cranium. Surrounding area shaved. Wound sutured.

The doctor referenced the numerous bruises on the young man's body and his mutilated finger tips. He was perplexed by the "burn" marks directly above and below each nipple. To confirm his suspicion he checked the man's scrotum. He found the same electrode burn and shook his head. He completed the chart with: Breathing, shallow. Condition: comatose.

Ackerman was accustomed to doctoring the bony and malnourished, the dying men of the Gulags who came to him with scurvy, tuberculosis, cancer, frostbite, bullet and knife wounds, self-inflicted mutilations, and physical exhaustion. The list was endless. But this young man was a fine example of physical fitness even with the severe bruises on his torso and extremities.

The doctor stood up, looked down at his patient and frowned. *I wonder what his condition will be a year from now?* Pity, he sighed. Excellent physical condition, but comatose. Someone of importance obviously, else the colonel would not have personally brought him here. Then he thought: what if he doesn't regain consciousness, what if he dies? It'll be my fault?

During the next four days Ackerman checked the patient's vital signs almost hourly. The colonel came by, frequently. On the morning of the seventh comatose day the doctor was beside himself. Six days was the limit. Sedecki was still unconscious with no sign of recovering. Ackerman knew his life may now be parallel with that of his patient.

The light was dim, but still blinding. Hooded eyes opened, closed, opened again, and traveled the barren walls and ceiling.

Ooooo, turning the head caused a sharp twinge. The eyes closed, tried to block the pain.

After a few moments the eyes again opened. The room was dingy white. A small wood table and chair set between his bed and the metal cot set against the opposite wall. A thin pad was folded on top of the cot. No sheets or blanket. He recognized nothing. *Where am I?*

He withdrew his right arm from the blankets and stared with alarm at the IV tube. He pulled his left arm out and saw bandages on his fingers. His eyes darted frantically about. The room had three walls that opened to a corridor. There was a similar room across the way. Some sort of ward, a hospital, where? He began to panic. Again he examined his arms. Trying to rise made his head hurt. What has happened to me? Where am I? He relaxed his arms, became quiet and listened. There were sounds of activity somewhere.

Presently a woman dressed in white passed by. He started to call to her but the words hung in his throat.

She noticed his movement and stopped, uttering words he did not understand.

"Where am I," he managed.

The woman raised her eyebrows and again said something unintelligible.

He repeatedly asked in Polish, German and English, becoming more panic-stricken when she did not respond.

Finally she held up a finger, smiled and left.

She returned shortly, talking jibber-jabber with a tall, older man wearing a white smock.

The man smiled, speaking in German, "I am Doctor Ackerman. It is good to see you awake. My nurse says you spoke in German and English." He sat down and checked his patient's pulse.

"Where am I," Sedecki asked in German.

"Suffice to say you are in the prison hospital," the doctor replied, produced a small light and looked into the young man's eyes.

Those eyes darted back and forth and his words came haltingly, "Prison hospital, *Prison?* What … what happened? What am I doing here?"

"Do not be alarmed. Let me ask the questions." Ackerman touched the dressing. "How did you get this nasty gash?"

Sedecki raised his hand but the doctor stopped him and placed both of his arms under the blankets.

"I, I do not know," Sedecki faltered, eyes frightful. "What has happened to me?"

"You arrived with a nasty laceration on your head," the doctor frowned. "It will heal in due time. You were unconscious when you were brought in here. You have been in a coma until now. I have been concerned. The facilities here are not the best. I did not know if you would come out of it. Now that is past, you will be all right." The doctor patted his shoulder. "I will remove the stitches tomorrow." Then the doctor sat back and smiled, "Can you speak other languages besides German?"

The young man hesitated a moment, "Polish … English."

"You do not speak Russian?"

"Nien," was his reply then quickly, "Russian? This is a Russian hospital?"

"I cannot answer those kinds of questions. I am only concerned with your medical condition," the doctor paused. "I do not understand Polish and my English is limited. So we shall continue in German." He picked up the medical chart. "Stanislaus Sedecki," he said, looking at the chart, then at the patient. "What hospital were you in?"

Sedecki's face became quizzical, his reply weak, "Hospital? I don't know any hospital. I do not remember any hospital."

"Sedecki, Stanislaus Sedecki. That is your name?"

The young man's eyes darted around before locking onto the doctor's. "I, I don't know ... My God doctor, I don't know!" Sedecki's facial muscles tightened. He tried to rise but the pain was too great.

The doctor held his shoulder. "No, no, relax, please relax. Do not sit up. You are going to be all right, but you must relax."

Sedecki tried, but could not.

The doctor continued. "Where did you get the head wound?"

"I don't know. I don't remember," His eyes blinked.

The doctor surveyed him critically. "Very well then, tell me what you do remember."

Sedecki was silent for a few moments then became agitated. "I cannot remember anything." His eyes were frantic. "I don't know where I was. I can't remember anything."

His hand came out of the blankets and he grabbed the doctor's arm, his voice becoming loud, "What has happened to me? How did I get here? Tell me doctor, what has happened to me?"

The doctor held him by both shoulders. In a firm yet soothing voice, he said, "Relax, do not panic. It is a temporary condition, this bump on your head. You must remain calm."

Sedecki closed his eyes, trying to think, to remember, to picture something, anything that would bring him out of this nightmare. *Sedecki, Stanislaus Sedecki, the doctor said.* He repeated the name to himself, rolled it over and over in his mind. It didn't mean anything, no thought, no image. The name meant absolutely nothing. His mind refused to cooperate. His whole body ached and mentally he was lost. The pounding in his head increased. Finally his shoulders slumped in resignation.

"I will take care of you. You will be all right," the doctor said. "It has been several days, this coma. It will take time."

Doctor Ackerman removed the IV tube and catheter. "I will be right back."

The nurse came with soup and bread.

The doctor returned and gave him an injection.

The next day Sedecki stood up and walked a little. He gave the bruises on his arms another puzzled look. Then he noticed the discolorations on his torso and legs. The bandage on the back of his head was gone. He felt the scar and stitches of his wound. He was confused by the bandages covering three of his left hand fingers. His touched one. The finger began to throb. *How did all of this happen?*

Later, when he was dozing, he opened his eyes to see the doctor and a heavy set man in uniform at the foot of his bed.

"I am Colonel Dakovnik," the uniformed man smiled, speaking in English. "I have come from Moscow to interview you and your comrades. How are you feeling?"

Sedecki wasn't certain how to respond, especially to a man in uniform. But the voice was pleasant, non-threatening. He rose on one elbow, grimaced, fell back and answered in English, "I, I'm not sure. My head, my hand … I hurt all over." He paused, looking up at the colonel. *Maybe this man knows. He looks important. A colonel he said. That's a high rank, isn't it? He must be in charge. He must know who I am.* "What happened to me?"

When the colonel answered his searching eyes bored into Sedecki's.

"Your injuries will heal in due time I am told. You are in very good hands." He nodded to Doctor Ackerman, and waved him away.

The doctor retreated down the ward to his office. His nurse was making tea. She poured a glass, handed it to him and asked, "Who is this patient who gets an NKVD Colonel to come to his bedside?"

"I don't know and if I were you I would not ask."

The colonel pulled the chair out and sat down. "When you are feeling a little better I will have you brought to my office. We shall have tea and a chat. Would you like that?"

"I ... yes, yes I would."

"All right," the colonel's smile broadened. "I had tea and a long conversation with your friends a few days ago. They are doing fine," he lied. His eyes narrowed, keenly watching for any change in Sedecki's expression. "Later perhaps you can join them."

"Friends, what friends?" the words came rushing from a puzzled face. "I don't remember any friends, I don't even know where I am, why I'm here. Please—"

Colonel Dakovnik held up his hand, "No more questions now." He smiled, turned and left.

The Colonel stopped at the office. "Doctor Ackerman, your amnesia diagnosis may have some merit. I want a written report. Take good care of him. I need him released as soon as possible—with a clear mind. Do you understand?"

"Yes citizen colonel."

The next morning Colonel Dakovnik received Doctor Ackerman's written report. Before returning to Moscow he gave a copy to Major Vlasov, the Troika Officer.

Trying for the hunderdth time, Sedecki grimaced and blinked. He could not remember who he was or how he got here. *I don't understand anything Russian, so why am I in Russia? And if this is a prison hospital, what have I done?* This doctor says the colonel and this hospital—this entire place—is Soviet State Security, Russian Secret Police or some crazy thing. So what is that all about?

His mind was on a treadmill. How could I have hurt my fingers, my head and get all the bruises I have, was I in some accident? Is the doctor right … a slight case of amnesia? What if it isn't slight? What if? He gripped his head with both hands and sat down on the bed. Some one knows and they're not telling me. I have to know who I am and why I'm here!

Doctor Ackerman came in the room and Sedecki's questions were immediate. "Doctor, you have to know something—you have to tell me who I am. *My God*, doctor, I have to know."

"Sussh. I don't know any more than you do," Ackerman softly replied in German. "Listen to me, my friend. This hospital is in a prison camp. I am ordered to treat you, nothing else. I don't know who you are, or where you came from, or how you got your injuries."

Sedecki frowned. His gaze became intense.

The doctor, old before his time, looked around before he said, "Your name, Stanislaus Sedecki, is Polish. You must be Polish. There are many Poles in the camps. Your concussion is severe. You suffer from amnesia. Everything may come back to you in a week or month or, who knows?" Maybe never, he thought, but didn't say it. "Your fingers and the bruising will heal. That is all I can tell you. That is all I know." His smile was thin. "Now you must rest."

Sedecki regained strength in the days that followed, walking up and down the ward and doing mild exercises in his room. But mental exercising did nothing for the clarity of his mind. The mauled fingers of his left hand were swollen, tender and scabbed over. The fingernails were black. The sutures had been removed from his head. Frequently he ran his fingers over the irregular scar.

Several evenings later Sedecki listened to heavy boots breaking the silence and coming closer. Two NKVD soldiers appeared. Doctor Ackerman stood behind them.

One soldier gruffly said something and tossed clothes on his bed.

"They want you to go with them," the doctor explained in German.

Sedecki stood up and looked at the faded shirt and pants, and green quilted coat. All of the buttons were missing. A piece of twine served as a belt. He started to say something but saw the doctor shake his head.

"Those are the clothes you were wearing," Ackerman said. "They're yours."

"*Skorei, skorei!*" one soldier hollered.

"They want you to hurry," the doctor urged. "Please get dressed. Do not waste time."

Sedecki looked at the two soldiers as he donned the clothes, trying to recognize their uniforms. As he slipped his left foot into the second boot one soldier ranted in Russian, grabbed his collar and jerked him to a standing position. He looked at the doctor's pleading eyes as they pulled him into the corridor. They shackled him then pushed him from the hospital into the prison yard.

A freezing cold wind smacked him like the jaws of a bear trap. Sedecki pulled his collar around his neck.

One soldier snickered, "It is warm and only a breeze."

"Wait till he goes north," the other said. "He will know what cold is."

Sedecki didn't understand a word but he did comprehend the rifle barrel poking his back.

He moved through the snow a little faster.

Once in the main building they led him down a long corridor, through several iron gates, made two turns and stopped in front of a door. The soldier knocked then led the prisoner in and put him on a wooden chair in the middle of the room.

It was a small, austere room, harshly illuminated by a light bulb in the ceiling. The walls were wood, yellowish color. No windows. Floor was heavy dark planking. A heater set by a side wall, but the room was cool. Sedecki looked at the three men standing behind a table. Wrongly, he assumed the men were military. The blue NKVD/MVD epaulets with their rank insignia meant nothing to him.

The two majors and the captain sat down and the questions began.

"Stanislaus Sedecki, is that correct?" the officer on the right asked in a stern voice.

Sedecki remained silent, staring blankly at the officers.

"You do not understand Russian?" the officer then asked in German.

Sedecki shook his head.

"Very well, since the English speaking officer who questioned your friends and talked to you in the hospital has returned to Moscow we shall conduct your interrogation in German. Do you understand?"

Sedecki's expression changed to perplexity, "What friends?"

"I shall ask the questions. You will supply only answers, understand?"

The other major watched Sedecki closely through half-closed eyes.

The officer on the right continued, "You are telling me you do not remember the two friends who came here with you?"

"I don't know any friends. I don't know how I got here." He scrutinized their faces as he spoke, "Why am—"

The Major on the left slammed his fist on the table and spat something in Russian.

Sedecki jerked and his chains rattled.

Major Sokoskaya continued in German, "A prisoner has no right to address anyone. A prisoner has no rights at all. You are a foreigner. We will overlook your ignorance—once."

Sedecki's eyes went from one officer to the other.

"Also understand," the major continued, softening his tone, "you only give answers, no questions." He paused, looked at his paperwork. "You maintain that you remember nothing?"

"I, I do not remember anything. I do not know about any friends. I do not know how I was hurt or why I am being kept here. I don—"

"Stop," the officer cut him off. "Do you know what we do with those who commit crimes against the state, and spies like you who hide behind a medical curtain and lie?"

The blood seemed to drain from Sedecki's face. He blinked several times. "I am not...."

The major held up his hand.

The interrogation ended without further explanation. The guards were given instructions and they led Sedecki away.

"I suspect he is fabricating this amnesia and I suspect he has the hospital fooled," Major Vlasov declared. "I watched him very carefully as he answered your questions. He is clever."

Major Sokoskaya walked around the table, lighting a cigarette. "I don't think so, Comrade Major."

Major Vlasov was quick to respond, "We don't have psychiatrists or neurologists here. Doctor Ackerman is an ordinary doctor. He is a prisoner himself, who I am sure can be easily fooled. He is soft and lenient with all prisoners. I tell you Nikolai this man is trying us."

Major Nikolai Sokoskaya almost smiled. He was conscious of Vaslov's self-importance and know-it-all comments. "Doctor Ackerman is more qualified than his Vienna credentials indicate and prior to leaving for Moscow did not our Comrade Colonel agree about amnesia?"

Vaslov made a face. "But, what if it isn't?"

Nikolai Sokoskaya lit a cigarette. "It is a moot point, Comrade Major," he kept his voice an even tone as he eyed Vlasov. "It is practically decided. The other two prisoners gave us all the information we could hope to attain. It coincided with the Chinese reports."

"Yes, Nikolai, but what if that information happens to be incorrect, or there is more?"

Sokoskaya exhaled blue smoke and faced Major Vlasov. "Did you not see the bandages on the hands of these three, and the bruises, the despair, the fear of interrogation in the eyes of the other two?" He turned, puffing his cigarette, "Perhaps you are not familiar with Chinese methods of interrogation—the bamboo fingernail treatment, or sitting naked on a chair with no seat while someone smacks your balls with a stick, or the three-wire electrical shock." He turned and faced Vlasov. "And the head wound of this last one, Sedecki—a three inch gash that has rattled his brains." He paused and puffed. "No, I think what information those two men gave us was all they had and this one can not give us anything in his present condition."

An irritated Major Vlasov gathered his papers, "Perhaps."

Sokoskaya squashed his cigarette. "Besides, you heard Comrade Colonel. There was nothing more to be gained from those two. The twenty-five year sentence to the Siberian north will hold them, if they survive, until their final fate is decided."

"That's another thing," Vlasov squinted. "It's not just the information we have or haven't obtained, it's the orders from Moscow, the special handling."

"Regardless, it is out of our hands," Sokoskaya said. "We will pronounce sentence on this one and send him on his way when Colonel Dakovnik returns. Whether he regains his senses or not, no longer matters. I don't think any of these three men will last very long anyway."

CHAPTER 4

In shackles Sedecki could not move very fast and the guards prodded him down the hall. At the first corner he started to turn the way they'd came and was knocked to the ground.

They jerked him upright, jabbered in gruff Russian and shoved him in the opposite direction. The muzzle of a rifle and course language moved him along. His leg chains echoed on the floors of the dimly lighted stone passageways. After making several turns they stopped by a metal door numbered cell 53. Two station guards were standing there under very bright lights. They removed his shackles, opened the cell door and shoved him into a blinding darkness.

Heat and a horrifying stench smacked him like a blast furnace and took his breath away. He gagged. The metal door slammed against him and knocked him to his hands and knees.

"Aaarrgh!" he screamed and immediately bolted upright, shaking his hands free of the slimy flesh—*cadavers!* He pressed against the steel door, overwhelmed. Bile reached his throat. He swallowed again and again. His eyes smarted and strained to see, but he saw nothing. The cell was deathly still. Revulsion and fear immobilized him. He dared not move.

Darkness gradually eased into a dim haze. The room came slowly into focus and a frightening death scene materialized before him. A hundred pair of eyes set in slick white skulls stared at him.

The cell was five meters wide and ten meters deep. In the middle of the ceiling a grimy low-watt bulb cast a dim yellowish haze over the mass of flesh and bones. He was about to retch. His vision was slow to adjust. He saw triple deck bunks stacked along the left wall. Those bunks and the entire floor were covered with naked bodies, drained of color. Some were positioned back to back, had knees crossed or feet tucked. A few were vertical. All were naked from the waist up, clad only in underpants. Some were totally nude. Every head in the room was bald and slick. Sedecki cringed. It was like the bottom of a graveyard.

Most of the putrid stench came from two half-keg *parashas*, almost full of feces and urine, which set on each side of the door. There were no windows, no air. Sweltering heat exaggerated the stench. He trembled.

He was forced to take a normal breath. It made him gag and swallow. He took shallow breaths, remained immobile against the door and stared at the silent, unbelievable scene.

There was movement on his right. A big, broad shouldered man with a large head was slowly getting to his feet. He looked even bigger when he stood erect. He said something Sedecki did not understand.

Again the huge man spoke.

Sedecki remained motionless.

Then the man said, "Deutsch … Sprecken ze Deutsch?"

Sedecki's face changed slightly.

"Ah," A smile crossed the big man's face. He held out his arm and continued in German. "Come. Come sit."

Sedecki stood still. There was no room to move. He looked down again and almost puked. He watched the big man slowly pick his way forward along the wall, spouting sharp words as he came. When he got closer Sedecki looked up at a giant that towered more than a head above him.

"Come, sit. Is all right," the big man said in broken German. "By me, sit. Come."

Reluctantly, Sedecki followed the man, extremely careful about where he stepped. They made room for him against the wall.

"Hot, take coat, make cushion," the big man's German was bad.

Sedecki realized he was wet with perspiration. He cautiously removed his padded coat, folded it and sat on it. Then he took off his shirt. The eyes were no longer staring at him. The ashen bodies, slick with sweat were not moving, but they were alive.

His fears began to subside, a little. The oppressive stench still assaulted him. He found breathing difficult.

"My German no good," the giant said. "Learn in war. Forget much. My name Viktor Stepanovich Zukovny," he smiled displaying a gap between his two front teeth.

Sedecki replied in German, "You speak English, Polish?"

"Engless, Polski? Aaah," Viktor's face lit up. He turned and spoke to someone. There were squabbling voices until the big man said something. The man next to Sedecki stood up. Then a young man Sedecki's size, wearing only shorts, rose from somewhere behind Viktor, gathered his clothes and made his way towards them. He swapped places with the other man, put his clothes next to Sedecki and sat down on them.

After a moment he spoke in English. "My name is Aleksandr Mikhailovich Leskov. Viktor said you speak English?"

"English … yes." he hesitated, "My name … umm, my name is Sedecki, Stanislaus Sedecki."

"Ssssh, speak quietly," Leskov said, looking at him carefully, quizzically. "Talking is not allowed. If the wolf's-eye opens stop talking and look straight ahead."

"Wolf's-eye?"

"Yes, wolf's-eye, the peep-hole in the door. They turn off the hall light. The guard slides the cover back, peeps in."

"Good God," Sedecki said and almost gagged, "you can't talk?"

"We must speak softly, and carefully." Leskov smiled, pleased with the opportunity to use his English.

Sedecki removed his wet undershirt and wiped his face.

Aleksandr Leskov noticed Sedecki's muscular build and weight, and the dark bruises. He could tell this man had not yet been in a camp. "You are new to the Gulags?"

"Gulags?"

"Yes, the Gulags, the camps, prisons," Leskov answered, suspiciously, "Your first time in prison?"

Sedecki wiped his face and eyes again. "I was in the hospital."

"And before that," Leskov asked slowly, "when were you arrested?"

Sedecki ran his undershirt across his face again. "Arrested? I don't know."

Aleks looked at him incredulously. "You don't *know*?"

Sedecki saw the look on the man's face and realized the absurdity of his words.

"I can't remember anything. I woke up in the hospital. I don't know why I'm here or what I've done. The doctor says I have amnesia, temporary amnesia."

Leskov had noticed the patch of shaved hair. Sedecki turned his head, allowing the man a close look at the vivid red scar in the shaved area.

"I don't know how I got this," Sedecki added, "The doctor said it caused the amnesia."

At the sound of metal on metal, everyone froze. The door swung open and in the blinding light stood four armed NKVD soldiers. The guard called off six names. Those prisoners stood, donned their clothes and stepped out.

The door closed with a clang. It took several minutes for eyes to once again adjust.

"Those *zeks* are goners," Leskov whispered in English.

"*Zeks*?"

"*Zek* is slang for a prisoner, and those zeks are goners—gone, won't be back."

"How do you know they won't be back?"

"They were told to take all of their things," Leskov replied. He liked the sound of Sedecki's voice and he found himself smiling, something he hadn't been doing lately. "Most of us are called by our patronymic names, but you can call me Leskov or Aleks if you like."

Sedecki offered his hand, which surprised Aleks. They smiled and shook hands.

"Call me …" Sedecki stopped, unsure of his words.

Aleks seized the opening, "Stanislaus is too much. I'll just call you Sedecki."

Sedecki shifted his legs, "Fine." Looking at the perspiring bodies surrounding him, he consciously tried to take little short breaths. It didn't work. Lungs did not receive the oxygen. He was forced to take a deep breath. He blinked twice, held his hand over his nose and turned to Aleks Leskov. "How does everyone stand it? This heat … the horrible stench!"

"Many don't. Some pass out. Some die."

"Die?"

"Yes, anxiety, stress, exhaustion, this unbearable hell," Aleks said rather matter-of-factly. "One man died several days ago, several passed out recently. Many of these men are exhausted, it doesn't take much."

Sedecki shook his head.

Aleks said "This room was built for twenty prisoners, thirty maximum." He turned to Viktor, spoke in Russian and turned back. "Viktor says there are now eighty-seven here. They have packed more than a hundred in this cell."

"Unbelievable," Sedecki said, looking around. "How long have you been here?"

"Two weeks. I'm awaiting trial again. This is one of the holding cells. Everyone is awaiting trial, most for the second or third time. Have you been tried?"

"Yes," Sedecki said, "No … I don't know. They talked about espionage and some friends and spying." He gently touched his scar. "Maybe it happened before I got this."

Aleks noticed the mauled fingers. "Where are your friends?"

"I don't know. I never saw any friends. I don't remember any."

Aleks scrutinized Sedecki as he spoke. Sometimes you learn more from a man's face and eyes than from his words.

Boldly he asked, "Are you a spy?"

"No...." Sedecki said then hesitated, looking at Aleks. "I mean, I don't think I am." He paused. "I don't understand any Russian. How could anyone be a spy in this country if you don't understand the language?"

"True, perhaps. There are many foreigners in the Gulags. Most speak some dialect of Russian, but there are some who do not." Aleks looked around, then leaned closer to Sedecki and spoke lower. "Talk is dangerous when there are so many ears."

Sedecki didn't understand, wasn't everyone here in the same boat? He looked at the solemn faces and languid eyes of those near him. There must be more to what Aleks said, he thought. He didn't understand anything that was happening so he remained quiet.

He leaned back against the wall with Aleks, trying to rest, trying not to breathe heavy, trying to keep the temperature down, to make the time go faster—trying to imagine being any place but here.

A few moments later Aleks explained that his friend, Viktor Zukovny, had been in cell 53 the longest, and was the *Starosta*, the Elder. He had been so elected by the others. A *Starosta* has the authority to rule among them: distribute the food, tell them where to sit, settle disagreements, detail slop bucket chores and other duties.

"When he leaves a new *Starosta* would be designated," Aleks said.

At 5 AM the following morning the door swung open, "TOILET." The sharp command startled Sedecki awake.

It was first call, a long awaited moment. The two *parashas* were almost overflowing. Viktor edged his mountainous frame to the front, spouting orders in Russian. Four men rose, put their clothes on and grasped the handles of the *parashas*. Very slowly and carefully they carried the slop buckets out as the rest of the group dressed.

"If they spill any they must clean it up with their own rags," Aleks whispered.

There wasn't sufficient latrine space for all the prisoners to use at the same time. Viktor divided them into three groups. Sedecki was in the second group with Aleks. There were a number of wash pans filled with water. No soap or towels. No one had towels. Some men had rags, pieces of cloth other than their ragged clothing—which they seemed to guard with their life. Aleks had the remains of a long rag. Sedecki rinsed his face and hands in the fetid water and like many others dried with his shirt.

At 7 AM the guards delivered to the cell a bulky breakfast of dark bread and tea. Everyone had to stand and Viktor distributed the ration of bread to each prisoner. The tea was nothing more that hot water colored with a substance resembling whatever. It was in large pails. Several tin cans were used as dippers.

"Is this all we get?" Sedecki asked.

Aleks turned to him. "That is it. Dinner is usually a half-liter of some type of weak soup and a small amount of millet or low-grade barley and bread. Supper is a half-liter of soup and bread. Dinner is the better meal. Better eat else you starve."

Sedecki ate part of what he was given and gave the rest to Aleks. He did the same with his dinner at noon and his supper.

Shortly after supper Cell 53 was given their exercise period. It was bitter cold but Sedecki did not mind, he was exhilarated. He thought he'd do it naked just to have a few minutes respite from that God-awful cell.

"Don't they leave the door open and air the cell out while we're gone?" Sedecki asked.

"No," Aleks replied. "Viktor says it hasn't been cleaned since he's been here, even though he asked for mops and water."

"Good God," Sedecki said as they walked. He walked with his

hands behind his back as required and inhaled deeply though his frosted nostrils. He gazed at the starlit sky and wondered what it would be like if he were free. *Where would I go, what would I do? Could someone help me, penetrate my amnesia, or will I ever know who I am? Couldn't one of those little stars float down here and save him?*

The fierce, guttural bark of a guard pierced the night.

Aleks whispered, "Keep your head down."

Twice during the night the Cell door opened. Prisoners were taken out for interrogation and returned.

"If you are called out," Aleks said in a low voice when the door closed a second time, "do not speak unless spoken to. If you address anyone, in any language, you use the polite term, 'citizen,' citizen guard, citizen whatever. Never use the word comrade. We are not allowed common courtesies. They'll beat you if you do not conform."

Sedecki watched various prisoners return to the cell grumbling. Some were completely shattered or crying about the additional sentences. Others never came back. So Sedecki asked if some were acquitted and released.

"No one gets an acquittal," Aleks answered, "there is no such thing in Stalin's system."

After dinner several days later it was Aleksandr Mikhailovich Leskov's turn. He returned to the cell shortly before the supper hour with a somber face, folded his clothes and sat down.

"Was it your trial, Aleks?"

"Yes," he answered with a pensive expression. "Five more years added to my sentence. I won't get out until 1963. I will die in the Gulags."

Sedecki tried to console him. "You'll get out, Aleks. You will."

Aleks quietly confided that in 1948 he was arrested while attending the university at Leningrad (referring to the city by its original name, St. Petersburg) and convicted of crimes against the state for articles he helped publish in an underground press. He was sentenced to ten years and sent to a *Spetzlager*—a special camp for political prisoners in the Ural Mountains.

Then, a month ago he was falsely accused of subversive statements by a prisoner who did not share his views and lied to get even. Aleks was interrogated but refused to confess. Now, he explained, another prisoner was brought before the Troika and gave false testimony.

"The provocateur was probably offered a trustee job, lighter work, or just better food for a month or two," Aleks grimaced.

"The who?" Sedecki asked as Viktor sat down next to Aleks.

"A provocateur, a fellow prisoner who spies or lies, for the secret police," Aleks whispered. "There are those among us who would sell their soul for more food, less work, easier duties, whatever. As I told you, there are many ears."

Aleks and Viktor began a conversation in Russian and Sedecki let them have their time together.

Before long the cell door opened. A guard yelled, "SUPPER."

Supper for Major Nikolai Sokoskaya, in the warm ambiance of the officers club on the evening of 15 January, was interrupted when he was summoned to the operations room. Such immediate calls to duty were not unusual but the urgency caused him to leave a half glass of exceptional German Riesling.

When he arrived there were several young officers in the room, including the watch commander, a captain, and Major Anton Vlasov.

"What is happening?" he asked, taking off his coat.

"There's been an escape at number 030 in the third section of Kem," Major Vlasov replied in his firm, all-knowing manner.

Sokoskaya frowned, "The new area, isn't that where the last shipment—"

"That's right, Nikolai," Major Vlasov cut him short, "the last shipment, which included the two men you were so sure of."

"How many escaped?" Sokoskaya asked.

"Twenty eight, according to the report," the watch commander answered.

"Names?"

"None yet comrade major, we are requesting more details."

"Don't request," Major Vlasov blurted, "demand!"

Sokoskaya, ignoring Vlasov, asked the captain, "Was Moscow copied?"

"Yes, comrade major, on the first communication," the captain answered, uncomfortable with two majors on his back. "Latest report, fifteen minutes ago, states that the twenty-eight have broken into three groups and tracks indicate they are all heading westerly towards the border."

"Have the Finns been contacted?"

The captain looked at Vlasov then said, "Comrade Major Vlasov gave the order immediately."

"Damn!" Nikolai said softly, scowling at Vlasov, "you could have waited for higher authority. It will take them several days to reach Finland, even if there is a chance they could make it through the heavy snow. No need for the Finns to learn of our problems."

Sokoskaya watched Vlasov purse his lips, take a deep breath and avoid eye contact. The silence was tense until the watch commander tore a message from the teletype. "Comrade Commander at Kem states that all escapees should be in custody by noon tomorrow."

"He had better be right if he wants to keep his head." Major Vlasov exclaimed.

At the Dzerzhinsky building in Moscow the following morning, Lavrenti Pavlovich Beria, director of the NKVD, read the message stating every one of the twenty-eight prisoners had been caught and shot. He slammed his fist on the desk, "Every damned one!"

His aide frowned, "Escapees are automatically shot even if they hold up their hands."

"I know the standard procedure, damn it," the director ranted. "Shoot them on the spot, or later with a firing squad so others can witness. But goddamnit, two of those prisoners were from the Chinese exchange."

Director Beria still fumed when Colonel Dakovnik was ushered into the office. The director did not even acknowledge the colonel's greeting. With obvious irritation he ranted at no one in particular. "So now we have but one left."

He turned around and looked at Colonel Dakovnik. "This"—he grabbed a paper—"this, Stanislaus Sedecki, the one with the head injury, he was the primary man, now he's the only one." The director paced behind his huge desk for several moments then faced the colonel. "I have a man that I want to go with you to Tayshet."

"Yes, Comrade Director."

Several hours later, Colonel Dakovnik picked up his passenger at the University of Moscow. They drove to the airport and immediately departed for Tayshet.

"TOILET."

It was 5 a.m. and Sedecki felt like he had just dozed off. Everyone dressed and was herded to the latrine in groups.

Breakfast was the same garbage as the previous day. The bread ration was smaller. He ate half of the soggy dough, could not force the rest of it down and insisted that Aleks and Viktor share the remainder.

The cell door opened again. From all the gibberish only one word was clear: "Sedecki."

Aleks touched his arm, "They want you to step out and take all your things." He made a face and added, "Goodbye, my friend."

Sedecki stood up, put on his clothes and picked his way to the door. Guards grabbed him by the arms and led him away.

Colonel Dakovnik and a short, chubby man wearing a dark suit, shirt and tie, were standing in the doctors office when the guards brought Sedecki into the hospital.

"Good morning," The colonel said in English. "I am sorry for the conditions you have been subjected to while I was gone. We will remedy that. You shall have a bath and clean clothes and this doctor"—he gestured towards the chubby man—"will examine you. I told you we would take good care of you."

The colonel smiled and left. Doctor Ackerman took Sedecki to his old room and spoke in German, "You are going to have a Russian *sanobrabotka*, a hygiene bath. My nurse will shave all of your hair. This prevents lice and other vermin. Do not worry, she does this frequently. Then you can bathe. "

Sedecki sat then stood nervously as the nurse shaved his head, armpits and pubic hair. Then she brought him a pail of warm water and two small towels. He washed the stench from his body and donned a hospital gown.

When he returned to the office the chubby man was wearing a white smock.

"I'm Doctor Chovskaya, from the University of Moscow," he announced in English. "I am here to help you."

Sedecki remained silent while the doctor examined the bruises and burns on his body and his swollen fingers. He checked his eyes, ears, nose and throat. He scrutinized the scar on Sedecki's head.

Sedecki was offered tea, which he accepted and a cigarette which he refused. He decided he liked the old gentleman who had a soft, pleasing voice and a nice smile.

Then the examination became oral with various tests and continued through the rest of that day and into the evening. The doctor had food prepared. Sedecki ravenously ate the best food he had yet tasted. He was even offered a glass of vodka.

He cooperated, replying to every question, problem, supposition and verbal query put to him. He did so with immediate and truthful answers to the best of his mind's ability. He pleaded with Doctor Chovskaya to ask him more questions, give him more tests—to please help him, tell him how he got here and why.

When the session ended at 9 PM Sedecki was returned to his hospital room knowing no more about himself than he did the day before. He felt hopeless. But he was thankful to be able to spend the night in a hospital room instead of that stinking cell. He sat down on the edge of the bed with his head in his hands. Maybe it will get better when we continue tomorrow, he told himself. They have to tell me who I am and why I am here. They have to.

Colonel Dakovnik sat in a swivel chair behind a desk. The room was slightly larger than the Troika room and much more accommodating. A filing cabinet, a small table, a hotplate, and two other chairs completed the Spartan office the NKVD Colonel was using.

Doctor Chovskaya took one of the chairs in front of the desk and thanked the colonel for the steaming hot tea.

"He is not faking," Chovskaya said after several sips. "He is suffering from amnesia, there is no doubt."

Colonel Dakovnik was skeptical. "How is it that he remembers three languages, but cannot remember anything else? He claims to know nothing about his activities in China, doesn't know anything about World War Two, the Berlin Airlift or the war that's raging in Korea—or about any other recent events; yet he can remember places in Europe and England. That does not seem right."

"What you say is true, comrade colonel," Dr. Chovskaya replied, "but in your discussions with him did you not observe that he cannot recall names or dates, or what he was doing in those countries, or who he was with? No, that he cannot do. Dates, names, specifics, they are blanks to him. It is a medical condition called 'Global Amnesia,' without doubt brought on by the severe blow to his head. The wound is obvious."

The doctor picked up his cup, sipped the tea and softly hissed, "Damnable Chinese."

Colonel Dakovnik was not pleased with the doctor's answer but he was well aware that Chovskaya was one of the most irrefutable men in his field, and privy to the highest echelons, including Director Beria. He decided to remain quiet.

Chovskaya went on, "He also has what is termed a 'closed head injury.' A massive blow to the head, like the one he sustained can, by abruptly moving the brain within the skull, damage one or many regions. I would further diagnosis his condition as 'Retrograde Amnesia.'"

Dr. Chovskaya paused to sip his tea.

The colonel made a face and was about to remark but the doctor continued.

"Retrograde amnesia, colonel, is selective loss of what he has most recently learned or experienced. 'Last in—first out,' is the general rule. That is why he has no recollection of what has been happening in his life for the past twenty years, more or less. I have seen many cases quite similar.

"He answers my questions eagerly, truthfully. In fact he implores me to ask more. He *wants* to know who he is. He *wants* to remember. He is not even sure that his name is Stanislaus Sedecki. The best he can recall is a time during which he must have been, I'd say, between the ages of four and five. He can evoke visions of schools, slates, certain furniture, buildings and houses, scenery and so forth. However, he cannot remember *where* those places are and he can not remember names, dates or time settings.

"He retains languages subconsciously, like he also retains motor skills and mannerisms, and other learned functions. And he will maintain many other talents learned from late childhood to this present day. I questioned him for specific details about the schoolrooms, furniture, houses and the scenery he describes. From those descriptions I can safely say that he was talking about places and things in Europe, most certainly in Poland and Germany. "

Dr. Chovskaya sat his tea on the desk before continuing. "It is quite interesting. He could describe, through a child's eye, areas that I know were of Berlin and Warsaw. I have been there. However, he has no idea as to what city or country these areas belong. He described those areas to me like they were *before* they were gutted by the war. I know pre-war Berlin and Warsaw. I have been there, studied there.

"He talked of little desks, chalk and slates. He attended school in one or both of those countries prior to World War Two."

The doctor took another sip of tea, set it down again and gestured with his hands. "That, colonel, is my report. Stanislaus Sedecki is like a babe in arms. He has no idea of who he really is or what country he is from and, as I was carefully instructed before we left Moscow, I did not enlighten him."

The colonel chewed on his lower lip, then asked, "How long will this amnesia last, what can be done to return his senses?"

"I would expect his amnesia to be permanent, or it could last only a few months, who knows. You must realize that he took a massive blow to the head. He was in a coma for seven full days. I am surprised the damage is not greater."

Doctor Chovskaya stood up, drank the last of his tea and faced the colonel. "I don't know of what use he will be to the Comrade Director or you. That is not my concern. I shall be leaving in the morning."

"I'll need your report before you leave."

The doctor looked at the colonel, "I'm sorry?"

"Your report," the colonel repeated. "I'll need your written report."

"Comrade Colonel, as I was personally instructed before I left Moscow, I telephoned Comrade Director with my report as soon as I finished the examination. It was his instructions that I give you the same report, verbally. My work is done."

At nine in the morning the two NKVD soldiers came to the

hospital for Sedecki. He hurried to dress under pressure as Doctor Ackerman watched.

Stepping from the room he said, "Thank you doctor," in German and offered his hand.

The barrel of one of the weapons came swinging down.

Doctor Ackerman grimaced at the sound of metal against flesh. The soldier did not have to do that. He would not have accepted Sedecki's hand—handshakes are forbidden.

Ackerman stepped back. One soldier held the prisoner while the other shackled him then pushed him forward.

Over his shoulder, Sedecki again said, "Thank you."

"Good luck," the doctor said softly as his patient was led from the building.

Sedecki was once again prodded through the hallways then pushed into a chair in the same bare-bones room as before, with the same two majors and captain. What did Aleks call this three-man arrangement, an NKVD Troika?

He blandly looked at them as they studied him. Then it began.

"If you sign," Major Vlasov said in Russian, holding the pre-drawn confession in the air, "things will go easier for you."

Major Sokoskaya translated into German.

Sedecki shook his head slowly. "I cannot sign for something I have not done. I have told you, I know nothing about what you ask. I can't remember anything."

"Yes," Major Sokoskaya said jadedly, "we have been informed of your amnesia. That is no longer a consequence. This is the final part of your trial."

"But—"

"Silence," Major Sokoskaya said, holding up two sheets of paper and turning them so Sedecki could see the writing and signatures. It meant nothing to Sedecki.

"These are the confessions of the other two prisoners who were brought here with you," the major lied, pointing to the phony papers. "Confessions of espionage which specifically implicate you whether you remember it or not. It will be better for you if you admit this and sign."

Sedecki looked down at the floor and shook his head.

"Very well," Sokoskaya said firmly in German. "You have been tried and convicted in a prior trial along with your friends, whether you confess or not is of little consequence now."

"I don't—"

Major Vlasov slammed his fist on the table.

Major Sokoskaya quickly raised his hand, stopping Vlasov before he could vent his fury. Then to Sedecki he calmly said, "You will speak only when asked."

Sedecki closed his eyes, let his mind float from this madness and drifted into silence.

The room was cool, almost cold, but beads of sweat appeared on Sedecki's forehead. His hands were clammy and the fingers of his left hand throbbed like a bad tooth. *Confessions and friends, what friends? What are they doing to me? I haven't done anything. Why can't I remember? My God, what is happening?* His mind kept coasting farther and farther away.

He heard a strange voice that seemed to be coming from a hollow chamber. He was not aware that Major Sokoskaya was reading from a paper in his hand.

"—for the crime of espionage against the Union of Soviet Socialists Republics, according to Article 58, point 6, of the Ukaz of the Presidium of the Union of Soviet Socialist Republics, dated June 7, 1943...."

Sedecki watched the movement of the Major's mouth through half-

closed eyes, trying to connect reality to the nonsensical German gibberish that seemed so distant. *This can't be real,* his crippled mind told
him. The yellowish glow from the single light bulb had turned the bleak
room into a bad dream: officers with scowling faces, the hellish cell, the
guards, the manacles, a trial, unknown friends, espionage—madness.

"—the court finds Stanislaus Sedecki guilty on all points and sentences him to death by shooting...."

Sedecki's mouth flew open and he bent forward like he was
smashed in the stomach. Tiny luminous spots danced before his
eyes. He swayed, losing his equilibrium, caught himself and tried to
straighten up. He could not focus. Bile burned in his esophagus and
he was about to vomit. His mind became a raging fire, sucking every
ounce of strength from his body. *Death by shooting, My God!*

His arms went limp in his lap. He slumped against the chair and
his head lolled backwards.

"—Death sentences being automatically commuted, on behalf of
the U.S.S.R.'s Presidium of June 1, 1947, the prisoner is hereby sentenced to 25 years *Katorga,* hard labor, in the penal working camps of
the Siberian north...."

Sedecki's brain continued to spin as his head rolled slowly from
side to side. With half closed eyes he stared at a vast expanse of nothing. The words were coming from some far away mountain top. His
brain, wanting to shut out the world, refused to listen—*A nightmare,
some damned crazy nightmare.*

"—such sentence is given without the right of appeal."

Sedecki's head went forward. He sagged in a stupor.

Major Sokoskaya called the soldiers in and gave them instructions. They took Sedecki by his arms and dragged the limp prisoner out of the room.

He was pushed and prodded as he staggered down several hallways in a state of delirium. They could shoot him right now and he would not feel it.

In front of cell 53 they unshackled and pushed him in. Hands came up to break his fall. Coughing, gagging, he numbly made his way through the perspiring mass of slick flesh and sat down by Aleks Leskov. He put his head back against the wall and squeezed his eyes closed.

Aleks was suspicious. His new friend's clothes were laundered, he had been shaved and he could tell that the man had bathed. That smacked of a provocateur. He thought of moving away from Sedecki and having nothing more to do with the man. But he sat there and silently watched the tears ooze from the corners of Sedecki's closed eyes. He began to feel the pain this man was enduring. There are some things that cannot be faked.

Finally he asked, "What happened? Where have you been?"

It was a while before Sedecki spoke, still keeping his eyes closed. "Death, by shooting," he uttered in a weak, whispery voice, "then they said twenty-five years … work in Siberia… no appeal."

Aleks waited while his new friend regained his composure, then he listened as Sedecki told him about yesterday's hospital stay, the colonel, the doctor, this morning's trial and the sentencing.

Aleks consoled his friend, but couldn't offer much. Being tried and sentenced for something you didn't do is devastating. It was something he and so many of the political *zeks* have endured and now live with. He could only imagine what it was for someone with a mind condition like Sedecki, someone who cannot remember anything.

From that moment on, Aleks and the *Starosta*, Viktor Zukovny, began to watch Sedecki closely. Their new friend no longer wanted to talk, did not want to eat and walked in a silent daze during toilet breaks and exercise periods. They agreed the distraught man needed help.

Viktor talked about their new friend. "I like this man, this Sedecki. He reminds me of you, Aleksandr Mikhailovich, when I first met you. In fact, now that his head is shaved he almost looks like you, same build and height, and features. He could be your brother, Aleks. We will make him our brother and take care of him like a brother."

At 5 A.M. four mornings later the same daily routine began, toilet-call then breakfast. The prisoners had no sooner finished eating before the door again swung open. Everyone squinted at a small cadre of armed NKVD soldiers standing in the blinding light.

A young officer stepped up to the doorway, coughed and stepped back. Finally, in a loud young voice he said, "When your name is called you will answer, gather your things, step out and go to my right, *Yasno*—clear?"

Sedecki didn't even look up.

Aleks held his hand in front of his mouth and nudged his friend with an elbow, "If your name's called, follow the man in front of you."

"No talking!" the officer squeaked.

The soldiers split into two groups. The lieutenant called off seventeen names. The eighteenth was Aleksandr Mikhailovich Leskov. Aleks patted Sedecki on the shoulder then stood up, donned on his cap and coat and left, whispering "Good luck" to both Sedecki and Viktor.

Three more names were called. The twenty-second and last name was "Sedecki."

The third time his name was called Viktor picked Sedecki up, helped him into his clothes, gave him his coat, whispered, "Good bye, my friend," in German and led him to the door.

Viktor said to the officer, "He doesn't understand Russian."

The lieutenant frowned suspiciously.

Out in the yard they were grouped in standard rows of five, with the two odd prisoners in the rear. The group of twenty-two was joined by men from other cells. Finally, five abreast, long columns of prisoners were formed.

Surrounded by soldiers the 185 prisoners, including 10 women, were led from the prison.

The blast of frigid air shocked Sedecki from his shell. He did not understand the shouts of the soldiers but he saw that everyone kept their hands behind their backs and their heads down, silent. Exiting the prison gate the columns turned south on the snow packed main street of Tayshet.

Sedecki glanced to either side as they marched. Wooden sidewalks were cleared of snow. There were stores displaying beautiful merchandise. NKVD men in uniform went in and out of a concrete building. That must be the officer' clubhouse. Aleks was right, NKVD personnel deserve the very finest—the bastards.

The columns came to a halt at the railroad tracks by the end of a train. Trying not to move his head, Sedecki glanced at a long string of black wooden boxcars.

As they crossed the tracks, turned and marched along the side of the train Sedecki looked down the main street of Old Tayshet. There were no sidewalks, just a smattering of small, ugly stores and single-story places. At the end of town were larger buildings. Beyond that and off to the side, he saw a massive complex of very high barbed-wire fences and watch-towers.

His group stopped near the middle of the train. They stood for a roll call and Sedecki watched long columns of prisoners coming from the barbed-wire camp. When the front of those columns reached the end of the train and turned towards his group prisoners were still coming out of the camp gate. There must be thousands.

The head of the train was pointing west. Whispers trickled

through the stretched out columns that it would be a long cold journey to the camps of the Siberian North—notorious camps from which
most would never return.

CHAPTER 5

Twenty-eight black freight cars were a stark contrast to the new fallen snow. Sandwiched near the middle of the rickety wooden cars was a coach for the NKVD soldiers. A baggage car next to it carried provisions of food and water.

When the last of the columns arrived the shipment totaled two thousand seven-hundred and eighty-five prisoners. Eighty-five women were put in the middle boxcar and one hundred men were crammed into each of the remaining twenty-seven cars.

Sedecki eyed a hole in the floor the size of a dinner plate as he and Aleks were entering the boxcar. At each end of the car on both sides were 4 x 8 inch slots with hinged covers. Any other light and air would filter in through the numerous cracks in the old freight car.

"This way," Aleks said, grabbing Sedecki's arm, "Up front."

"There's plenty of room in the rear," said Sedecki.

"We'll sit up here," Aleks replied, hurrying to claim a spot. "The air will be better here once we start moving. Any place from the toilet on back will smell God-awful before nightfall."

"Toilet?"

Aleks almost smiled when he rolled his eyes. "The hole in the floor, you don't see any door marked toilet do you?"

Sedecki made a face.

A box of dark bread was put in each car, along with two pails of *kipyatok*—hot water, and a dozen 8-ounce tin cans for dippers. The *zeks* were told to elect an elder for distribution.

"It doesn't take long for the water to get cold, does it," Sedecki remarked as he dipped a tin. "I wonder how it is for those guys back at the end."

"By the time they get hot water it will have ice on top," Aleks replied with a worried look. "We should not be shipped in these old cars in the winter. These are bad. Most are too far from the kitchen car to get anything before it turns cold. Like always, it is crazy."

The sliding doors slammed, locked and the train began to move west towards Moscow.

The train stopped twice each day and buckets of gruel were distributed—some kind of mashed barley, millet, or God-knows-what. Remembering Aleks' previous admonishment, he forced himself to eat.

"Well, well," Sedecki said when the *starosta* passed out pieces of fish. "It was cabbage soup the other day, fish today, maybe things are improving."

"Yeah, but the cabbage leaves were black, spoiled," Aleks commented. "And a few tins of water or soup a day is not enough."

Outside of Moscow the train turned due north towards Murmansk. The men closed the vents and huddled closer together. A day later the train passed the rail juncture that went west to St. Petersburg. As it continued on north the temperature dipped to three degrees below and turned colder by the hour.

The next day dawned like an omen. The train was nearing the Arctic Circle. "It's snowing," one man said, peering through one of the slits. "It shouldn't be snowing, it's too damned cold. It must be 20 below and the wind's picking up."

"Never too cold to snow in Russia," someone bellowed.

Suddenly, like turning on a faucet, the weather went wild. The wind became stronger, the snow heavier. The rapidly accelerating wind began screaming like an infuriated banshee, *Skeee, skeee, skeee,* driving the snow horizontally across the frozen tundra. It turned into a complete whiteout. The density and power of the ferocious storm obliterated all traces of light, changing daylight into complete and sudden darkness.

Skeee, skeee, skeee….

"My God," Sedecki raised his voice over the eerie noise, "what's happening?"

"It's a *purga*," Aleks answered apprehensively, "A sub-arctic blizzard. Nothing stands in its way, nothing." He shivered. "This could get bad."

Sedecki looked at him. "It could last awhile?"

"Pray that it doesn't, my friend. If we become stranded we will freeze to death, all of us."

"How long can it last?"

"A day, a night, a week, who knows?"

Sedecki listened to the uncertainty in some voices change to fear. The fierce storm drove the wind-chill to 50 degrees below zero. Moaning and grumbling surged through the car. Everyone bunched together for heat, for life.

"I'll bet those Goddamned guards aren't freezing," someone murmured through chattering teeth. "They're sitting next to a warm stove eating borsch and playing cards."

It wasn't long before the train began to slow against the relentless *purga*. The ear piercing *skeee, skeee, skeee* became terrifying. Slower and slower the locomotive chugged against the violent storm until finally it surrendered in a clanging standstill. Nothing could move in such a storm, nothing, unless the storm itself moved it.

"What do you think?" Sedecki said as the cars jerked to a stop.

"I think we may be stranded," was Aleks' understatement. They huddled together.

The intensity of the merciless whiteout continued as the hours passed. The screeching noise and darkness bewildered Sedecki. Time seemed to be an endless dark tunnel. He rubbed Aleks' arm as they huddled together.

"We haven't eaten," Aleks said. "If this continues and we don't get something, some guys aren't going to make it."

Sedecki rubbed Aleks more vigorously. "Maybe help's on the way."

As wretchedly cold as he was, Aleks smiled at the endless optimism of his new friend. It reminded him of his college days, of St. Petersburg and of old friends. He's so naïve, one of Sedecki's traits that he admired. He turned his head toward his friend. "There'll be no food or water until this is over. No one can get out in a *purga* like this. It would knock you down, blow you away—bury you." He repositioned his arms by his chest. His voice took on a lower octave. "Everyone had better pray that this lets up soon, very soon, otherwise we will all certainly die."

Aleks coughed, turned over and made Sedecki turn over. He huddled against his friend and began rubbing Sedecki's arms. "The skin is the largest organ of the human body. It is like an enormous radiator, and is subject to the same physical laws as those that govern an automobile's radiator. As exposure continues it calls rapidly on its reserves, the skin and the body must be protected." Aleks stopped and coughed then spoke closer to Sedecki's ear.

"The body will burn calories furiously in an effort to counteract heat loss. It will even cannibalize itself to do so. But it cannot escape the first law of thermo-dynamics very long. As a consequence, that is why death by hypothermia comes with such astonishing rapidity."— more coughing—"The body's first warning is usually pain followed by shivering and numbness and eventually disorientation. Then the body will initiate a very rapid and sequential shutdown of all but essential functions. Within a short time thereafter, it simply fails." Aleks went into a coughing jag.

"You seem to know a lot about it," Sedecki said over his shoulder.

"I did go to college, remember?"

The *purga* continued through the day, the night and into the next day, overwhelming numbed minds and bodies. Old-timers had passed the word to others: Continue to shake the comrade next to you, rub him. Don't go to sleep or you will die. But it was difficult to remain awake. Some men stood up, stomping their feet, rubbing their bodies—anything to circulate blood. Some yelled and screamed. Others huddled in groups, massaging each other, telling their comrade to stay awake. Some tried to create a pile for warmth. There was constant shifting and swearing.

Sedecki and Aleks spent most of the time trying to stay awake by talking. Aleks was teaching him rudimentary Russian, grinding out basics and having him repeat the words, trying to take their minds off the vicious cold—trying to stay alive.

Thirty-two hours of screeching wind and brutal cold was an eternity, even though no one could determine how long the blackout lasted. Movement among the men had subsided. Talking had long since trailed off into the wind. Some men no longer moaned.

Suddenly there was an unexpected jerk and a metallic clang.

Sedecki rose up on one elbow. His numbed mind started to clear. He began to realize that the *skeee, skeee, skeee* no longer assaulted his ears.

The wind had slowed. The snow almost stopped. As suddenly as it began the *purga's* assault had passed. Several men got slowly up. One man was at a slot and began to babble.

Sedecki shook Aleks, pulled him to a sitting position and continued shaking him until Aleks protested, coughing,

"What is he saying?" Sedecki demanded.

Aleks was blinking. "Snow drifts up on the sides of the cars," he translated into English.

Sedecki shakily got on his feet and finally got Aleks upright. They both began stomping, and rubbing their arms.

The man at the slot said, "We are stranded. The train is like a snow fence. We're on a curve and packed tight in solid drifts." He peered through the slot again. "It's got to be morning, but can't tell. It's dark."

"Sure, dummy," someone yelled, "we're beyond the Arctic Circle, you never see the sun in the winter."

The couplings clinked as the train jerked again. They sat down.

"He's trying to get us moving," Sedecki exclaimed.

"He'd better," Aleks said, "or we're done."

In the NKVD car the commander yelled in the radio. "Are you sure about how far we have to go?"

The engineer looked at his fireman and said, "How many times do I tell this bastard?" Then into the radio he said, "One hundred ten or twenty miles, major, can't be certain."

"Sonavabitch!" the major bellowed, more to himself than anyone. "I told them to give me cars with stoves. Now it's impossible to get food to the cars and I'm the goat."

A few deaths were acceptable, and he could care less, but this train was his responsibility. There is a limit as to the number of bodies Command would accept, *purga* or no *purga*. Finally he stopped ranting and clicked the radio. "Well, let's get moving!"

The engineer set his radio down and snapped at his fireman, "Damnit keep stoking!"

Again and again he tried to ply his train loose from the grip of the drifts. He brought the engine forward then reversed. He kept repeating the procedure.

Finally, with some leeway gained, he slowly walked the engine forward, wheels slipping and then grabbing, until at last the train was inching forward.

Sedecki and Aleks huddled together again. Aleks' condition alarmed Sedecki. "Are you all right?" he asked.

"I'm, I'm fine," Aleks weakly replied, coughing, "Just … just cold."

The train did not stop until it reached camp #30 just north of Kem, three and a half hours later. Blowing the whistle the engineer pulled onto a siding not far from the White Sea. When clear of the main line, he stopped.

It was four o'clock in the afternoon and dimly gray. Everyone in the cars were stamping their feet and yelling.

The clamor seemed the loudest as the deputy camp commander and his guards arrived. He saluted the major and tried to say something but the din was too loud. He turned and gave an order to one of his guards. The guard pointed his submachine gun in the air and triggered off twenty rapid-fire rounds.

Sedecki shuddered as if every round penetrated his body.

The cars became silent.

When the boxcar doors opened the prisoners began moving out. Sedecki and Aleks were among the last in their car. Near the door Sedecki stopped in quiet shock. At the middle of the car by the latrine hole were nine frozen bodies, completely nude. Their blue-white skin, covered with husky black frostbite blotches, was evidence of their painful death.

Dull, glazed eyes stared silently back at Sedecki.

Turning to the doorway he looked down to see guards pushing, shoving, and clubbing.

As prisoners jumped from the cars there were sharp sounds of brittle bones snapping. Some prisoners could not get up no matter how the guards threatened. Several shots ripped the air before the major screamed for the killing to stop.

Aleks and Sedecki's column of fives began slogging through the snow. It was some distance to the prison camp. The march was silent, arms behind and heads down.

As they approached the main gate a mummer rippled through the columns.

Then he saw it.

"Good God!" Sedecki whispered, wide-eyed.

Spread eagled and wired to the fence above the snow was the frozen body of a naked man. Below him was a crude sign.

Before Sedecki could ask, Aleks translated, "Last Escapee. All others shot."

Sedecki shook his head. "What kind of depraved place is this?"

After a long roll call they entered the camp, had a toilet break and were fed. By nine that evening they were assigned barracks. Bunks in most barracks were a premium. Men had to sleep on the floor.

Sedecki and Aleks felt lucky to find a bunk. They crawled in exhausted, still numb.

A short time later Sedecki was half awake, scratching. Then something fell on his face. He brushed it off and another fell on him, and another. Something was biting, eating him alive. He came fully awake and grabbed the edge of the bunk to swing out. His hand squashed something. He jumped out and stood, straining to see.

Aleks came out of his bunk.

"What is this?" Sedecki cried, flinging bugs off his face and neck and squashing others.

"Bedbugs," Aleks said, "the place is lousy with them."

CHAPTER 6

It penetrated his skull like a bolt of lightning when the maul hit the rail—the standard wake up call. Sedecki made an attempt to move but nothing happened. He was on the floor, on his stomach, head turned to the side. He could see activity nearby but he couldn't move. His eyes were glazed, staring. The mind cried for help but the body would not respond. Paralyzed!

"Get up, Sedecki, get up." Aleks cried, violently shaking his friend.

Cold, stiff, uncertain and with the help of Aleks he began to stir and finally got to his feet.

The stove had died to nothing. Sedecki was disoriented. "I', I'm okay," he said, unsteadily. "I thought I had frozen to death."

Once more the *starosta* slammed his maul on the steel rail.

Again Sedecki's brain exploded.

"All right, listen up," the *starosta* roared, issued the day's instructions then left.

Aleks turned to Sedecki. "He said we can go to the toilets with the rest of the men, but not to the kitchen. We'll be fed after the others leave for work." He held his friend by the shoulder and looked at him. "Are you all right?"

Sedecki appeared dazed. "We're going to work?"

"No we're not, that may be the problem," Aleks said. His brow furrowed. "In camp, you don't get free days. Something's going to happen."

Once the work gangs had cleared the zone and the gates closed, the new prisoners were marched to the mess hall. It looked like any other building except several stove pipes jutted from the roof. The kitchen was walled off with three waist-high small openings. The rest of the building contained long rows of narrow tables and benches. The exit was at the far end.

When Sedecki and Aleks got to the first window the food smelled too good to be true. They each took a bowl. At the second window their bowls were filled with what looked like porridge and at the last opening was a piece of fish. When they sat down a one-armed kitchen worker placed a large hunk of bread in front of them. Will wonders never cease?

Aleks pulled a short wooden spoon from his boot and stirred his soup. There were actually pieces of something solid other than the fish. Then he realized Sedecki was watching. "I'm sorry, my friend, I forget, you don't have a spoon. I'll lend you mine in a few minutes."

Sedecki smiled. "That's all right I can drink from the bowl and finger out the chunks of whatever." His smile widened. "What I can't eat I'll rub in my hair. I'll never waste another morsel of food."

Aleks appreciated his friend's sense of humor, but knew he was also serious.

Afterwards they lounged in the barracks, being called outside only for a period of exercise. The dinner meal at noon was even better and contained more fish. Improving all the time, Sedecki thought.

Meanwhile, the camp's normal work brigades toiled at their job sites. The gong that would end their ten hour work day would not sound until 5 PM. Then a march back to camp.

At four that afternoon the gong in the barracks pealed again. All of the new arrivals formed outside. They were led to the mess hall, told to eat quickly and get out. The working brigades would return to camp by six.

The supper offering was not as large as the noon meal, but was surprisingly substantial. Aleks and Sedecki cleaned their bowls and because of the rush decided to take half of their bread back to the barracks.

Upon returning to the barracks Sedecki sensed the pensive mood.

Aleks would talk only when he was ready. He was learning much about his friend, but he was having great trouble understanding the rudiments of this strange life of which he was now a part. He realized if he didn't have Aleks he would be lost in this nightmarish ordeal that had twists and turns and a new set of circumstances each day, each hour.

"Fatten the hog before you stick him," Aleks mumbled once they were alone.

"Eh?"

"I have never had food this good before, in prison or in the camps. I have never been left to laze around like this, except for an occasional day off—once or twice a month."

Sedecki tried to set his mind to his friend's thinking. "Aleks, maybe they're making up for all those that froze to death in the cars yesterday and the shape they found us in."

"No," Aleks shook his head. "No, that's not it. It doesn't work that way. Never has, never will." They stood near a stove and Aleks put his hand on Sedecki's shoulder as he spoke. "The system works only in one way. Stalin and his government created these camps for criminals and for the moral breakdown and psychological destruction of political prisoners—those who oppose him or his thinking—and for the opportunity to have free labor, forced labor. All of these camps and these prisons, their commanders and their staffs, the camp guards and the NKVD soldiers, they are instructed, programmed to do exactly that. They don't care if we live or die. They can replace us many times over in an instant. What matters to them is their own comfort and survival and to maintain and follow the doctrine Stalin has mandated. If they don't, if they mess up, they will be in here just like us before you can say Rasputin."

Sedecki frowned, his tone serious. "I hear what you are saying, but I have trouble fully understanding all of it. Is it like this all over Russia … these camps and prisons?"

"You have no—" Aleks stopped short and turned his head as a

rush of men entered the barracks.

At 10 PM—lights-out, Aleks and Sedecki settled down in the aisle close to the stove. It was quite different from the previous night. There was wood and coal.

The shrill sound of the gong at 5 AM shattered the silence and caused an immediate uproar from the permanent prisoners. "It's Sunday, our day of rest!"

Prisoners were supposed to have two Sundays a month for rest. Men in every camp always grumbled that they should have every Sunday off.

Aleks and Sedecki, stiff and cold, stood up slowly.

"Listen up!" The camp guard yelled. "Listen up. All prisoners who arrived the day before yesterday will fall out for roll call immediately. All other prisoners will remain in the barracks until further ordered!" He repeated the orders.

Aleks translated as he looked at Sedecki.

"*Skorei, skorei!*" the camp guard began yelling.

Aleks and Sedecki got up scratching old bites. As they headed for the door calls of "Good bye" and "Good luck" came from the men behind them.

Once outside NKVD soldiers replaced the camp guards. "Rows of fives—make fives."

It was cold and dark but searchlights on the birdhouses lit the compound with a blinding glow. An officer stood with papers in his hand.

Once the twelve new arrivals from their barracks were formed and the roll call completed the NCO in charge said, "You will go to the toilet. After that you will be taken to the kitchen and then reformed for another roll call. Move out!"

Aleks translated in Polish as quietly as he could.

"Quiet! No talking," a guard shouted as they marched towards the latrine.

Morning constitutionals completed, they were led to the mess hall. The breakfast meal was again better than Aleks expected. Sedecki did not agree. "It's better than what they gave us at Tayshet," he admitted. "But it's still slop."

Outside, the twelve men formed fives. Other men joined their group.

Aleks turned to his friend and softly said, "They're saying the camp hospital and a barracks floor are flooded with sick *zeks* from our train." He glanced around, "Hundreds of men and women with broken bones and frostbite. Burial details say there are hundreds of frozen bodies."

Two *zeks* got in line behind them and heard Aleks.

"We just got the word," one man said, "More than three-hundred men and some twenty women froze to death. About a hundred and eighty others have severe frostbite and are losing hands and feet."

"And a lot of those are dying," the other man added. "It's just as well. If you lose two limbs you can no longer work. You'll be shot."

When all men from their group were assembled and names checked they joined other rows of fives already formed. At the main gate they stood a roll call by dossier—name and picture. Then they were formed into three groups of forty men each. When it was again confirmed that all one-hundred and twenty prisoners were present the gate was opened, they were passed through and the officer in charge signed for his prisoner detail.

A non-com jumped on the rear of a vehicle and addressed the group.

"Listen up," he shouted. You are being moved from this camp. You will obey the commands of the guards at all times. They have been instructed to shoot without warning if anyone tries to escape. *Yasno?*"

"Yes," everyone except Sedecki cried in unison.

They were marched into the biting cold. It was 8 AM and dimly gray. Two trucks with head lamps turned off drove on each side. Guards with dogs straining at their tethers kept a vigil. A mile later they reached the railroad tracks. But there was no waiting train.

Mumbling could be heard in the columns. Guards called for quiet.

They crossed the tracks and continued east for another two miles before stopping at an embankment that dropped twenty feet down. Beyond it the snow disappeared into the gloomy darkness. An ominous sound emanated from the gloom.

Confusion and panic spread through the columns. The dogs became agitated and pulled against their harness.

The NKVD sergeant yelled for quiet.

Aleks and Sedecki were in the third file of the first group and could clearly see past the two rows in front. "It's the sea," Aleks said quietly. "It's the White Sea."

The sergeant gave a command and the trucks on each side of the columns turned on their headlamps.

On the dark frozen sea that stretched beyond them three large trucks and several small vehicles idled. These trucks also illuminated the area with headlights.

The columns were sent sliding down the bank onto the ice. Forty men were packed into each waiting truck. The trucks were covered with heavy tarpaulins.

Chains covered the dual wheels of each six by six. A driver and two armed guards were the only ones in the cab of each truck. Two smaller, enclosed vehicles, carrying guards and dogs followed the three trucks as they headed east into the darkness of the frozen White Sea.

Once the trucks began moving and the prisoners knew they were alone the conversation became rife. "What if we fall through the ice?" someone cried. "The ice is thick," another man answered. "The guards wouldn't be with us if there was a chance we'd drown."

That quieted some men.

"We're going to the edge, where the sea is open. Then they'll shoot us and toss us in," another voice of panic yelled and everyone became silent in thought.

"I thought salt water couldn't freeze, or couldn't freeze very thick," someone said.

"Must be a peasant from the Black Sea of Georgia," was the gruff response, and a ripple of laughter. "Don't you know where you are, peasant? This is the Arctic Circle. Everything freezes solid up here—including your *kipyatok* (hot water) and even your balls."

Aleks Leskov spoke up. "We're going to the Solovetsk Islands. There is no reason to panic."

There was silence for a moment then a voice asked, "Yeah, how do you know so much?"

"My friend and I saw the tracks of packed snow in front of the trucks," Aleks answered. "They have made this trip many times before. The Solovetsk Islands are directly east of us, the same direction which we are heading. That is where we have to be going." There was mumbling, so Aleks added, "We can be thankful they did not make us march across the ice all day."

"How far is it?" a man asked.

"I don't know, twenty, thirty, fifty miles," Aleks said.

Someone gave a low whistle.

An uneasy quiet came over the forty men. They settled down, listening to the truck's chains grinding on the ice, glad to be packed like sardines in the frigid twenty degrees below.

Traveling at a carefully slow pace the small convoy reached the island just before eleven o'clock. Darkness had given way to a weird sunless gray. The prisoners were off-loaded and marched up the short embankment to the main gate of the zone.

No different from any other camp or prison, the prisoners stared at the nineteen-foot high fences of barbed wire and birdhouses that encompassed the compound. Once inside the compound the commander of the camp came forward and gave a concise address:

"Welcome, convicts, to the great Solovetsk Islands. This is Multavo. We are located thirty-eight miles from the main island. This island is a mile and a half wide and almost two miles long. No one has ever escaped from Multavo. No one ever will. Anyone who attempts to escape will be shot without warning. You will obey our rules and you will obey all guards."

They were led to a bath house for another *sanobrabotka,* where all hair was removed. They stood with chattering teeth until their ragged clothes were treated and returned. Then they were taken in groups of twelve to cells located in two story buildings.

"So we are not going to a camp," Aleks remarked as they entered the building. "We will be in prison, until summer."

"What do you mean until summer, this isn't a camp?" Sedecki whispered.

After they entered the cell, Aleks answered, "It's a prison. When and if, you leave these islands you are shipped out. I mean you leave by ship to northern camps. They don't put you in the Solovetsk unless you are going to die or be shipped to the far north."

"I thought this was the far north," Sedecki protested.

"There are places further north, more extreme, much worse."

There were twelve men to a cell that was 10 by 20 feet with two sets of bunks set end to end along one wall. Each set was three tiers high. Each bunk was five feet wide, accommodating two men. There was a small window. Everything was wood—floors, walls, bunks, as well as the thick door. On the wall between the door and the first tier of bunks was a rectangular slot with a sliding flap through which food was passed.

"How about this one," Sedecki said climbing onto the top bunk on the end next to the window.

"Looks fine," Aleks replied, looking out the second floor window.

Sedecki turned to Aleks. "You really think they'll ship us somewhere else?"

"Of course, but shipments go to the far north only in the summer, when the ice has broken up. Ships have to navigate the Barents and Kara Seas. If they had room for us they would put us in some camp until summer and get some work out of us. It is obvious there is no room at the camps in Kem, just this prison. If we make it until summer, we will be shipped out."

One man began fooling with the small stove and already one man was urinating in the *parasha*. "Can't you wait?" someone yelled at him. "It will fill up soon enough. You should have pissed in the bathhouse."

A single light bulb was suspended in the center of the room, near the stove, where everyone was trying to warm their hands.

"Well, we've got mattresses," Sedecki said, patting the long sacks filled with straw, or maybe hay.

Aleks looked at the box beside the stove, half full of coal and pieces of wood. "We might even stay warm, if they let us have enough to keep it going."

Each two story building contained fifteen cells, seven downstairs and eight up, housing 180 prisoners. In front of the cells on each floor was a long hallway with an open wash area on one end. The first floor was different. A semi-kitchen was located at one end. Food brought from the main kitchen was reheated in the mini-kitchen. The latrine was outside.

The trucks went back to the mainland and returned with another load of one hundred and twenty prisoners. They repeated the journey several times a day for the next two days until a total of 920 prisoners had been transported.

This was a new part of the prison, constructed during the summer by the 1,780 convicts already here. Aleks and Sedecki's group of 920 filled the prison to its 2,700 prisoner capacity.

As the sunless days dragged on Sedecki began to feel somewhat comfortable in his new surroundings. He simply didn't know any better. He had no relative comparison.

The days were strange twilight zones. Four months of winter when the sun never rises and it would be four months in the summer when the sun never sets. Sedecki found it difficult to acclimate to this twenty-four hour phenomenon of no sun. But he was thoroughly fascinated with the northern lights. The continuous bombardment of charged solar particles traveled along the earth's magnetic lines of force in ever changing displays of brilliant color. For hours he'd watch the fascinating aurora borealis.

The striking of a heavy hammer on a rail was the clock by which all camps lived. The day in Multavo began at 6 AM, much later than the working camps.

"Toilet," was the first command after rising. Food was delivered at 7 AM, noon and 5 PM. Exercise was floor by floor, for thirty minutes each morning and afternoon in areas close to their building. Emptying the smelly *parasha* each morning was an alternating two-man detail.

Also, two men from each floor, accompanied by guards, would assist in bringing the food from the main kitchen to the mini-kitchens. Teams changed each day.

"This is great," Sedecki said one day, "to be outside, carrying food, doing something."

"We are lucky," Aleks replied, "we don't have to work and we don't have to put up with criminals in our barracks."

A frown crossed Sedecki's face. "What do you mean we're all criminals aren't we?"

"Sedecki, there are two types of prisoners, a political and a criminal. Politicals like you and I are those accused of crimes against the state: counter-revolutionary activities, espionage, political opposition, or anything that is contrary to Stalin and his government.

"Many of us are serving sentences for crimes we did not commit, or maybe we did. We are automatically convicted and sentenced by an NKVD Troika. People like us are no danger to society but, we represent the greatest threat imaginable to Stalin and his regime.

"Convicted criminals are just that, murderers, thieves, crooks, rapists, felons of the worst kind. They are a threat to all of society, including us—even while we are in prison. A hardened criminal will prey upon a political, steal from him, intimidate, beat him and even murder him. A political is easy—he usually does not fight back. Politicals who have tried are dead. Criminals band together. They are organized and dangerous. They run most camps."

Bewilderment showed in Sedecki's expression. "But when things like that happen what about the guards, the camp officials?"

Aleks made a wry face. "In most camps the guards are criminals from within that camp. Sometimes they are men who have served their time and have become "free men" but stay on as guards. Either way they are bad news. Multavo is different. It is a prison, like Tayshet. Guards here are NKVD soldiers."

Aleks kept his voice low. "There are many things you must learn. The vernacular and vulgarity of the camps you will learn. You must in order to survive. But the proper language, the flowing language of Russia I will teach you. The beautiful dialect of Belarus, my home, I will teach you." Aleks smiled, "I will make you a Belorussian, my friend."

The weather during February was more frigid than January. The snows were heavy. Aleks kept pounding the Russian language into Sedecki relentlessly. Sometimes he would answer Sedecki's questions in Russian, refusing to use English. It would drive Sedecki wild, but it caused him to think and learn. Even the other *zeks* in their cell began to speak to him more slowly, in more simple Russian terms to help him learn. They were older men and they liked the two young men. Besides, it was something to do and to pass time, almost like a game.

"You are doing very well," Aleks said one day as they carried large boxes of bread from the main kitchen to their building.

"You're a taskmaster."

Aleks laughed. "Well, I am the teacher. The Russian language is not that easy to master. You learn and adapt more easily because you already speak other languages. You are doing well, but you must do better. If you are out somewhere and a guard tells you to do something and you don't respond you could be shot. We could be separated when we leave here and you may be own your own."

"I know, Aleks, I know. I'm trying, and the books really help a lot."

"We're lucky. This is one of very few places that I have seen any books at all. Read and study every one they pass on to our cell. They do help."

Initially Aleks and Sedecki had their private talks when they could not be overheard by the guards, or other *zeks*. But gradually all of the men in their cell began to speak more openly about the system and their experiences without fear that one among them could be a provocateur.

The other men in the cell were aware of Sedecki's amnesia, more reason to offer help.

One day the shortest Russian of the group asked, "What can you remember about China?"

"China?" Sedecki answered.

"Your thick, quilted coat, it's a Chinese army coat. The collar area where the insignia was is not faded. Chinese wear such coats in the northern regions. So maybe you were in China, eh?"

Sedecki thought about that for many days but could remember nothing about China. So many times he wanted to pound his head to jog a memory. His attempts to remember were always the same: Flashes of a stone bridge over a small canal; patches of indeterminate scenery; narrow winding streets; dark gray stone buildings; houses with balconies, flower boxes and windows of lead and glass. All of this would flit quickly in and out of his mind. Schoolrooms, with slates, chalk and erasers and different kinds of little desks would blur in his mind's eye.

He saw words, many words, written on the blackboard. Polish words and German words. No English words. *Why? I speak English. How did I learn these languages? Why can't I picture my mother and father? Why can't I understand where I am from, what I have done, and how I got here?*

Images of young boys wearing short pants crossed his mind, some wearing leather shorts with halter-type suspenders, and a girl, a blonde haired girl danced across his mind. But they had no names. They were just children, young children in various modes of dress with vague, imperceptible faces.

One afternoon early in March, while walking in the exercise area, Sedecki said, "So these islands are where your uncle was, where all of those horror stories took place."

"Yes, my friend," he softly replied. "You are very naïve, Sedecki. Wait, do not take offense listen to me. Naïve only because you can not remember anything, thus you cannot associate. You cannot compare any of this to reality."

"I know," Sedecki countered. "I understand, but it just seems that some things are too outrageous to believe."

"Believe it, my friend, believe it." Aleks began to relate things he could never forget, stories embedded in his mind like concrete. Stories of his uncle's years in the Gulags and some of his own Gulag experiences—and the painful loss of his entire family.

"My father graduated from the Frunge Military Academy with honors in 1925 and received his commission. He made a career of the army, became a colonel and was to be promoted to General when he was killed early in the war. He was a great patriot. But he was not a fanatic like uncle Grigory.

"Uncle Grigory was younger than my father. Father persuaded Grigory to join the army. He did but soon tired of it. He got out as a captain. He became a very successful trader of imports and exports between our country, Poland and Germany. Our home was in Brest, a railhead town in Belarus, on the Polish border. Uncle Grigory also mingled in high circles. He met and married the beautiful Polish Countess, Zofia Szorenia Stodenowski.

"She had a sumptuous home outside of Warsaw. When they married in 1935 they bought a large mansion in St. Petersburg. Uncle Grigory was such a communist zealot that he and Aunt Zora used to argue about it. Then suddenly Uncle Grigory was tossed into the Gulags. When the Germans invaded, my mother and I were visiting Aunt Zora in St. Petersburg. We stayed there."

Sedecki didn't understand. "If your uncle was such a good communist how'd he wind up in the Gulags?"

"Uncle Grigory was considered brilliant within the party. My father tried to tone him down, but uncle Grigory had a strong will. In 1936 our most glorious leader, Stalin, began his great purge. Staunch party supporters who disagreed with Stalin, and some who didn't, were arrested and thrown in jail. Josif Stalin purged not only the country and his enemies but those in his own party. It was madness. Uncle Grigory was one of the unlucky ones."

"What did they charge him with?"

"Because he was in the import-export business they claimed that he said German and Polish products were superior to Russia's. The charges were totally false but you see, it doesn't matter."

Sedecki shook his head.

"Tens of thousands at first, then hundreds of thousands of false arrests were made. They created camps and prisons in the Siberian north and other areas where there was no industry or activity, nothing. They erected the barbed wire and *zeks* lived in tents until they could build barracks. They put them to work in whatever that area could produce: mining, timber cutting, farming, factories, making bricks, you name it. The numbers turned into millions."

"Millions?"

Aleks nodded, "Millions. Uncle Grigory was among the first to be falsely convicted and sent to the Solovetsk Islands."

"Where we are now?" Sedecki exclaimed.

"Yes, but some distance from our island of Multavo. He later told of the atrocities that were epidemic here in this archipelago. Someday I will tell you."

They walked with their hands behind their back. The air was sharp, an invigorating change from the closeness of the cell. Thankfully, talking was not forbidden in Multavo.

Aleks went on. "The German invasion was at first uncontrollable. My father was killed. Russia needed every man. Uncle Grigory was released from the Gulags and put back in the army as a captain. His unit came down to St Petersburg in July of 41. He told me the Gulag stories. Then the bombardment began and Uncle Grigory was also killed.

"The siege of St. Petersburg began in early September of 41 and lasted more than two years—900 God-awful days. My mother and brother were both killed at the same time in a bombardment during December of 1941. When it was over in January of 44 only Aunt Zora and I survived. It's said a million and a half Russians died. More than six hundred and fifty thousand civilians were in that number. Many died of starvation, disease or froze to death. I saw it. It was horrible. I was only twelve. I will never forget those numbers or those days."

Aleks found it somewhat difficult, explaining such facts to someone who had no comprehension of war or of the tragedy and scope of what he was trying to relate. But he found it refreshing to talk to someone with such an unaffected mind. Tears welled in his eyes but he did not cry.

"I am sorry, Aleks," Sedecki said, shaking his head, "terribly sorry, my friend, for the loss of your family."

"It was long ago," Aleks shook off the personal memories and continued. "You don't know the history, the facts, but before, during and after the war, *zeks* built most of the railroads in Russia while living in camps that only had tents."

Sedecki glanced sideways at him.

"That's right, my friend, *zeks*, like you and I, millions of us. In the beginning the camps were for criminals. But Stalin soon discovered prisoners could produce while in prison in what became known as labor camps. Then it escalated into a way to imprison and do away with not just criminals but dissenters, those who disagreed or challenged Stalin—hard core communists or not. He not only got rid of the old party leadership and socialism, he found a way to obtain cheap labor at the same time. It is penal servitude—hard labor, which you and I will do.

"When they want engineers to build the railroads, a canal or do anything, Stalin has the NKVD arrest however many of them it takes. Just whisk them off the streets, boom, you're gone. Whatever the project requires, plant managers, agronomists, geologists, engineers, technicians, laborers, even doctors. If Stalin needs them the NKVD people go out and arrest them. Beria's NKVD is much worse than the German Gestapo ever thought of being.

"The word is there are twenty million of us in the Gulags right now and at all times—twenty million! Most Russian citizens do not believe that, they don't know. Thousands die, or are killed every day and they are replaced. So figure that out."

Sedecki pulled up the edges of his collar and his face took on an incredulous frown.

"How can they get away with it?"

"Power, control and terror, Stalin and Beria's NKVD wield it with ruthless abandon. Like you, Sedecki, you were convicted and sentenced and you don't know what you did. A closed Troika convicts and sentences you. No lawyer, no jury. They say there is an appeal, but that's a laugh, appeals are denied. It's over and done. There is no justice."

Sedecki pursed his lips and considered what Aleks said.

"Form fives!" was the gruff command.

The exercise period was over.

In March Aleks and Sedecki were struggling through falling snow with loads of wood for their building when the guards produced a coil of rope, tied it to the stanchion by the entryway and told them to pull the rope to the next building.

"*Purga*," Aleks said.

"What?"

"There must be a *purga* coming. They string ropes from building to building to keep anyone from getting lost in a snowstorm."

They talked as they played out the rope.

"If we should ever part do not be so naïve my friend," Aleks said, "I realize your amnesia makes everything a surprise to you. But this is the Gulags. You are in the system and you will not be getting out any time soon. You must be careful, always on guard."

Sedecki grimaced, as they reached the building and secured the rope. "Damn, I feel like a lost kid. It's just that everything is so, so unbelievable."

"Sedecki, my friend, I—"

Aleks stopped in mid-sentence as guards came out of the kitchen and gave them another roll of rope. "Take this to the guard barracks," the tall one pointed. "Secure it then follow the line back here immediately. We will wait for you. Go!"

When they reached the guard barracks two soldiers watched them secure the rope.

"Stop!" one NKVD guard commanded as they started to return. He pointed to Aleks and waved his hand. "You go back."

Then he looked at Sedecki and motioned him forward. "You stay. Come here."

"We were told—"

The guard cut Aleks off. "Never mind, shut up. I tell you what to do. GO."

The other guard squinted and Aleks reluctantly retreated.

When Aleks arrived at the kitchen alone the guards there were immediately alert. He explained that Sedecki was detained.

"We will check." One said, cranking a field phone.

Sedecki was taken into a barracks that was very warm. No rationing of coal here. He saw single bunks with footlockers and coat hooks. There were two potbelly stoves producing plenty of heat. The barracks was divided near the center by a three-quarter partition.

Led past the partition Sedecki found himself in a recreation room with a round poker table, chairs and two picnic-type tables. Shelves of books lined the wall by the window. The opposite wall held posters and pin-up pictures of women.

The guards removed their coats. One disappeared.

"Take off your coat," the other guard said. When Sedecki didn't respond he spoke in English, "No speak Russian? Take off coat."

Sedecki welcomed the opportunity.

The other guard returned with glasses of tea and a bottle of vodka. He set everything on the table then poured vodka in each glass. The other guard took off his shirt.

"Drink, get warm," he said, handing Sedecki a glass of the hot, vodka laced tea.

Sedecki watched the smaller guard pick up a glass, take a gulp, set it down and begin taking off his short jacket and shirt. He was surprised when that guard also spoke in broken English. "Speak Russian no good?"

"Ah ..." Sedecki hesitated, unsure which language to use, "I'm learning," he finally answered the smiling faces.

The taller guard poured a little more tea and a lot more vodka.

"You work ... guard barracks?" short-one asked in halting English, pointing down. Then he spread his arms and smiled, "Warm, food good, tobacco, hard work no ... life good, sleep here, guard barracks. Drink, drink tea."

Sedecki frowned. He didn't trust the smiling faces. He raised the glass to his mouth and held it there a moment. He took a sip as he eyed the guards, now sitting in their undershirts. Sedecki was sweaty also. The barracks was too warm. Why have they picked me, he wondered? *Be an orderly in this guard barracks, for you slobs? Huh uh, not me.* Would be easy, no doubt, always warm, plenty of food, NKVD really eat well, many other perks. Just sweep the floor and clean boots. No. Screw you, you bastards.

Over the rim of his glass he studied the smirking faces, flush with the warmth of hot tea and vodka. But what happens if I refuse? These slobs look like they could become unhappy, and if there's two of them there must be more. Damn.

"I will think about it," Sedecki said, and very slowly set his glass down.

The smile disappeared from the face of Shorty. He stood up, looking at his comrade, and then at Sedecki. He held his right arm up, flexing his bicep, pointing to it with his other hand. "Good muscle, you?" he asked, smiling. "Can work, yes?"

"Yes, but—"

"Stand up. Up, up!" he bellowed in English, "Take off shirt."

Unsure of what to do Sedecki complied as the guard moved closer to him.

"Undershirt," Shorty said in Russian, then in English, "Off."

Sedecki stood there, frowning, and started to say something.

Shorty yelled, "Off, off, see muscle."

Sedecki stood looking at the man until the taller guard, sitting on the other table edge, stood up and menacingly said, "*Skorei!*"

Sedecki peeled off his undershirt. The smaller guard covered Sedecki's right bicep with both his hands. "Good, good," he smiled.

He led Sedecki to the other table. The taller guard now stood at the far end.

Shorty looked at Sedecki's pectorals. "Good," he repeated, "muscle, good." He smiled and ran his fingers through the hair on Sedecki's chest.

Sedecki flinched.

"Stand!" the tall one shouted, "Turn. Table … turn!"

Slowly, Sedecki turned facing the table's far end and stared at the smiling face of the tall guard. Shorty stepped back a few paces and firmly commanded, "Take off pants."

Sedecki's heart skipped a beat. He turned to look back at short-one.

The taller man leaned over the far edge of the table, withdrew his sidearm and pointed it Sedecki. "Take off your pants," he said in guttural Russian.

Sedecki was trapped. His mind whirled. He wondered if he would live or die right here.

"*Skorei!*" tall-man hissed.

Tall-man and the pistol were out of his reach, even if he lunged. If he went for the short-one he would be dead before he made the turn. Slowly he untied the twine around his pants and pressed his legs against the end of the table.

"Off, off!" Tall-man said pushing the pistol a little closer.

Sedecki leaned away from the table. His pants fell to his ankles.

"Underpants," Shorty said in Russian.

Tall-man in front waved the gun up and down, his smile becoming uglier.

Sedecki dropped his shorts and stood there naked.

There was a thud behind him and he turned his head enough to see Shorty had tossed his munitions belt and holstered pistol on the floor, and stand there with his pants down around his ankles.

"Bend down, put your arms on the table," Tall-man said slowly in Russian.

Sedecki did not move.

"Forward, on the table," Tall-man hissed, "or I will shoot you right now like a dog trying to escape."

Sedecki didn't identify every seething Russian word but knew he was about to be shot.

Click … Click.

The metallic sound of the pistol being cocked was electrifying.

Tall-man leaned forward, put his pistol closer to Sedecki and motioned him downward with his other hand.

Sedecki slowly bent forward with his hands on the table.

Tall-man gestured, further, further forward.

Sedecki stretched his arms out until his chin touched the table. He was in a crouch, bent at the knees. The edge of the table was wedged in the top of his groin.

Tall-man leaned forward, grasped Sedecki's right wrist and pulled it to the table's edge.

Sedecki's eyes strained upwards to see the pistol within a foot of his forehead. He closed his eyes then slowly opened them and concentrated on taking slow easy breaths. With the pistol at his head he had no choice but to hold still and wait for what he knew was coming. He heard the shuffling feet of Shorty behind him. He could sense the close presence of the man.

Shorty put a hand on Sedecki's hip.

Sedecki flinched.

Tall-man with the pistol sniggered.

Arms outstretched, chin on the table, head slightly turned, Sedecki read Tall-man's giggling thoughts. *You think you're next and you can't wait.*

Laugh on bastard, I'll die before you ever dick me.

With a greasy hand Shorty again slapped his young prey on the butt. Sedecki flinched once more and took a deep breath.

When Shorty's erection touched his cheeks Sedecki let out a blood-curling scream of faked a penetration. Using his right hand on the table's edge as a fulcrum his left hand shot up with lightening speed, grabbed Tall-man's wrist, twisted it away and down and pulled him forward on the table. If Tall-man squeezed the trigger he would shoot his partner. In the same instant Sedecki jerked his right wrist free and smashed the heel of his hand in the man's face. Tall-man screamed and his pistol clattered on the floor. Blood gushed from his torn nose.

Sedecki released Tall-man's wrist and spun around swinging a bloody, knife-like right hand for Shorty's neck. It glanced off the Shorty's shoulder and they collided. Sedecki's forward momentum and the pants about their ankles caused both of them to hit the floor in a sprawling mixture of naked arms and legs.

The force of Sedecki's drive carried him on top of the would-be rapist. He swung a haymaker at the man's face and they both rolled, bringing short-man on top. Unwittingly, it saved Sedecki's life—temporarily.

Shorty being on top prevented his partner from firing. But Sedecki's stay of execution was short lived.

His fingers closed around the little man's throat and he stared up to see Tall-man hovered above them, blood spewing from the hand at his nose and the other hand clutching his pistol.

Tall-man bent down slowly, pushing his weapon past Shorty's head with his trigger finger about to make Sedecki's next breath his last.

Sedecki relaxed his grip on short-man's throat, stared at the tall man and waited for him to squeeze the trigger.

The boom pierced Sedecki's brain with such a shattering impact that his entire body constricted. His eyes bulged. He knew his head had been blown open like a shattered melon, yet in absolute bewilderment he could still see the bleeding tall-man and the gun.

The reverberating noise sounded again. Sedecki finally realized it was an exceptionally loud, gruff command, coming from the other end of the room. His eyes never left the pistol but he could hear and feel the elephant-size vibrations of the two men tromping towards them.

His would-be rapist collapsed at his side gagging then scrambled to get up and gather his shorts and trousers. Tall-man with the pistol straightened up.

The NKVD sergeant of the guard stomped heavily towards them with a subordinate at his side. He stood over Sedecki's naked body looking for a wound to go with all of the blood that covered his chest.

"What happened?" the sergeant demanded, looking at his two guards.

"He attacked me," the smaller guard exclaimed. "He was choking me to death."

"He attacked you with your pants down—while he was naked?" The sergeant screamed. "You blundering, fucking idiot! I've had about enough of your deviate escapades. You can't even accomplish them without fucking up."

He turned to Sedecki, decided he was not wounded, motioned to the table and said, "Get up and sit down."

Sedecki rose, pulled up his shorts and pants and sat down on the table bench, eyeing the taller guard who had holstered his pistol.

"Clean this *zek* up," the sergeant told his subordinate. The guard snickered and hustled to the kitchen for a rag and a pan of water.

The sergeant glared at the tall guard, "Tell me what happened,"

The tall guard held his bleeding nose, looking down.

"The truth damnit, quickly."

"Aah," tall-man mumbled, "Anatoli was just having some fun—"

"Idiots." he cut him off. "A *purga's* coming, we have much work to do, and you two can't keep your cock in your pants."

Shorty opened his mouth to speak.

"Shut up!" the sergeant roared. "Put your shirt on."

The subordinate, Yuri, returned with a rag and water.

"Get this *zek* cleaned then take him to the punishment cell," he ordered. "He gets five days. After that report directly back to me."

He looked at his two soldiers, "If either of you fuck up one more time, I'll have *your* ass in a punishment cell and it won't be for just five days."

The metal door banged shut. Sedecki crouched in total darkness, unable to fully stand or turn. He squatted, partially sideways on his knees. The cell was a little wider than his shoulders. It was not tall enough for him to stand up and not long enough for him to lie down.

From the end of his thumb to the tip of his index finger his span was just over ten inches. He knew he would be here awhile. He began to measure his cell.

The snow continued after Alex returned to the barracks without Sedecki. All of those in his cell were discussing their missing friend's plight when the *purga* began.

Skeee, skeee, skeee, the powerful wind tore at the building, trying to drive snow into the wood like nails.

Aleks' thoughts of Sedecki almost blotted out the sound of the screaming violence.

Of the ten other men in Aleks' cell, one was a Romanian, one from Latvia and the rest were from various parts of Russia. All feared the worst for Sedecki. His non-presence acted as a lynchpin of camaraderie. Guessing what fate Sedecki has met they recalled the fate of other men. In this common mood they began to talk openly.

The Russian named Arkady, a communist party functionary in his Ukrainian home town, verified some of the stories that were being told about the nearby islands.

"My friend was sent to Kem in 1939 and I can tell you that the killings in these Solovetsk Islands are true. His brigade worked on the docks in the summer off-loading barges of bricks, wood, coal, livestock, hay, fish and other things. The story about monks and nuns is true.

"He told me about the monks and several hundred nuns imprisoned in the monastery after the NKVD took it over. The nuns were sent from the main island to Mukselya and placed in punishment cells. They refused to work for what they called the 'Antichrist.'

"One day they were led into the yard and lined up. They knelt in prayer. The camp commander with a pistol asked one nun, 'will you work?' When she replied, 'I will not work for the Antichrist,' he pulled the trigger.

"All of the nuns began to pray loudly as he stepped to the next woman, asked the same question and was given the same answer. He shot that sister. He continued shooting and when his pistol was empty he walked over to a squad of soldiers and once more shouted his question to the remaining nuns. When they did nothing but continue to pray he gave the command to fire.

"This man told me that he and all of the other *zeks* had been lined up on the opposite side of the yard and were required to watch as all of the sisters were executed. He was also part of the detail that dug the trenches and buried them."

The cell was very quiet after Arkady finished his story.

Later that evening the Romanian, who had not been very talkative, asked, "Where is this island of Mukselya?"

To everyone's surprise, Aleks answered, "The other side of the main island, about forty miles or more from here. There are several other islands, including Sekirnaya Gora."

All eyes turned to Aleks, the quiet man who had been deep in thought.

"You are too young to know of such things," one man admonished.

"I was too young," Aleks admitted.

The mind-altering skeee, skeee, skeee and Sedecki's dilemma and the openness of the others pushed Aleks into the discussion.

"My uncle was imprisoned on Mukselya in 1937. The camp warden was a monster. My uncle told me of the many barbaric incidents: The piles of dead bodies on the stairs of the monastery; the inhuman punishment cells; the cries of pain that could be heard every night; and the hundreds of nuns that were murdered. Some of it he saw, some he heard from those who were witnesses. He told of those sent to Sekirnaya Gora, never to come back, and of things your mind would not believe."

"How did he tell you of these things," one man asked facetiously, "you could visit him?"

"No. He served four years, was released in 1941, put back in the army and was killed during the bombardment of St. Petersburg. I was in St. Petersburg with him, my mother, my brother and my aunt."

"You mean you were in Leningrad during the siege?" the Rumanian said.

"St. Petersburg," Aleks said, "It's St. Petersburg, not Leningrad." He paused and stared through the window.

"Yes, I was a boy but I was there during the entire time. I was given a rifle but I never fired it. My uncle said *zeks* were arriving so fast at these islands there was no place to put them. Thousands were sent straight to Sekirnaya Gora, shot and tossed into the sea. No one ever came back from there."

There were no more questions. With the screaming of the ferocious *purga* and their roiling thoughts no one rested that night.

On the fourth day the relentless *purga* vented its last ounce of fury, ending as quickly as it began.

Just before noon of the sixth day the cell door swung open and Sedecki walked in.

The men came bounding out of their bunks. He was dirty, pale, looked terrible. He told them of the solitary confinement. Finally, unable to evade the question of why, he told them of the attempted rape.

"I saw a guard yesterday with a bandage covering his nose," the bald-headed Russian blurted. "Good, good."

"They're getting soft here," the Romanian said. "Anywhere else the sergeant would have stood there and watched, or got in the action. You are a lucky man, Sedecki my friend."

The days continued to lengthen and became more bearable and lighter as spring approached. Sedecki, under constant pressure from his determined tutor and the prompting of his cellmates continued to make strides in his ability to read, speak and understand the Russian language.

"You are doing exceptionally well, my friend," Aleks told him. "You must have been a linguistic scholar in college."

Sedecki gave him a blank expression, trying to recall his school days.

"I am sorry, my friend, if I push too hard," Aleks put both hands on Sedecki's shoulders and looked directly into his eyes. "You are like the brother I once had. You'll need every bit of what I can teach you and then some before you leave here."

"And you're sure we will be leaving here?"

"We will all be leaving here. Not everyone to the same destination perhaps, but all of us will be leaving."

The months rolled by. On the morning of 22 August 1952 the Romanian returned to the room from a kitchen detail. "Well, my friends, our little vacation is over. This prison has been heaven compared to where I had been. Now it's back to the Gulags we all know.

"A shipment is coming. If we should all go different ways let me say now, it has been a pleasure to have met you, my friends, every one of you."

CHAPTER 7

It was anchored in a deep part of the White Sea. Prisoners from Multavo and other islands were being ferried to the ship on motor barges.

Looking back at Multavo from the barge, Sedecki said, "That is beautiful."

They passed another. "Look at this one, it looks like a floating oasis."

"Russia is a beautiful country Sedecki, in winter or summer," Aleks said. "Take a good look. This may be the last beauty you'll see for some time. From here on north nothing grows, just snow and frozen tundra."

Sedecki was quiet until they approached the ship.

He read the large letters, "What's S.L.O.N?"

"*Solvetsky Lager Osoboyp Naznacheniya*—Solovetsk Islands Special Camps," Aleks said, grabbing Sedecki's arm as the barge bumped the ship.

They moored alongside an open hatch. The grime and filth on the rusty plates was disquieting. It was an old bucket of iron in ill repair.

"Crummy and stinking old tub, isn't it," Sedecki said.

"It looks like an old freighter that's been converted to a *zek* transport," Aleks replied as they were herded into the ship and to their deck.

A five story wooden structure had been built in the hull with bunks stacked close together on each level. Half-keg *parashas* were placed at the end of various rows. Two open stairwells in the hatch amidships connected each level to the open deck on top.

The bunks rapidly filled. Men were crowding in the aisle. Irritated soldiers with batons smacked those who would not stay by their assigned bunks.

"If the other levels are like this one," Aleks said, "I'd say there are five-thousand of us."

"Maybe more," Sedecki replied, "we're like sardines."

"If this thing ever starts to sink," Aleks added, "we wouldn't stand a chance."

Sedecki tried not to visualize that.

It was almost evening before the ship pulled anchor. Like everyone else, Aleks and Sedecki had already shed their coats. "Well, at least it's warm down here," Aleks said.

"The heat is great," Sedecki answered, "But this tub stinks almost as bad as Tayshet."

"Wait till we get going," The man next to Sedecki said in Russian, "and *parashas* spill. You will love this trip."

Pails of water were brought to each row. Sedecki and Aleks broke out the pieces of fish and zwieback they had been given on the barge. They savored every crumb, knowing that this second meal was the last of the day.

"Two pails of water per row, three times a day, that's not enough," Aleks said.

A *starosta* was chosen for each area.

The next morning at first latrine call everyone rushed to the staircase. It was one-way traffic up and one-way down on the other side of the hatch.

It took Sedecki and Aleks almost an hour reach the top. Many prisoners got in line just to get a breath of fresh air.

"God," Sedecki gasped as they moved. "I don't know if I can stand much more of this stench."

"Hang on," Aleks smiled, "your lungs will acclimate."

The smell of human misery was compounded by men who were

seasick. All of this was magnified in the stairwells that tunneled everything upward.

"I can think of no worse torture than being on this ship in these conditions," Sedecki said, "It must have been planned by a madman."

"I know," Aleks answered. "No convict, even criminals, should be subjected to this kind of debasement. It's overwhelming." He turned to look at his friend. "I am proud of you."

"Proud?"

"Yes, you have been speaking only Russian since we left the island and speaking very well."

On top deck Sedecki breathed deeply and looked around.

Positioned between the bow and the superstructure at the rear of the ship were four large hatches. The first hatch near the bow and the fourth hatch at the base of the superstructure were covered with a raised wooden platform. NKVD armed guards stood inside the platform railings. The second and third hatches in the middle were open. They had come up through the second hatch and were waiting to use the latrine. Aleks pointed to the Icebreaker in the far distance.

"Stay in line," The guard with the baton cracked, "Wait for your turn. Move off the toilet as soon as you're done. No loitering!"

The line from the hatch moved back along the port side.

"Well," Aleks said, "the line is long enough that we'll get a little more fresh air."

The column of men moved on and Sedecki couldn't believe it when he saw the latrine. "I thought the latrine would be inside," he whispered.

"The guards and crew have inside toilets," Aleks groused, "Our 'inside toilets' are the *parashas*."

Sedecki stared. Where the port rail met the superstructure a latrine had been built out over the side. It would allow thirty men at a time to sit. Three steps led up to a welded, metal frame that extended over the side. Boards were spaced just wide enough apart to allow a man to sit and have a body function. The four-foot backing had strands of barbed wire above and on each end. At the gunwale was a place where the *parashas* could be emptied.

"Well," Sedecki jokingly whispered, "at least you can't fall overboard."

"Or escape," Aleks quipped.

"Who'd want to escape into this sea of ice?"

"You would be surprised. Now be quiet."

It was the fifth day before they saw a corpse being tossed overboard.

"Only one today," the big man in line behind them said. Then he added in a matter of fact tone, "two yesterday."

After many long days and nights sailing the Barents and Kara Seas the ship navigated down the delta of Siberia's great Yenisey River.

It was summertime and three o'clock in the morning, yet it was so light Sedecki thought it could be noon.

Disembarking, Sedecki and Aleks pulled their coat collars up.

"It's cold," Sedecki said and studied the horizon across the river. He saw nothing but a flat, endless expanse of snow and small weather-beaten houses that rose like little black bumps along the opposite shoreline.

"My God, where are we?" Sedecki asked.

"Dudinka, I heard someone say."

"Christ, Aleks, it's the middle of summer and nothing but snow."

"I know," Aleks hunched his shoulders. "This is as far north as you can get. The next thing north of us is the polar ice-cap."

They were loaded into a train that ran the narrow gauge railroad from Dudinka to Norilsk.

Riding in an open gondola Sedecki watched the flat landscape of the Yenisey delta change to rolling terrain then small mountains. He was entranced. Not a tree, a bush, or an animal could be seen, nothing but a vast wilderness of snow. It held a certain reverence, perhaps a silent death call. "It's so beautiful, so white and eerie," he said, "like some invisible spider is hiding out there, just waiting for a foolish fly to violate his pristine surface."

Aleks smiled. His friend was like a schoolboy.

Sedecki's enchanted state of mind quickly turned to reality when the train stopped at Norilsk, the northern-most populated town in the world. "This place is uglier than Tayshet," he said.

The civilian part of town set on the south side of the tracks. Streets packed with grimy snow and rutted. Low unpainted wooden buildings looked like black globs of coal. Beyond the town Sedecki saw factories, smokestacks, warehouses and a conglomeration of other buildings.

"Metallurgy plants and coke factories," a round-faced prisoner said, as if anticipating Sedecki's question. Then he smiled. "This town is only fifteen or eighteen years old yet they say it has a graveyard bigger than all of those in the Ukraine."

"There are a lot of camp sections here," Aleks said. "Norilsk is supposed to be the largest single Gulag in Russia."

"And that doesn't include the townspeople," the stranger said.

"People in their right mind want to live here?" Sedecki asked.

A small bald headed man in his forties said, "Some came here hoping to strike it rich when the mines were discovered, only to find that the government lured them here with lies. Many left when they had the chance, that first summer. There are only two ways out, by plane or by boat down the Yenisey in the summer, if there is a boat. Quite a few living here now are free-men, ex-prisoners."

"Free men?"

Baldy smiled, "Many of those who survive and are finally released from the Gulags stay in the towns near the camps. They are called freemen, but they're not really free—you never are. They tell you that when you are 'released,' but then they tell you where you are going to live, as a free man." He laughed. "Free, ha. You live in exile somewhere in Siberia. They keep an eye on you. Some are given jobs and kept here in Norilsk."

"He's right," Aleks injected. "I was told the population of Norilsk is about 300,000."

"Probably is now," the little man answered. "Before the war when my friend was here it was less than thirty thousand."

They were offloaded on the north side of the train. Main Street, in the original part of town, changed drastically on the north side of the tracks. This side had raised board sidewalks cleared of snow. Many elegant shops lined the streets. Houses and other structures spread out behind them. Off to one side was a huge complex of three-story concrete buildings.

"That's where the elite NKVD bloodsuckers live," the man standing next to Sedecki said as they formed fives and the train pulled away.

Glancing back at the south side Sedecki said, "It's like night and day."

"There will be no talking and all heads down" the officer said.

The march went up the main street past the nice looking shops and concrete buildings and turned east at the far edge of town towards the foothills of the Taymyr Mountains.

It was two in the afternoon when they stopped. In any direction you looked there was nothing but a high barbed wire fence with watchtowers. Inside was nothing but barracks—the enormous compounds of the Norilsk Minlag, the most notorious mining camp in the Siberian Gulags.

There were 135,000 prisoners, more or less in that part of the compound Aleks and Sedecki were assigned. There was another roll call, a check against their dossiers and pictures. Once cleared, they were marched to section ten.

"These barracks seem newer than the others," Sedecki whispered.

"Don't talk," Aleks murmured

They stopped at a huge processing bathhouse for another *sano-brabotka*. They were stripped completely and their clothes tossed on one huge pile. All hair was shaved off. They were sprayed with a disinfectant and processed through showers of almost lukewarm water.

Naked, they funneled down a hallway. Sedecki gave his name. The guard pulled a dossier, looked at the picture and called loudly to the other guards, "Sedecki, Stanislaus."

"Number seven nine one," the man up ahead yelled.

N-791 was marked on the roster after Sedecki's name.

"*Skorei, shorei,* faster," The guard on the right was calling and motioning. Sedecki hurried ahead. On each side of the room there were stacks of clothes, two sizes. Sedecki held out his arms and was given a pile of clothing. The number N-791 was painted on the knees of the pants, the back of the jacket and coat, and on the front of the cap. No belts or buttons. On top of the stack was two pieces of cord to use as belts, plus a rag. He was told to move forward and dress.

Supper hour was over but they were taken to one of the mess halls and hurriedly fed.

Slurping his soup in extra loud fashion, Sedecki said, "I can see that this is going to be a real vacation."

Aleks did not share his light-hearted banter. "It will be no picnic. Always be careful, watch yourself and don't talk."

"You're in a good mood, mister seven-ninety-nine," Sedecki answered. "I like your number, N-799."

Stopping at a barracks on the left, Sedecki and Aleks were the last of six men assigned to barracks 5. Sedecki was surprised to find the interior looked like new wood. He surveyed the barracks as the others scrambled to claim a vacant bunk. He judged the building to be twenty-two or four feet wide with open rafters.

The other four men quickly claimed a bunk. Those in the barracks began pumping questions at the new arrivals. Aleks and Sedecki shrugged them off as they tried to find an empty bunk.

There was a maximum of one hundred and fifty-three men per barracks, three work gangs of fifty men each, plus the *dnevalny*—barracks janitor, and one or two crippled helpers, men who were unable to do normal work in the mines.

Sedecki looked at the six-bunk sets jutting out from each wall. They were actually two sets of bunks, each three tiers high. They were joined side by side with an eight-inch board dividing them at each level.

"There are three or four bunks down there," the *dnevalny* said, pointing and trying to be heard over the jabbering questions of keyed up prisoners. "But be careful, the last third is a mixed barracks."

Aleks was immediately alarmed as they made their way down the wide aisle.

"Did you understand what the *dnevalny* said?" Aleks asked, looking at the bunks on each side as they walked down the wide corridor.

"Yes, I heard," Sedecki answered. His Russian had improved drastically with the tutoring that Aleks and his cellmates had put him through. He now spoke only Russian, except when he and Aleks talked privately.

Criminals or politicals, they were all convicts were they not? He had thought about this several times in the past upon hearing the gruesome stories his cellmates told about criminals. He felt that Aleks sometimes embellished his stories.

He noticed that the barracks seemed to be divided into three sections by the two pot-belly stoves located a third of the way from each end of the building. Where the stoves set in the middle of the aisle there were no bunks by the wall. Instead there were large boxes for wood and coal and brooms.

Near the door at each end of the barracks was a smelly half-barrel *parasha*.

"Go slowly, my friend," Aleks cautioned. "Criminals and politicals do not mix."

Aleks and Sedecki walked past the first stove and beyond the middle of the barracks without finding an empty bunk.

At the second stove, two-thirds of the way down, Sedecki noticed the unit of six bunks on the right. The two top bunks and the middle bunk facing the wood bin appeared to be vacant but rags and other things were draped over the edges. A heavy set, ape-like man leaned against the bunks. Maybe they're taken Sedecki thought.

When he walked on past the stove Aleks whispered that they were treading into criminal territory. Sedecki paid him no heed. But as he walked on he became aware that the barracks jabbering had subsided.

Some faces were smiling. But the more faces he saw the more he realized that the smiles were not warm greetings. He maintained a false half-grin and continued down the last third of the barracks. Aleks was beside himself but nervously followed his friend.

Reaching the end of the barracks they saw one bunk apparently empty. They needed two bunks, together, or close. Sedecki turned to start back down the corridor and almost ran over Aleks. Going back they walked side by side. Aleks whispered softly in Polish. "Please Sedecki, be very careful."

"Sure."

As they walked back up the aisle the barracks was quiet. Sedecki could now feel the criminal presence that had Aleks so scared. The watching eyes seemed more intense.

Aleks stayed close to Sedecki and didn't meet any of the stares.

When they got back beyond the stove Sedecki stopped.

Aleks went a few steps further before he turned to say, "Come on."

Sedecki didn't answer. He just stood in the middle of the aisle, by the stove, looking at the three bunks that appeared to be vacant. The huge, burly looking man, clad only in pants, was now sitting on the edge of the bottom bunk facing the open area between the stove and wood bin. Both arms were covered with black tattoos.

Sedecki looked around at the men standing by the other side of the stove. More criminals had followed them up the aisle and were quietly watching.

Aleks spoke quitely in Polish, "Let's go back and talk to the *dnevalny*."

Sedecki replied in Russian, "These must be three of the four bunks the *dnevalny* was talking about. They're the only ones left. Two bunks on top and one middle bunk on this side"

The only voices that had spoken since they had walked down the criminal third of the barracks and back were theirs.

There was a quiet shuffling. The criminals were crowding the far aisle and climbing onto top bunks for a view. They loved excitement and this might become the show of the day.

The politicals in the remaining two thirds of the barracks were stone-faced. A few walked down and stood near Aleks while others watched from whatever viewpoint they could find.

We're newcomers, they're curious, Sedecki thought. He realized he was standing at the dividing line of the barracks. This had to be the end of the politicals' domain; therefore, these three vacant bunks have to be in political territory.

Sedecki stepped to the end of the six-bunk set and continued to speak in Russian.

"These two top bunks look vacant," he said, taking off his coat.

He tossed his coat onto the top bunk facing the opening. "I'll take this one you can take the one on the right."

Aleks didn't have a chance to answer. His mouth hung open as he watched the burly man rise from the edge of the bottom bunk. He was an inch or so shorter than Sedecki, but he was enormous. His head set on top of wide hairy shoulders, his bull neck almost invisible. He had a massive barrel chest supported by thick stubby legs. His arms were like tattooed hams with hands the size of bear paws. Small dark eyes were set in a shaved, cue ball head. *Oh my God, he'll kill you, Sedecki. Get the hell away from there now.*

Burly-man stood in the open area between the stove and the coal bin. Then he stepped to the end of the bunks and glared at Sedecki, like a bull about to snort. Aleks watched him snatch Sedecki's coat off the top bunk, take one step towards the stove, throw the coat on the floor and look at Sedecki with an ugly smile.

Aleks retreated several more feet up the aisle with a cold, sinking feeling in his stomach.

"Sedecki ... please," he turned and whispered, "forget it, lets go back up front."

His friend did not answer, only stood staring down at his coat. Then his head came up and he looked intently at burly-man. *My God, he doesn't realize, he's totally crazy!*

Sedecki stepped forward and retrieved his ragged coat. Keeping his eyes on the burly man he stepped back to the end of the bunks, pointed with his finger and speaking in Russian, said to burly-man, "Yours is the bottom bunk, isn't it?"

The political *zeks* couldn't believe it. No one, no one who wants to live that is, stands up like that to a criminal, most certainly not this criminal.

Burly-man planted his feet and grinned, showing his ugly gaping teeth. "Bottom bunk, middle bunk, top bunks ... all mine. Get your shit outa here."

Sedecki stood gazing at the beady eyes and yellow-toothed sneer as if he were looking right through the ugly man. *Screw you, screw 'em all.* His injured mind started to whirl. I can't remember who I am or why in hell I'm here. Stuff me into an overcrowded prison ship and transport my ass to this god-forsaken ice-age and now you, you ape-like idiot, you want to play games and tell me what to do. Well, screw you, and screw all of your buddies too.

Sedecki's face had a strange expression. After a few moments he spoke slowly in his very best Russian, "The bottom one seems to be yours. You can also have the second one but we are taking the two upper bunks."

With that he tossed his coat back on the top bunk.

You could hear men sucking a breath through their teeth.

Aleks' heart was in his throat. He just knew he and Sedecki were about to die. If they don't kill us they'll beat us to a pulp. He couldn't believe what Sedecki just did, and what he *said*. Scenes like this he had witnessed before and watched men die. He started to speak but the words stuck in his throat. It was too late.

Burly-man suddenly rushed forward with both arms extended for a bear hug that could crush any man. Aleks watched with open-mouth amazement as Sedecki deftly grabbed the charging man's right wrist with both hands, stepped back, planted his foot, pivoted, and used burly-man's weight and momentum to swing him around and slam him backwards into the end of the empty bunks. It happened within a blink of an eye.

Boards creaked and popped and splintered under the thundering impact. The wall shuddered. Burly-man stood motionless, like he was impaled.

Without hesitation, Sedecki drove a fist into burly-man's solar plexus. Air whooshed from the beefy Russian's lungs and he doubled over. Sedecki closed his right hand around his left fist and brought them down between the man's shoulder blades.

Like a sack of potatoes burly-man hit the floor with a thud.

Aleks stood wide-eyed with the rest of the barracks, stunned by his friend's foolhardy display of power, and trying to believe what he just saw.

Aleks came out of his trance when two men begin to move from the far side of the stove.

"Sedecki...." he gulped.

He watched Sedecki step back from the crumpled body and gaze at the two men who were coming slowly around opposite sides of the stove.

A couple of whoops and hollers came from the criminal end then it was quiet again.

Aleks caught the gleam of a blade in the hand of one man. He was ready to run for the door but realized his friend would not be running with him. Instead of backing up Sedecki moved one step to his left and assumed a strange-looking stance.

Aleks was in total shock. One criminal on the floor, bleeding, maybe dead, and two more advancing on his friend with a knife—and his friend is just standing there. It's incredible. This can't be the same man I have been tutoring. This is not the friend I have accepted as a brother, he doesn't look the same, he doesn't talk the same and he doesn't act the same. He is about to die and shows no fear for his life. He is crazy!

Sedecki watched the two criminals advanced around the stove at a slow-motion pace. He moved one more step back and stood in the middle of the wide aisle, maintaining his relaxed stance. The criminal with the knife made no effort to hide it now. He kept his arm at his side and wiggled the knife back and forth.

The other criminal was about to step over the crumpled burly-man.

"ENOUGH."

The sharp, electrifying command shattered the silence.

Sedecki's eyes flicked past the open area on the right to see a man sitting on top of the first set of bunks. The man sat like a statue of a mini Buddha, legs crossed hands on his knees. He was clad in an undershirt and black pants, a pale, wiry sort of man with swirling tattoos on both upper arms and a lightning strike on the inside of one forearm. His pallid appearance contrasted with his closely cropped black hair, which narrowed to a widow's peak. He had a serious smirk on his face.

After staring at Sedecki for several moments the man made a quick motion with his head and the two criminals retreated.

The pale man's face became solemn, his voice strong. When he spoke the words were clear, sharp as a razor.

"What!" he said loudly then more softly, "is your name, number … seven-nine-one?"

Sedecki straightened himself and stared at the odd looking man. He must be the boss.

"Sedecki, Stanislaus Sedecki and," he turned, "this is my friend, Aleksandr Leskov."

"Where are you from?" boss-man asked, paying no attention to Aleks.

Sedecki hesitated, not sure how to answer then said, "Kem."

"I know that, but *where* are you from?" Boss-man said without changing his expression.

Sedecki was silent for a moment, but his eyes were asking: who in hell wants to know? Finally he said, "I don't know."

Aleks emerged from his petrified shell, "He has—"

Boss-man's ice-cold glare cut him off then returned to Sedecki.

"You don't know?" he mockingly chuckled, looking around.

Ripples of laughter came from the criminal end of the barracks.

Boss-man's voice changed to a lighter, more knowing tone, "Stanislaus Sedecki, umm … that is Polish. You have a slight accent. You are a Pole."

"Maybe, I don't know. I can't remember where I'm from but I speak Polish, English and German, and now Russian."

"Ah haaa, languages," boss-man held his hand in the air, "a real intellectual."

More laughter from the criminal end.

"My compliments, you speak Russian well."

He clapped once, pointing. Two men from the crowded aisle gathered burly-man Ivan and dragged him to a sitting position on the floor against the coal box. They tended his bleeding. Boss-man watched, sadly shaking his head.

"*Makhorka*—tobacco." he said sharply.

From the bottom bunk below him a man quickly jumped out, grabbed a piece of paper and some rough-cut tobacco from the empty middle bunk, rolled a cigarette, struck a match and handed the lit cigarette to his boss.

Boss-man blew smoke in the air and looked at Sedecki. "What is your sentence?"

"Twenty-five years."

"Oooooo, big-timer," Boss-man smiled. Criminals chuckled.

"What is your crime?"

"I committed no crime. My trial was espionage," Sedecki answered, deciding to go with the flow rather than fabricate. "They said I am a spy, but that is not true."

"Ahh, a political, an intellectual political and also … a spy."

The snickering stopped when boss-man held up his hand.

"You are pretty brave for a political." He appraised Sedecki sternly. "A political of many languages but can't remember where he is from, how very interesting."

With piercing eyes boss-man gazed long and hard at this wild young Pole. He has just vanquished the strongest man in this complex then has the audacity to stand up to two others with a knife like he could take on the entire barracks. What kind of man is this upstart who has such a death wish and doesn't know where he is, a very smart political or a man who is too brave and foolish for his own good?

The barracks remained quiet while boss-man puffed, pondered

and blew smoke to the rafters.

Finally he said, "A political that fights like a tiger," then paused. "I like that."

Boss-man looked towards the criminal end of the barracks, "Sergei!"

A man edged his way through the crowded aisle.

"Move your things to Ivan's bottom bunk," he commanded, "and take Ivan's things down to yours."

The man grumbled something.

"Do it, now."

Sergei moved quickly forward to gather Ivan's things.

Ivan, the burly man, was coming back into the world.

"Ivan," boss-man called.

Ivan's head moved but was unable to focus. His face remained blank.

Boss-man snapped his fingers and waved his arm. The same two men came forward and half dragged, half carried Ivan down the aisle to the end bunk that had been Sergei's.

Boss-man turned his attention back to the new political upstart.

"Stanislaus Sedecki … so, you don't know who you are? Well, I know who you are. You are a very lucky man. Do you know that?"

Sedecki said nothing.

Boss-man paused, thoughtfully squinting at Sedecki. He blew a cloud of blue smoke to the rafters and softly added, "Very lucky, indeed."

Sedecki remained quiet.

For what seemed to be an eternity, boss-man sat in his cross-legged position, slowly blowing smoke, making rings. Finally, his eyes again turned to Sedecki.

"My name is Boris Eduardovich Viskaya." He knocked the ash off his *makhorka*. "I don't care for politicals, but I like you, Sedecki. You are foolhardy, but you have balls." He took another puff and blew more smoke. "You will have the top bunk, and your friend can have the other top bunk. The line, as you politicals call it, is here at the stove even though Ivan claimed all of those bunks. That's why the middle and top bunks were empty. You politicals don't like to be too near us criminals," he smiled, looking around and added, "They might catch something."

All criminals laughed.

Boss-man handed the last of his cigarette to his gopher and returned his attention to Sedecki. "The middle bunk below you will remain open. Do not worry," he announced and his voice became louder, "you and your friend will not be bothered. Anytime you leave the barracks, your possessions will not be disturbed."

Boss-man Boris Viskaya paused, looking up and down the silent barracks, then added, "I have said it."

Sedecki nodded a "Thank you" and punched the burlap sacks of straw, or hay, several times. He only hoped that the mattress was not crawling with vermin. He looked at Aleks and motioned him nearer.

But two of the political prisoners linked arms with Aleks and guided him towards their end of the barracks where they gathered around the other stove and talked.

When Aleks returned he played with his mattress, constantly looking around, still fearful that Ivan or someone would sneak up behind them. Quietly he said to Sedecki, "You know who that is, don't you?"

"The leader of the barracks, or the group I guess."

"The barracks or the group," Aleks mocked, shaking his head, "Sedecki, you amaze me. You are so calm about it. The leader. Ha. He is the *Pakhan*—the boss man. Some of the others just told me that Boris Viskaya is not only the boss of the criminals in this barracks, or all these sections, he is the boss of this compound area—that's one hundred and thirty or forty thousand men. Do you understand? He is also the number two *pakhan* of the entire Gulag."

Aleks got no response.

"You are crazy to have even tried such a stunt. We both could have been killed right then and there and no one would have dared to say a word. The one who had the knife is a *Blatnye*, a major criminal, a murderer, they tell me."

"He didn't look so major to me."

"Holy Christ," Aleks whispered, rolling his eyes. "Well, he should. He can kill you, and he won't forget. And, Sedecki, just be very careful with this *pakhan*. With a snap of his fingers he causes life or death," Aleks glanced around. "They say he is a three time murderer and thief and that he is 'connected,' which means the mafia or something big."

"He can't be too connected he's still here in the Gulags."

Aleks closed his eyes, "Sedecki, for God's sake. He's serving time for three murders and who knows what else. He may be forced to smoke that stinking *makhorka* instead of standard cigarettes, but he doesn't have to work and he is fed better than us. He doesn't have all the money and things he wants, but Sedecki, he *is* powerful.

"No matter who you are, who you know or who you're connected to, if you are convicted you serve your time, but by camp standards he serves his in style. Camp commanders, even some NKVD people fear him. The *zeks* up front told me about this man. He gives an order and it appears. He gives another order and something, or someone disappears—poof, just like that."

Sedecki crawled up onto the bunk next to the open area. Aleks climbed into the bunk on the other side. Keeping his voice low Aleks turned to his friend. "The guys in this end of the barracks like you. They think you're crazy. Where did you learn to fight like that? I've never seen anyone act so quickly before."

"Aleks, I don't know," Sedecki breathed a sigh. "I am surprised myself now that it's over. It just … happened."

He had been searching the corners of his mind but found no explanation. Now he was somewhat uneasy as the impact of what he had done was sinking in—but he wouldn't let Aleks know.

"I wasn't going to let him bully me. But I had no idea of what I was going to do. It just happened. His momentum helped. I simply reacted."

Aleks slowly shook his head, "Simply reacted. The way you were ready to take on the guy with the knife. The way you stood, your arms out like that, your hands. It was unreal. Someone said it was oriental, judo. Maybe that guy at Multavo was right about the insignia marks on your coat collar. Maybe you were in China."

"Maybe, and maybe it means nothing, Aleks," He began to feel tired. "Let's get some sleep."

But Sedecki could not sleep. For hours he thought about his Chinese coat and how he could have come by it; about burly-man Ivan and how he had handled him; and about how and where he might have learned to fight the way he just did. He looked at his hands, now conscious of how he had held them and the stance he had involuntarily taken. It surprised him and also scared him, not knowing who he was or what he was. He dug through his sick mind but came up with nothing.

He thought about the *pakhan*, this Boris Viskaya, and how he intervened. That man may be a criminal but he is no dummy. The way he talks, the words he used tells me he is an educated man.

At last his eyelids became heavy. He thought about what tomorrow would bring and he drifted off.

CHAPTER 8

Sedecki was startled when the maul struck the steel rail at 5 AM. The barracks door flew open and two men came tromping heavily down the corridor banging their clubs on the ends of the bunks and shouting crude obscenities.

"Who in hell were they?" Sedecki asked Aleks, putting on his boots and walking around to Aleks' side.

"Camp police," a gruff voice answered, "criminals, selected to make sure everyone goes to work. They'll come back in five minutes. If you aren't out of your bunk they'll jerk you out and beat you.

"I am Mikhail Sergeyevich Vilkin," the deep voice added. "You two are in my brigade, brigade thirty-three. Toilet, then eat and come back to the barracks."

Aleks and Sedecki grabbed their coats, starting down the aisle.

"You got bowls?"

The words were sharp and somehow familiar. Both of them stopped then turned.

Pakhan Boris Viskaya was standing by the stove. "If you don't have a bowl where will cookie pour your soup, in your boot?" His big grin faded. "Nikolai, two bowls."

Sedecki and Aleks looked at each other as Nikolai came scurrying with two tins.

Boris handed them to the newcomers. "Here in Norilsk you must have your own bowl. You have any money?"

"No," Sedecki said.

"You owe me five rubles."

"Five rubles, that's outrage—" Aleks immediately checked himself.

That was no way to talk to a *pakhan*.

Sedecki looked at Boris. "We'll have to owe it to you, but we will pay you."

"Oh, yes, Stanislaus Sedecki, you will pay me. I know that," Boris smiled. "Go."

As they left Aleks grumbled, "Criminals, did you notice how quickly those two police went on through their end of the barracks, almost no noise. Five rubles. Damn."

It was a bright sunny morning, no clouds. Although the temperature was only a few degrees below zero it did not seem cold. Strange, how things can seem so bone chilling one day and so relative the next.

The kitchen set between barracks two and three, feeding seven hundred fifty men of the first five barracks. The cook ladled measured amounts of soup to each can. Holding out his tin, Sedecki received a ladle of thin soup and stood staring at it. The cook let out a curse. Sedecki moved on. Near the end they were given bread and pieces of salt fish.

"This slop is no better than on the ship," Sedecki said, "maybe worse."

"Give it time, it might get better," Aleks smiled, "and then it could get worse."

When the next gong sounded at six all of the work brigades began forming in front of each barracks. They lined up ten men to a file, five columns, fifty men to a brigade, less only if someone had died or was sick.

Aleks and Sedecki answered when Brigadier Vilkin called 33's roll. Within minutes Sedecki could hear the reporting of brigades down the line becoming louder.

Then Brigadier Vilkin called out, "Brigade number thirty-three, forty-eight men strong, ready for work."

The deputy commander walked on by as his subordinate made entries on his chart.

"I didn't see the *pakhan* come out," Sedecki whispered.

"A *pakhan* doesn't do menial things," Aleks said. "In fact this *pakhan* doesn't have to do anything." He paused, wiping his nose on his coat sleeve, "That's why our barracks is warmer than others, so they say."

Sedecki just shook his head.

Aleks made a face at Sedecki and whispered, "If any *pakhan*, especially Boris Viskaya, says 'shit,' anyone within hearing distance had better pull down his pants and squat."

Sedecki's eyebrows raised and the corners of his mouth turned down then up.

"Funny, but not really," Aleks said. "If the guy doesn't do as told he's a dead man."

"Quiet!" Brigadier Vilkin growled.

When all brigades were accounted for the compound gates opened and the brigades began marching to work. The ten-hour workday had begun.

Snow squeaked beneath their feet.

"Someone guessed the temperature to be ten below," Aleks whispered.

"Ten, my ass, feels like fifty below and this is summertime," Sedecki exaggerated and looked at the gray sky. He now regarded the cold differently after the warmth of the breakfast area. "How can people live here during the winter?"

"Keep the scarf up around your face," Aleks told him. "It's ten. When it's fifty below zero spit freezes before it hits the ground. No one has to go to work when it's fifty below."

"Quiet in there!" a guard snarled.

Sedecki adjusted the rag that wrapped around his face. They trudged on for the next thirty-five minutes to the base of a hill. The mine superintendent took a count and passed brigade 33 into the mine.

The temperature changed dramatically and none too soon for

Sedecki as they picked up incandescent kerosene lanterns. Inside the wide entrance three tunnels angled off in separate directions. Tools were at the work stations where they were left yesterday.

Sedecki and Aleks' crew were led along the narrow iron tracks of the middle passageway to where the rails split into a Y. Two small gondola cars set there side by side. Beyond the Y was a six foot wide open shaft dropping down twelve feet to a lower vein. A tripod with a pulley and rope hovered over the shaft. A two foot wide passage area went around one side of the opening and the high tunnel continued further into the mountain.

The brigadier sent two men into the tunnel straight ahead. Then two men lowered themselves hand over hand down the rope to the lower vein.

"You three will load and push the gondolas," The brigadier said, turning to Aleks, Sedecki and the last man. "You pull the buckets up and load the cars. When one car leaves you continue loading the other one."

Brigadier Vilkin paused and glared at his two new men. "Listen carefully. Brigade 33 works hard. We have a quota and the bread we get or do not get for supper depends on whether we meet our quota. You understand?"

They all nodded.

"Then get to work."

There were a number of buckets. As soon as Sedecki emptied one and sent it back down a full one would be waiting. The men working straight ahead would alternately carry a full bucket back. Aleks and Sedecki and their partner had to hustle.

At the end of the long day their hands were raw and bleeding. Shoulder muscles were tied into knots. Aleks found it difficult to stand up straight. Although the same height and build, Sedecki was much stronger and more muscular than Aleks. But even Sedecki had muscles that hadn't been used in this kind of intensive labor.

When the sledgehammer hit the rail, resonating throughout the tunnels, the brigades came out of their warrens and lined up for the march back to camp. The brigadier noticed the bloody rags and the hands of his two new workers. "You are lucky," he bellowed. "We are just maintaining our quota. Wait until we receive a new quota you'll learn what work is really like."

Weeks passed into months and blisters turned into calluses.

One Sunday Aleks came into the barracks carrying a box.

"What is that?" Sedecki asked.

"A package from Aunt Zora," Aleks grinned, coughed and motioned. Sedecki came around to Aleks' side of their bunks, away from nosey criminals.

"It's finally caught up to me," Aleks said, setting the package on the bunk below his. "Every year or more she sends me a package and some money."

"A package and money?"

"Only fifty rubles, that's all they allow. If she sends any more they confiscate the rest. I received a box more than a year ago, before I was sent to Tayshet. This is the first since." Aleks rummaged through the box and constantly glanced around to see if anyone was watching. "This one's the usual, lard, sugar, hard crackers, jerky and some tins of fish and meats and cheese. Dogs, dirty dogs!"

"What's the matter?"

"They took the candy. Aunt Zora usually includes a bar of chocolate."

"How does she know where to send it?"

"She doesn't. All Gulag mail goes to a Moscow address. From there it is routed to wherever you are, hopefully. They would never let anyone know which camp you are in, or even that you are in the system." Aleks looked up and smiled. "I got the rubles from the office. There is a camp store, such as it is. You can spend your rubles there if you have any."

"Great," Sedecki replied, examining several items. "What's this?"

he asked, rummaging in the box.

Aleks looked the small flat box wrapped in plain brown paper, like the tin of fish he had just opened. He tore off the paper to reveal a packet of English cigarettes. "Well, well, well, how did this get by those idiots? I can't believe it. I never smoke but Uncle Grigory had told Aunt Zora to always send foreign cigarettes. Do you know how much this is worth?"

Sedecki shrugged, "Fifty, a hundred, a thousand?"

Aleks smiled, "Much, much more than that my friend. This is like gold."

Sedecki shrugged. He and Aleks munched on the tin of fish and a few of the crackers.

Later Sedecki was listening to the *pakhan* holding court the other side of the bunks. He always kept his ears open and had paid attention when others told stories about Boris Viskaya and his power. There are many things a *pahkan* can do. But he smiled to himself even a *pakhan* must have limits.

Sedecki listened to more of the high and mighty rhetoric then he faced his friend. "Aleks, let me have five rubles, we owe the *pakhan*, remember.

"Yes, I remember," Aleks said and counted five rubles.

They ate till almost stuffed before Sedecki made another request. "Aleks may I have the box of cigarettes?"

Aleks was dumbfounded, "The cigarettes?"

"Yes Aleks, the cigarettes."

Aleks noticed the far away look in Sedecki's eyes. "But this, my friend, is a pack of cigarettes, a pack of real English cigarettes. It's gold!"

Sedecki locked eyes with his comrade, "Aleks please trust me, let me have the pack and you will not be sorry."

Sedecki would not offer a reason. Aleks thought long and hard. He trusted his friend and finally handed him the pack.

Sedecki opened the flat little box, removed half of the cigarettes and gave them back to Aleks. He took one cigarette from the box and put it in his left pocket. The box of remaining nine he put in another pocket.

Boris Viskaya, number one criminal, number one boss-man of the compound, was sitting atop his bunk still holding court like a king in his usual attire—undershirt and black pants, as if to say the cold does not bother me.

It shouldn't, Sedecki smiled, at seventy degrees this barracks is warm.

The *pakhan's* legs, as always, were folded. His back was ramrod straight, his hands rested on his knees. If he turned his palms up he would be in the Lotus position.

Sedecki stood on Aleks' side of the bunks, laid his arms on the edge of the top bunk, put his chin on the back of his hands and gazed at this unusual man. Boris must be in his early forties he guessed, with a slim, wiry build—very deceptive. His face was pasty white and he had a thin smile that showed a gold crown edge around one tooth.

But it was the eyes that Sedecki watched, piercing eyes that moved quickly, seemingly focusing on nothing, yet absorbing everything. Aleks was right—nothing would get past this *pakhan.*

Boris Viskaya would snap his fingers and man in the lower bunk would roll one of those horrible *makhorkas*, light it, take a drag (his reward) and hand it to his boss.

Sedecki thought it almost comical. He had witnessed this scene time and time again as he lay in his bunk. Comical, seemingly uncomplicated and off-hand, but he realized the terrible supremacy it represented. That was sobering.

A number of men in the compounds had been killed or just plain murdered, since he and Aleks had arrived. Scuttlebutt said most if not all, were on Boris Viskaya's orders, including all of the other anomalies that occurred weekly. Since the incident with burly-man Ivan, Sedecki had received no further favors from the man that he knew of, but then no one had bothered him or Aleks and nothing had ever been missing from their bunks. Twice he had tested by leaving coveted items like bread in plain view.

Camp Commanders feared him and NKVD people looked the other way. Can this *pakhan*, this Boris Viskaya, be that powerful? Sedecki wondered. If so, he is truly a man to be reckoned with.

Still standing on the political side of their bunks, Sedecki watched the *pakhan* inhale and blow streams of blue smoke at the rafters. The criminals were laughing, responding to his remarks and antics. At last Sedecki smiled, stepped back and slowly walked around the end of the bunks to the stove.

The *pakhan* spotted him. With a flourishing hand and loud voice he said, "Ah, how is our intellectual friend this evening?"

"Well. Very well," Sedecki answered in Russian—the only language he used now—and returned the grin. "The day has been warmer, I have a full belly, not happy, but full and there is one less day on my sentence."

Boris Viskaya chuckled. Those around him laughed weakly.

"You are truly an astute, interesting man, Sedecki, probably the wittiest spy in all Russia." He smiled, looked at his criminal element with a mock scowl. "I should retain you to educate some of my comrades."

"Point made," Sedecki smiled. "As for my being educated and witty, that's conceivable, but, a spy? Hmmm, could be and then maybe not."

"It is of little consequence," Viskaya waved a hand. "You'll serve your time regardless."

"Perhaps," Sedecki wryly smiled, reeling out the bait, "perhaps."

"*Perhaps?*" Boris Viskaya mocked, frowning at this young man's calculating manner, wondering if there was any meaning behind the words. Is there more to this Pole than I think?

"But never mind that," Sedecki, quickly said now that he had the *pakhan's* attention. "I have come to pay you the five rubles as promised for the bowls."

Approaching the bunks he pulled out the five rubles and laid them on the foot of Viskaya's bunk. Then he stepped back towards his bunk, leaned his butt against the coal bin and looked up at the man.

The barracks became quiet. Viskaya stared at the money for what seemed an eternity. His bland expression made others uncomfortable. He gazed at the rafters, stared at his ashtray then finally he looked down at Sedecki.

"I knew you were an honest, educated, understanding man," Boris said looking away for a moment then returning to Sedecki with a serious face. "But you know very little in the ways of finance, my friend. Have you never heard of interest?"

"Interest, Boris … interest?"

Boris? There was an intake of breath in the barracks then a hush. No one ever addressed the *pakhan* by his first name, no one.

Boris Viskaya did not flinch or move a muscle. His smile did not fade. He just stared at this inexplicable Pole with the cool blue eyes and the hidden strength. *He's an arrogant political, upstart sonavabitch with the audacity to stand up to anyone.* Is he too young to realize how foolhardy his actions are, or is he really ignorant about where he is, what he's doing and who he is toying with?

Sedecki, fully aware of the nerve he had touched, broke the strained silence.

"Yes, my good friend, I do understand interest. Interest is for bankers and money grabbers," he waved a hand. "I am not a banker. You are not a banker or a grabber. I do not pay interest. I do not collect interest. I am a man of honor who deals with men of honor, men such as yourself; but you know, Boris"—there it was again, *BORIS.* The name

was like a knife in the side of every criminal. All of them stiffened, but
no one dared speak—"there is something else I have wanted to talk to
you about, as one friend to another, it's that damned horrible smelling
makhorka that you smoke all the time."

Boris Viskaya froze. Some criminals began to move but at the
slightest motion of the *pakhan's* finger they froze.

Good God Almighty! Aleks thought, standing on the other side of
their bunks. I can't believe this. Does he want to die? It's one thing to
have bested burly-man Ivan and got away with it. But to challenge and
then insult a *pakhan* is like signing a death wish. Aleks wanted to speak
but he found no words. In shock, he could only stare.

He watched Boris Viskaya glare at Sedecki then shift his gaze
down to the ashtray by his legs. The man appeared calm and cool, but
Aleks could sense the fierce churning inside of him. No one insults
such a powerful man. This *pakhan* might take care of Sedecki's termi-
nation personally, and mine too. Damn it, Sedecki, you crazy bastard,
what have you done?

He saw Boris Viskaya's piercing eyes narrow, the forehead wrinkle
and the mouth become a thin line of roiling irritation as he silently
stared at his tin ashtray.

The *pakhan* stubbed the butt of his cigarette in the tin in front of him.

"Ah thank you, my friend," Sedecki quickly seized the moment
again, pushed off the wood bin and wrinkled his nose. "That *makhorka*
is so stinking terrible."

Boris Viskaya's expression became a frown, his eyes narrowed and
his face flushed.

Aleks was about to cry.

Sedecki didn't miss a beat. "If I were a smoker and a man of your
stature and great taste I would smoke only the best."

With a grandiose wave of his hand he slowly reached in his pocket and withdrew the single English cigarette. "This is what I would smoke."

He held the cigarette up between his thumb and forefinger.

He closed his eyes and with exaggerated showmanship ran the length of the cigarette under his nose, deeply inhaling the aroma. "Ah, yes. What bouquet. What excellence. Those English, they know how to make a real cigarette."

He stepped closer to the *pakhan's* set of bunks and leaned towards the boss-man's gofer sitting on the edge of the bottom bunk. He put the cigarette to his mouth and snapped his fingers.

The sharp crack was electrifying.

The *pakhan's* astonished gofer jerked as if Viskaya himself had called. Without hesitation he fumbled for a match, struck it and lighted Sedecki's cigarette.

Sedecki stood up facing the stove and as theatrically as he thought appropriate, took a puff, careful not too draw too much lest he choke or cough. He held the smoke in his mouth, looked up and slowly blew two smoke rings like he had studied Boris doing time and again.

"Ah yes, truly a most delightful smoking experience."

He held the cigarette up, looked at it then turned towards the *pakhan.*

"Boris, (sic) my good friend, you will appreciate this cigarette much more than I, so why don't you try one of mine." Sedecki stepped forward and offered him the cigarette, "With my compliments."

Boris Viskaya hesitated for the longest moment and scrutinized this daring young Pole.

Finally, the English cigarette was too much to refuse, even if irritated. He accepted and examined it, noted the brand and took a deep drag. When he exhaled his expression was still insipid. He took another long puff, exhaled through his nose and blew a thin stream of blue smoke to the rafters. After a moment he looked down at this rude, young antagonist.

Sedecki returned the stare then quickly spun around and stepped away, keeping his timing just right. He wasn't through yet.

He stopped, turned and faced Boris. "Now some people might consider that cigarette to be the interest Aleks and I owe you. But I don't, no sir," he waved his arm. "I don't deal in interest. I offer you that cigarette as a token of our gratitude and our friendship, even though it is worth much, much more than what you could ever calculate as interest."

Viskaya's expression did not change, but his color was slowly returning. He took another drag, held the cigarette up and gazed at it.

At last he looked down at this wild man.

"Sedecki," he said, "your debt has been paid."

What had been gut-wrenching disbelief throughout the barracks became sighs of relief.

Aleks began to breathe again.

But the first-name insult still lingered with the criminals, and perhaps with Viskaya.

When the chatter died down Sedecki once again took center stage and made an even more stunning gesture, "Boris, my friend," he said, pausing for greater effect, letting the name *Boris* penetrate every mind. "I do consider you to be my friend, nothing more, nothing less, Boris, just my friend. Because you are my friend, and because I like dealing with men such as yourself, men of honor, I would like cement our friendship with a trivial token."

From his other pocket he pulled the box of English brand cigarettes.

"Oooos," echoed throughout the barracks. Everyone assumed it was a full pack or only minus one. But what matter—a box of English cigarettes!

"Actually," he went on, "this pack belongs to me and my other friend, Aleks." He looked at Aleks then back to Viskaya. "We would like for you to have this."

Then he stepped over to the bunk and offered the pack of cigarettes to the astonished Boris Viskaya.

The *pakhan's* eyebrows arched as he recognized what this arrogant man was handing him. He accepted the packet. He opened it, stared into it then smiled at the irony because he counted only nine cigarettes this clever Pole had given him, not nineteen. But never mind, here was nine beautiful English cigarettes. He removed one, held it up, saw the brand name was the same, closed his eyes and passed it under his nose, twice. Then he looked down at Sedecki, put the cigarette back in the pack, smiled, almost chuckled, laid the pack by his ashtray, maintained his smile, bent his head and stared at the cigarettes.

Next, to the surprise of everyone, he bounded off the bunk and still clutching his burning English cigarette he grabbed Sedecki by the shoulders and kissed him on the cheeks three times, Russian style.

After that, he stood back and said, "Sedecki, my friend, you are amazing, an amazing magician, an artist ... and damn, you do have guts."

He turned to his criminal element with a sweep of his hand and in a voice loud enough for everyone to hear said, "This is my friend."

He turned back to Sedecki with a big grin, "From now on you may call me, Boris."

When they were alone Aleks said, "My God you are unbelievable. You scared the hell out of me and everyone else in the barracks."

"Me too," Sedecki said then grinned. "I discovered there were no foreign brand cigarettes in the Gulags, only Russian brands the NKVD soldiers could purchase, and those are very low quality. The *pakhan* could occasionally obtain two or three of those, but ninety-nine percent of the time he has to smoke that stinking *makhorka* crap and they roll *that* in whatever paper is available. I knew what I was doing with your gold. You just have trust me, Aleks."

Summer turned quickly to fall. Aleks became more easily fatigued and he was coughing a great deal. The work quota was a monster, constantly changing. If they met the higher quota level they could not maintain it. When they failed to meet the quota the brigade's food rations would be reduced—supposedly. But strangely enough those reductions never did occur in brigade 33. Boris controls the bean counters at the mine. It pays to know a *pakhan*.

Men became weaker. The elderly man in their work group could not maintain the staggering pace and he died. Other men throughout the compound became sick, especially the frail and elderly. Many died. Some were shot when they fell from the ranks while marching and were unable to rise. The camp guards were cruel.

Winter came with a vengeance like all Norilsk winters then eased into spring and now turned into another summer. One day Sedecki and Aleks were leaving the mess hall when a marvelous thing occurred.

"Aleksandr Mikhailovich!" the words thundered through the building.

Aleks Leskov froze, turned and couldn't believe his eyes. Standing in line with a bowl in his hands was a giant towering head and shoulders above the other men. Those big eyes were wide and that grin, showing the space between the two front teeth, was spread from ear to ear.

"Viktor!" Aleks shouted in complete surprise and went into one of his coughing spells.

Viktor Zukovny, the *starosta* at Tayshet left his place in line and embraced his lost friend. Then he gave Sedecki a huge hug.

Aleks stopped coughing. "When did you get here old friend?"

"Just came up the Yenisey River on the first boat of the year."

"What brigade are you in," Sedecki asked.

"Thirty-six."

"Maybe we can get you into our brigade," Aleks said.

A camp policeman came from nowhere. "Move out! No standing around."

****

It was September when Aleks spent the last of his rubles at the store.

"I'll take a bite of that," Sedecki said, "If you don't mind."

"What's mine is yours."

Sedecki wandered off chewing as Aleks and Viktor talked.

When Sedecki returned he was wearing a big grin and just blurted it out, "Viktor will be transferred to Brigade thirty-three before the week is out. What do you think of that?"

"I don't believe it!" Aleks exclaimed.

"And how will this happen?" Viktor asked.

"I have no idea," Sedecki replied. "I only know that, like Aleks told me, *Pakhans* are powerful people."

"The *Pakhan* told you this?" Aleks asked.

Sedecki nodded.

"For nothing in exchange?" Aleks said in a voice of disbelief.

"No," Sedecki answered, "I had talked to him last week about Viktor. Today he enjoyed the last one of our ten cigarettes."

Aleks and Viktor looked at each other.

"I am a magician. I do miracles. I am his friend," Sedecki laughed. "But wait, there is more. Viktor can move into the bunk below me, how about that?"

CHAPTER 9

The winter of 1952-53 was typical of the Siberian north, harsh and extremely cold, adversely black and white and always dreary. Malnutrition, scurvy, tuberculosis, and pneumonia took its toll. Some men did not make it to the hospital. Many that did were turned out too soon because there was no room. Thousands died in Norilsk. But what matter, when summer comes, like all the previous summers, thousands would replace them. Stalin's Gulags never lacked for labor, as Aleks had often said.

The daily march to the mines in temperatures minus 5 to minus 30 was normal. Only at fifty below zero would work details be cancelled. The evening trek coming back was the killer. They would leave the forty degree warmth of the mine and freeze in the mind-numbing march back to camp.

"Grab him!" Sedecki yelled as Aleks collapsed.

Viktor grabbed one arm, Sedecki the other. They pulled Aleks up between them and began carrying him along.

"Heist him up on my back," Sedecki said. "The going will be easier."

"I can carry him," Viktor replied.

"We'll switch off," Sedecki countered.

The guards watched Sedecki and Viktor alternate in carrying Aleks all the way back to camp. Because it was Sedecki and Viktor they said nothing. Aleks was put in the hospital.

Weeks later, in January of 1953, a rage that had been festering for so long was coming to a head. Someone had to die.

Viktor, and Jacob, the Jew from Moldavia who replaced old man Kosko, were in the lower level of the mine. Sedecki and Nicholas, the Romanian taking Aleks place, were working the buckets and gondolas. One man was up ahead in the main tunnel. The crew was shorthanded.

Nicholas was pushing a loaded gondola towards the entrance.

Sedecki was busy filling the other one.

Nicholas yelled, "Sedecki!"

Sedecki turned and came down the tunnel. In the glow of the kerosene lamps he saw Nicholas take a backhand smash from burly-man Ivan. The bear-like Ivan lumbered on towards Sedecki with a wild sneer on his face. Sedecki held an empty bucket and he hurled it at Ivan. The beefy man brushed it aside and slowly kept coming.

Ivan Petrovich Blücher would never defy the orders of his boss, it would be his undoing. He had waited, sure that the young smart-ass Pole would make a mistake and fall from Viskaya's grace then he, Ivan, would once more court his *pakhan's* favor. He waited and he waited. But the bond between Boris Viskaya and the Pole showed no sign of weakening. He had waited so long, he could wait no longer. If my *pakhan* thinks killing this Pole is wrong and I must pay, so be it.

Sedecki moved behind the empty gondola then rushed forward, sailing it down the track.

With an awkward yet quick-footed movement heavyset Ivan flattened against the wall like a ballerina. The speeding gondola raked across his stomach and sailed on. With a huge paw he wiped his belly and looked at the blood on his hand. His sneer changed to a nasty snarl.

One slow foot at a time Ivan advanced like an animal on prey that was finally cornered. This time he was smarter, he would not rush his opponent as quickly as he had in the barracks. I have him trapped he told himself. I will wait until the last moment.

****

Sedecki had a big problem and his mind began to spin. The tunnel behind him was a dead end. The shaft and the channel down below was a dead-end.

He backed up to the wide area where the track split for the gondolas. But it wouldn't be wide enough to allow him to stay out of the madman's reach.

He glanced around. The open shaft was but three yards behind him. To step around it meant he'd be trapped in the tunnel's far end. If Ivan charged while still on this side of the open shaft there would be no room to maneuver, we both might go into the shaft together. Damn it, what other choices?

Sedecki assumed Burly-man would take his time and come slowly. That will give him the advantage. I need to put him off balance, outfox him into making a mistake, but what?

Sedecki took a weird stance, bent his legs at the knee, held his arms akimbo, wiggled his hands frantically and made the most gruesome, contorted face he could muster. Then with a fierce growl, in his most guttural Russian he jeered, "Go away, don't bother me you slimy, dogs-blood idiot. You bastard son of a whoring bitch!"

Then he spat at Ivan.

Upon seeing the man take a bizarre stance Ivan became wary. However, everything changed when the insult came and Sedecki spit at him. All caution evaporated. Ivan's fists opened and closed. His breathing increased like a snorting bull. The words bounced around his simple mind, *Slimy dogs-blood idiot? Bastard? Whoring bitch?* No man had ever insulted him like that, no man. You have spoken your last words you lousy fucking Polack.

The area behind Sedecki seemed to become smaller to Ivan's eyes. There would be no squirming room for his opponent. The shutter of his mind clicked. With arms open, enraged and growling he trudged forward like a lumbering elephant.

Sedecki watched the space between them diminish to four yards … three yards. His mind whirled faster. He knew the man would eventually lunge. He considered a knife-handed chop. But even if it hit its mark, if such a blow would render this raging bull unconscious, the sheer force of burly-man's three hundred-plus pounds would … He purged the thought.

Suddenly, Ivan charged.

Sedecki turned sideways to take two calculated strides, but his foot rolled on the loose gravel. His next step was several feet short of what he wanted. He had to take three steps. Then he summoned all of his strength and made a desperate leap up and over the shaft reaching for the tripod's pulley wheel.

Burly-man was surprisingly fast and Sedecki had lost ground. As Sedecki turned and slipped, the charging Ivan saw his opportunity and thought he had to attack—now. With all the power his stubby legs could muster he rushed forward and lunged.

In midair he caught Sedecki just below the knees with a vice-like grip.

Ivan's weight caused Sedecki's outstretched hand to miss the pulley by several inches. Just below the pulley wheel the rope slapped his right hand. He closed his fist. Then simultaneously he grasped the woven hemp with his other hand and held on.

But his weight plus Ivan's was too much. They would both go into the shaft.

The short end of rope whizzed through the pulley for two feet then the knot jammed in the pulley block. Their plunge into the shaft stopped with a sudden jerk and their momentum swung them both like a pendulum. Sedecki hands slid down the rope and he slammed into the far edge of the shaft on his stomach. The wind gushed out of his lungs, spots appeared before his eyes and everything went black.

Two feet below, clutching Sedecki just below the knees, Ivan crashed into the solid rock wall of the shaft at an angle, head first. The 300-plus pounds of impact shattered his skull, forced vertebrae upon vertebrae and Ivan Petrovich Blücher's neck snapped. He was dead before he hit the rock slab below.

"Hang on!" Nicholas yelled as Sedecki gasped for air.

Bounding to the far edge of the shaft, the Romanian grabbed the semi-conscious Sedecki and pulled him up and away from the edge.

Viktor had heard Sedecki shouting. He looked up in time to see Ivan slam into the wall then plummet and splatter on the slab beside him. He looked back up the shaft and saw Sedecki's legs dangling. "I'm coming," he shouted, climbing hand over hand up the rope. He reached the top as Nicholas pulled Sedecki off the edge.

Hours later Viktor and Nicholas half carried their battered friend during the long march back to the camp. Sedecki's lower ribs, stomach and hips were painfully bruised, his hands were rope burned.

Lying on his bunk that night Sedecki listened to Boris Viskaya hold court regarding the very unfortunate accident that befell his trusted man, Ivan Petrovich Blücher. Saying all the kind, obligatory words about his strongman the *pakhan* was putting an end to the incident; however, the word was out, everyone already knew what had really happened.

"Let this be a lesson for all of you," Boris said, ending his decree for all those in the barracks to hear. "You must take care at your work stations or you too can become an accident."

A short time later Viktor stood by Sedecki's bunk. "Did you understand?"

Sedecki looked at him painfully.

"The *pakhan's* little speech," Viktor said, softly. "He was in fact saying Ivan was wrong, it was his mistake, leave the Pole alone."

"How did he have it declared an accident?" Sedecki murmured.

"The mine supervisor, his subordinate, immediately realized who was involved and very wisely reported it as another accident."

"The camp commander believes that?" Sedecki grimaced in pain.

"You still don't understand?" Viktor shook his head. "Camp commanders allow this *pakhan* plenty of latitude. It was just another death, a criminal death at that."

Sedecki made a facial expression.

Viktor smiled, "As long as the *pakhan* trusts you, you can do no wrong."

The seventh day of March 1953 was a sad and a very glorious day, depending on where your alliances were placed. On this day Josif Vissarionovich Stalin died. Most were encouraged by the news. Everyone stood with their caps off in a moment of silence.

Also on this day Aleks returned from the hospital. Sedecki commentated on how pale and thin his friend still looked.

"He doesn't seem to have the energy he had before," He told Viktor. "He still coughs."

"I know," Viktor replied. "But he says he's all right, so you talk to him."

Upon entering the barracks several weeks later Sedecki said to his friends, "I hear talk about a new regime, of sentences being commuted, of better times to come."

"Believe nothing of what you hear," Aleks said, "and be careful of what you repeat. Stalin may be dead, but the regime is still very much alive."

Rumors were rampant. Everyone wanted to believe that things may change, but deep in their gut and heart they knew it wouldn't.

Life in the Norilsk Gulag did not change and the rumble that had been festering for months was rapidly spreading.

One night while lying in their bunks Aleks asked, "Have you ever seen England or America?"

Sedecki was surprised by the question. He thought long before replying. "I don't know," he said, squinting as if peering into a dark hole. "What does it matter anyway?"

"When I was a boy, before the war," Aleks said softly, staring at the ceiling. "I went to England and America one summer with Aunt Zora. England was great, but it rained too much. I loved New York, California and Florida. We crossed the entire country both ways on a train. Two months of my life that I will never forget."

"Your Aunt Zora was rich?"

"Yes, she was, and so was Uncle Grigory. Aunt Zora is not as rich now as before the war, I'm sure, but she has means and she is still a Countess."

Aleks went on to relate his American trip in great detail, almost boring detail.

"And, another day I'll never forget," Aleks said, "June 22, 1941. That's the day Germany invaded. We were visiting Aunt Zora in St. Petersburg and were about to make the trip home to Brest. They overran everything and continued their onslaught until they reached St. Petersburg. Just before the siege at St. Petersburg we received news about my father being killed in the initial German assault.

"All of my family died in the war, my mother, my father, my brother, my uncle … and my beautiful city of St. Petersburg laid in ruin. How Aunt Zora and I survived I'll never know. Aunt Zora is the only thing, the only person I have left. And the only way I know she is still alive is because I receive a package from her once a year or so."

"Aleks, I'm sincerely sorry about the loss of your family," Sedecki tried to sooth his friend's loss. "I wish—"

"It's all right," Aleks waved his hand, coughing. "There is nothing to say or do. Now it is my turn to die."

Sedecki started to interrupt but again Aleks waved him off. "It's true. I don't expect to get out of the Gulags alive. It is my fate, my entire family's fate, what is to be will be."

Sedecki and Viktor tried to console their friend. But Aleks' depressing mood was like the darkness that prevailed over the sunless winter months.

The rumblings that were heard during February and March continued to grow louder. In late April the administration was giving the matter serious attention.

"Did you hear about the Moldovian that was knifed last night?" Viktor asked coming from the mess hall. "He was a provocateur. They were telling me this during supper. There's talk about the demands being changed."

Sedecki voiced his opinion, "Everyone's quietly talking about something that's going to happen."

"It's not just talk now," Viktor said. "They are thinking crazy. A committee has been formed to represent the demands everyone has agreed upon."

Aleks sat up. "Demand all we want it won't matter. Like I said before, none of the demands of the past two months will ever be met. It just won't happen."

"Who are they?" Sedecki asked.

"The committee, there are six of them," Viktor replied. "One is an ex-Army Major who was highly decorated in the war. I really believe things are about to blow."

May Day 1953 was a harbinger of disaster. A depressing solid gray sky reflected the mood of the camp—a gloomy camp of black weatherbeaten barracks contrasted in the snow and surrounded by nineteenfoot high barbed wire fences and bird houses. Even smoke from the stovepipes drifted listlessly in the stagnant air.

"I wish they'd either shut up or do something," Sedecki said.

"They can't do anything but mouth off," Aleks said. "You can't change the system."

"The demands are too strong," Viktor said. "One day off a week instead of every two weeks. Cut work by two hours a day. Third: Better food. I go for that; fourth, more contact with relatives and so forth. It's like pissing in the wind."

The commandant of the camp and the NKVD would agree with Viktor.

"Who do they think they are?" the civilian camp commander mumbled in his office, "We have run the Gulags for twenty some years and never has anyone been able to demand anything." He scoffed at the audacious fact that the men even formed a committee.

"Then stop this rumbling before it gets any worse," the Colonel replied.

On the second day of May the commandant threatened to increase the work quotas if the prisoners did not forget about their demands.

"It's set for tomorrow." The word passed like wildfire through all of the barracks that night.

"Do you actually think it will happen?" Sedecki asked Aleks.

"It-will-happen," Viktor softly emphasized from the bunk below.

"It scares me," Aleks added. "I am surprised the committee has been permitted to exist this long. They are brave men." He began coughing, "I expected to see all of them shot days ago."

In the morning the overcast had moved out. It was sunny but cold. Five AM came and the camp guards tromped through the barracks banging their truncheons on the bunks. Today everyone came awake with anticipation and a certain amount of fear.

"Let's go," Sedecki said, shaking Aleks.

Viktor was awake and grinning like a big bird, "Today is the day."

"Com'on, let's go eat," Sedecki said, "Aleks?"

Aleks grumbled, "Take your time we're not going anywhere"

"What's the matter with you?"

"I didn't sleep a wink last night. I—" Aleks coughed.

Sedecki looked at Viktor.

Aleks finally said, "I'm … I'm all right. It's nothing."

Later Sedecki got Viktor alone.

"You and Aleks have been telling me that nothing is wrong. That the truth Viktor?"

Viktor hunched his shoulders, "He doesn't tell me everything."

Sedecki eyeballed Viktor, "Well, I think they let him out of the hospital too soon."

"COLUMNS OF FIVES," The commandant yelled through the bullhorn at 6 AM when no formations were being made. "Form columns of fives!"

The prisoners in each compound all gathered near the fences and gates chanting, "No work! No work!"

The commandant became livid. He continued barking through his bullhorn to no avail. NKVD soldiers gathered en mass along the fences and the gates. On the commandant's order the soldiers opened the gates. The prisoners stood their ground, glaring at the soldiers.

The soldiers wisely stayed outside of the open gates. They were few, the prisoners were many.

The standoff continued until the commandant finally realized there would be no work that day. The gates were closed. He returned to his office to confer with the NKVD colonel.

That day, the next, and the next continued to be a standoff. The commandant met with the prisoner's committee and their demands remained the same.

The camp gates were opened only to deliverer the daily rations of food.

Near the end of the second week of no work Sedecki said, "Well, I think the food seems to have improved a little bit."

"Damned little," Viktor said.

When the work stoppage moved into the fourth week the unexpected happened. The city of Norilsk shut down: The coke plant, metallurgical plants, rail yard, everything. All of the workers, the majority of whom had once been prisoners themselves, just stayed home in sympathy with the Gulag.

Most were "free men," paid wages for the work they did; free to mingle with the rest of the citizenry; free to stay home; free—but freedom was not a word in the Russian lexicon.

Problems for the camp commandant and the NKVD increased ten fold. It was a totally unforeseen development. Three hundred thousand Norilsk citizens had joined the hundreds and hundreds of thousands of prisoners inside the fences. It was a total catastrophe.

The almost hourly telephone calls to and from Moscow reached the point of panic.

Daily flights carrying soldiers and supplies from Moscow increased. At the end of the fourth week of rebellion, several trucks were pulled in front of the camp. The commandant stood on one, raised his bullhorn to announce that the delegation standing with him had arrived from Moscow to confer with the prisoner's committee and settle the matters at hand.

The prisoners jeered him and his Muscovite impersonators off the truck.

Weeks of nothing to do had given rise to prisoner discussions on everything.

"You say this can't continue because they're losing money?" Pavel asked. "That's crazy. One Gulag cannot harm the country."

"You don't understand the Russian economy," Aleks replied. "I've been to England, America, Poland and other countries. They have appliances and things we can only dream of, millions of cars, on-time trains, airplanes, the list goes on. Russia doesn't make a tenth of what any western country produces. What we do make is by comparison pitiful in quality. Our local economy produces nothing.

"The multitude of minerals, copper, coal, cobalt nickel; the wood from our forests; and many other items Russia sells to foreign markets, where does it all come from? It all comes from the Gulags.

"The cost to feed and house prisoners in the Gulags is simply a pittance, but the Gulags produce billions and billions of foreign dollars in return. The Gulag is the most profitable industry in the Russian economy, in fact my friend, it *is* the Russian economy. Moscow can't afford to have Norilsk shut down, let alone allow word of such a rebellion spread to other camps. It would be total disaster."

Aleks began coughing and said no more.

Into the sixth week the unprecedented stalemate dragged on. The government in Moscow, under Malenkov, Khruschev, or General Zhukov, no one really knew who was in charge, had lost patience. Work must be resumed and quickly. News of the rebellion was leaking. Gruesome tales of Stalin's barbaric methods were beginning to surface, including Gulag conditions. This had to be stopped.

Was it day 52, 53, or 54? Sedecki couldn't remember, but someone was keeping tally on the barracks wall. The committee had been called to the main camp office and what they brought back to the compounds was an ultimatum.

"The commandant has agreed to several points," the committee spokesman said, and went on to cite the two minor items the commandant would agree to.

"That is nothing, nothing," the prisoners shouted, almost in unison.

Nikolai Korolov, the committee chairman, raised his arms, calling for quiet. "I know. I know," he shouted. "We met with an NKVD General from Moscow. He is not an imposter like the last one, he checks out. He said we must return to work."

The committee's pitiful results fueled the fire.

The men began chanting, "No work, No work."

"This vacation has to end," Aleks said. "We're not going to get any further,"

That afternoon trucks rumbled up to the front of the camp and foot soldiers marched with them. The General and two other officers climbed up on the truck and waited for the catcalls and insults to subside. Then he raised his bullhorn and spoke.

"Tomorrow morning the gates will open and you will resume your work schedules."

The General's last words were drowned out by the defiant shouting of the prisoners. The raucous raving and ranting continued unabated and finally jelled into chants of "NO WORK! NO WORK!"

The sharp chatter of a machinegun brought silence. The General again held the bullhorn before him.

"You will answer role call and form fives tomorrow," he bellowed. "If you do not form fives and proceed to work I will send in my men with fixed bayonets!" These words were echoed from trucks in front of the other compounds.

Wild hollering erupted once more followed by chants of "No Work."

"Tomorrow morning, be ready for work!" the General shouted over the cacophony.

"I told you!" Aleks spat. "I knew it."

"You really think he will do that?"

"Sedecki, my friend, life is cheap. They have nothing to lose but a few workers, a few bodies. We lose thousands upon thousands every year anyway. There are plenty more where those came from."

"Aleks is right," Viktor added. "I too am surprised that this work stoppage hasn't been crushed by now. How long has it been now, seven, eight weeks?"

"It's the eighth week," Aleks intoned.

"An NKVD General does not give orders he's not ready to back up," Viktor said.

Five o'clock the next morning Sedecki woke to the ear-splitting sound of the gong and truncheons pounding on the ends of bunks. It was such a change to the past weeks that he momentarily forgot about the word that was passed the night before: Get up, go do your toilet, eat, go back to the barracks and remain there until work call is sounded. But we will not form fives and we will not go back to work.

The camp guards had orders to leave the compounds after the wake up call. They didn't hesitate to comply. From this point on it was an NKVD operation.

After the prisoners finished breakfast the brigadiers sounded the work gongs. The men began filing out of the barracks with determination and apprehension, but no one formed fives.

"Go easy," Aleks said, "stay as far back here as you can."

Prisoners en masse came surging forward to the big open areas between the front line of barracks and the fence.

At the main gate of the middle compound the camp commandant and the NKVD General climbed up on the bed of a truck. NKVD officers clambered onto trucks in front of all other compounds.

All of Norilsk and the Gulag were ominously quiet. The streets in town were deserted. The factories, warehouses, workshops, rail yards and the Gulag, all stood as mute as a death pall. No one stirred except several thousand soldiers standing in front of the compounds with their bayonets fixed.

It was a Norilsk morning. The dull gray overcast pressed like a mantle over the now quiet town and the silent throngs of rag-tag men standing in the Gulag snow.

Sedecki, Aleks and Viktor stood by the front row of barracks. They were too far away to see the general. But the officer in front of their compound would relay the general's orders.

"FORM FIVES!" was the command roaring from the general's bullhorn.

Officers in front of the other compounds repeated the order.

No one moved or said a word.

The general surveyed the zone.

"If you do not form fives and be ready to march to work I will send in my troops!" the general roared over his bullhorn.

Officers on the other trucks repeated the order.

Sedecki saw heads glancing about and heard soft mumbling, but no one moved.

The general turned and waved his arm. Soldiers stepped forward at each compound and unlocked the main gates.

"Form fives!" the general growled again. The bullhorns repeated it.

Sedecki saw heads and eyes dart around. It looked to him like the men were going to start forming. But he was wrong. Movement stopped. Silence prevailed.

The general raised both arms above his head, held them up for several moments then quickly brought them down like sabers slicing the heavy Siberian air.

Instantly, the quietude was shattered by the shrill blasts of whistles from officers at every gate. Main gates flew open and more than half of the soldiers rushed into the compounds with bayonets fixed. The rest remained as a blockade, ready to go in if called.

The running the screaming and the dying began.

****

Sedecki, Aleks and Viktor were almost knocked down by the stampede of fleeing prisoners. Many fell, becoming easy targets. Bayonets sliced into flesh and bone. The shrieking and pleading was horrendous. Sedecki couldn't believe it.

They backed against the front of the barracks as hordes of men rushed by. "My god," Aleks cried, "this is butchery!"

"Quickly," Viktor yelled over the shrieking voices, "get out of here!" He grabbed Aleks by the arm. They turned and became part of the fleeing mass.

Sedecki was riveted on the barracks stoop looking over the heads in front of him. His mouth was agape, eyes squinting in disbelief. Men were being viciously bayoneted. Stumbling, falling and yelling they scattered, trying in vain to avoid the cold steel.

It was a massacre.

Sedecki was dumfounded when some men tore open their coats and proudly stood their ground. With bare chests exposed they defiantly let the soldiers run them through.

Other men in the wild melee saw what their comrades were doing and stopped running. Some regrouped, linked their arms together and stood six or eight abreast as soldiers charged. Like defenseless sheep in a slaughtering pen they were left dying in the blood stained snow.

Something surged within Sedecki like a firestorm—something that wanted to make him scream above all other screams. It reached the throbbing in his neck, coagulated and died in his dry throat. He gasped, swallowed and realized that he had no weapons, no sane defense and if he did not move quickly he would face a bayonet.

He turned into the barracks and ran to the other end. Men were cowering in bunks, underneath the bottom bunks and balled up against walls in sheer terror, hoping, praying, to somehow be spared death by a slashing bayonet.

When Sedecki exited the rear door soldiers had entered the front and were randomly stabbing at the whimpering prisoners.

Once outside he saw soldiers darting everywhere like hunters chasing rabbits. But there were no warrens in which the rabbits could hide.

He ran past the second line of barracks and kept running.

Shots rang out.

Sedecki glanced around. My God, they can't run fast enough to catch someone so now they're shooting? It's already like fish in a barrel. This is madness. He could not see Aleks or Viktor anywhere. He looked around the corner to his right then ran to the end of the next barracks then the next.

He stopped against the far end of a barracks, glanced to his right and saw Boris Viskaya by the perimeter fence. He turned in that direction and got as far as the stoop when a soldier with a bloody bayonet came around the corner behind him.

If he ran he would be shot. Stand still very long and a bayonet would gut him. Looking at the bayonet and the intense face he quickly gauged the soldier: Maybe in his mid twenties, several inches shorter, a little heavier in stature. Bulky coat, or is it extra pounds from sitting around? Well trained? No doubt, but how quick to react?

The soldier stepped ever so slowly to the left, bayonet poised.

Sedecki backed against the barracks rear stoop.

He crouched forward, flexed his legs, holding his arms out in a wrestler's stance like burly-man Ivan did. He watched the eyes of the man who wanted to kill him and saw the grin. *That is a mistake.*

Sedecki rocked just a little from side to side. The soldier's grin became a smirk. *Your second mistake.*

Sedecki moved his right foot slightly to the rear. The soldier started to shift forward. With a blood-curdling scream, Sedecki threw his arms up in the air like a wild man. The startled soldier responded with a short, reflexive jab of his bayonet. *Your last mistake.*

Sedecki spun to his left and dropped, landed sideways on both hands swinging his right leg in a sweep that took the surprised soldier off his feet. Sedecki sprang upright and grabbed the rifle barrel. With his right hand he aimed a knife-like chop at the soldier's neck, but it was partially blocked. The blow landed on the man's ear and he screamed. Sedecki yanked and the rifle came free.

He stood holding the rifle, not sure of what to do next. Part of him said go ahead kill him, yet part of his wounded mind said, No, no, no.

He looked down at the defeated soldier who was pleading with his arms out, palms open, eyes wide with fear.

Suddenly the soldier rolled away. On the second roll his right hand was in his coat and as he came face up he was pulling out a pistol.

With one lunge Sedecki stuck the bayonet in the soldier's chest.

Most prisoners were running chaotically trying to evade the charging bayonets while some tried in vain to stand their ground. Groaning men, dying men and dead bodies littered the snow packed grounds. The killing spree ran into every area of the Gulag.

Sedecki saw Boris Viskaya with five men gathered around him, still by the side fence three barracks away. The six of them were being stalked by three oncoming soldiers.

"Go, go!" the *pakhan* shouted to his men as he backpedaled to the rear area.

The five men in front of him fearlessly rushed the three soldiers. Two of them were immediately stuck with bayonets.

The *Pakhan* retreated along the fence until reaching the last row of barracks. He stepped away from the fence and progressed through the area in front of the last row. He got to the left corner of the first barracks when a soldier appeared, blocking his way.

Boris and the soldier both stopped and stared at each other. The soldier began to slowly advance.

Holding his arms out as if he was walking a tightrope Boris moved cautiously backward and to his left along the front end of the barracks—cat and mouse in slow motion.

It was obvious to Boris the man didn't want to shoot—he wanted to gut him. Good, I can take you, you sonavabitch. Just get close enough to make your lunge and it will be your last act. Boris was no stranger to cold steel. The muscles of his shoulders flexed. His breathing was softer and each step was more deliberate, more cat-like.

Suddenly, off to his left near the fence another soldier emerged, one of the three soldiers his men had just attacked. For an instant a huge grim appeared on the *pakhan's* face. But he had little time to appreciate the fact that his men had eliminated the other two soldiers before they themselves fell.

Boris kept his back ever so cautiously against the front end of the barracks. The two soldiers moved to within three yards of Boris. They had him flanked.

With stark finality Boris Eduardovich Viskaya realized that he was about to die. He thought he could take one of them but not two.

The game of life for him suddenly changed, his eyes darted from one somber face to the other as he moved. The soldier on his right smiled, faking a jab. Boris flinched to his left, caught his heel on the edge of the stoop, fell backwards and down on the stoop. The other soldier moved forward. They had him. On his back with nowhere to go Boris courageously grinned in final defiance knowing that his time had come.

The sharp crack of the rifle was so much louder than the rest.

The soldier on his right dropped his weapon and crumbled. The bayonet almost sliced into Boris' leg. The second shot hit the other soldier with such force it drove him against the barracks, where he collapsed.

A stunned Boris Viskaya quickly sat up and gawked around.

A gigantic smile spread across his face. Standing at the rear corner of the second barracks from him was a man with a rifle at his shoulder—Sedecki!

****

Another shot pierced the air, splintering wood next to Sedecki's ear. Sedecki jumped back around the corner and counted. At the count of ten he peeked and quickly drew back again.

The *ptichniki's* that perched like birdhouses at every corner of the compound and along the nineteen-foot high perimeter fence were, he confirmed, made of wood. They were not designed to protect the soldier manning them. It wasn't necessary. No one would ever be shooting at *them*.

Sedecki shouldered the kalashnikov and on the count of three took a deep breath, stepped quickly around the corner, aimed and fired. High above the fence in the rear corner of the compound the soldier in the *ptichniki* slumped over the railing.

Was it peripheral movement or just instinct? It didn't matter. Sedecki was on pure adrenalin and some inner sense left no doubt. He spun to his left and dropped to one knee as a bullet whizzed by his ear and hit the barracks. His rifle was shouldered. He fired. One hundred and fifty yards down the rear fence line the soldier in the next birdhouse was blown backwards.

Boris Viskaya scrambled to his feet with wide eyes and a huge grin on his face, and he came running.

"Sedecki, Sedecki, son of a bitch, you are great." He shouted. He grabbed Sedecki by the shoulders and kissed him three times, Russian style. "You are my man!"

Then awareness set in. "Come on," Boris yelled, "Let's get the hell away from here. Trust me Sedecki, it's about over. Throw the rifle away, don't get caught with it. Let's go."

They ran down the corridor between the last two rows of barracks, away from the area that had almost cost them their lives.

Like a *purga*, the slaughter ended as quickly as it began, and so did the rebellion.

The ringleaders and a thousand others considered instigators of the failed uprising were labeled "traitors against the State" and marched to barracks hastily separated by additional barbed wire at the far end of the main compound. This included the number one *pakhan* of Norilsk and the number two, Boris Viskaya, and the third ranking criminal, simply because they were the top three *pakhans*.

But that did not satisfy the NKVD General.

"Round up another thousand," he said. "No, make it fifteen hundred. Get them from the same compounds the instigators came from."

The additional roundup included Sedecki, Aleks and Viktor, and five others from barracks Five. They, and the other fourteen hundred and ninety-two, were put in barracks next to the hard-core rebels, but separated from them by barbed wire.

"Why are we down here with these guys," Sedecki complained.

"It's because of the *pakhan*," Viktor replied, "Did you notice that they did not take everyone from our barracks to begin with? After singling out the three *pakhans* they came back and took just a few of us."

"Boris Viskaya told me you saved his life," Aleks said, coughing. "What happened?"

"I don't want to talk about it," Sedecki replied.

Aleks and Viktor exchanged looks.

Details of prisoners removed the dead bodies that afternoon. Work brigades were reformed and barracks assignments changed. The next day prisoners formed fives to be marched off to work, but not before they were given the opportunity to witness what happens to "traitors of the State."

In front of the main compound where Aleks, Viktor, Sedecki and the hard-cores were now held, four stakes were set up outside the perimeter fence for the four members of the rebel committee that had survived the slaughter. All rebels were ordered out to stand and watch.

The cold morning air was crisp, sounds carried forever. The sun hung like a washed out balloon on the rim of the horizon, the blood-stained snow of yesterday a grim Gulag reminder.

Sedecki watched three of the ringleaders march to the stakes holding their heads high, accepting their fate. The fourth, an ex-Army Major, was screaming, pleading for his life.

The volley of rifle fire echoed throughout the compounds.
Sedecki flinched.
A second volley followed then another and finally one last nerve-shattering blast.

Every work brigade in the Gulag had to march past the four men slumped awkwardly against their ropes. After the last brigade passed all rebel prisoners were ordered back into their barracks.

"The word is, it was the Major," Viktor said rubbing his hands by the stove.

"What was?" Sedecki asked.

"The provocateur on the committee," Viktor answered. "That's how they knew about everything that was planned. The camp commander and the NKVD double-crossed him. Shot him anyway."

"It was a losing proposition from the beginning." Aleks said. "They never would have given in to any of our demands."

"I just got the word," the last man coming into the barracks yelled. "More than twelve hundred *zeks* were slaughtered. But also, twenty-eight bloodsuckers died."

The fifty-five day Norilsk rebellion that began in May became history.

The mines began to once again disgorge ore from the bowels of mother earth and the metallurgical complex returned to its usual hum. All of Norilsk went back to normal like nothing more than another snowstorm had passed.

CHAPTER 10

June warmed into July and the fate of the twenty-five hundred rebels remained in limbo.

Being confined to their barracks allowed Aleks to rest but his coughing was worse at times, not better.

"Damn!" Sedecki said. "Something has to be done. He needs a doctor."

Viktor nodded. "I know, I know, but they refuse. Only dead men get past the gate."

Three o'clock came suddenly one morning in July. Twelve of the rebels had died since the rebellion. The remaining twenty-four hundred and eighty-eight were rousted from their bunks and given a latrine call while bread and warm water was delivered to the barracks.

"What in hell is going on now," Sedecki said to no one in particular.

"It's coming to an end," Aleks sputtered.

Shortly after that the steel gong pealed again.

"Everybody out, out, FORM FIVES!" the bullhorn announced.

Roll call was taken. Under heavy guard they were marched to the railroad tracks and jammed into boxcars.

The train stopped at the Yenisey River near Dudinka. Through the slit Sedecki gazed at the same austere little houses that he had seen before. The vast flatlands were still snow covered.

She was moored to the pier like some god-forsaken ogre. Black, rusty and so cruddy the big letters SLON were almost indistinguishable. She brought new prisoners in, now she would take old prisoners out.

"Good God," Sedecki said, "that's the same old bucket we came here on. She ought to have sunk by now. Look at the crud. And the same shithouse built out over the railing."

"I think it's the only SLON ship operating these waters," Aleks coughed and spit.

They were herded over a gangway onto the ship.

Viktor said, "It looks like we'll have the ship to ourselves."

"That won't make the accommodations any better," Sedecki grimly joked. Empty or not the ship still smelled of feces, urine and human misery.

Aleks stopped doubled over coughing, trying to catch his breath. They stopped with him.

"Move!" a man behind them gruffly hollered.

Viktor straightened up, looked down, "Go around, you idiot."

The man backed off.

Two stairways, up and down, ran on opposite sides of the open hatch. A twelve-foot square opening was between the stairways on every deck, the same as before except the stairway to the bottom deck was blocked.

"What in hell...." Sedecki said, looking over the railing of deck number two where they were assigned.

Three decks below, they lounged around in the open area. Some were half clothed but most were completely naked. They offered big smiles, seductive poses. The daylight filtering down wasn't much, but the milk-white skin against the murky background was clear enough to discern the mass of human bodies: big boobs, small boobs, arms akimbo, some with legs spread apart, pubic hair accentuated by white, sweaty skin. It reminded Sedecki of Cell 53.

"My God," he said, staring bug-eyed. "They're as bald and ugly as we are."

"Yeah," Viktor grinned, looking down at the women taunting everyone who could see them. "And they're hornier too."

"Sure, but you'll never get close enough," Aleks rasped and coughed.

Viktor said, "Well, I'll bet someone will."

The next morning the three of them emerged on deck for a toilet break.

"Look," Sedecki said softly, nodding to the other side of the deck.

Boris Viskaya was in a line with the rest of the hard-cores. His head was down but he turned just enough to make eye contact and smiled.

"I thought they were being kept separate," Sedecki said.

"They are," Viktor whispered, "they're up front near the bow, first hatch. I guess they get their toilet break along with us but in a separate line."

"Okay," Sedecki whispered, "now I see."

"What?"

"That board sticking out near the middle, see? It separates the latrine, hardcore on one end, us on the other. A rope runs from the board to that last hatch"

Aleks went into a coughing spell. A soldier watched him until he stopped.

"Damn it was cold," Sedecki said going back down to their deck. "If I hadn't had to crap so badly I would have said to hell with it."

"We're going east," Aleks said.

"Son of a bitch," Viktor pounded his fist in his other palm, "I kind a thought so. You're right, Aleks. That's why that Icebreaker is still in front of us. We're going east, a direction they don't take from the Yenisey. There is no place to go when you go east of the Yenisey and the Kara Sea that I know of. All that's left is the Artic Ocean, and the Bering Sea, and you can't get through it." He turned, looking at Aleks, "Can you?"

Aleks shrugged his shoulders.

It was slow going through the heavy sea ice that even in summer extended from the polar cap all the way down to Taymyr Peninsular, the most northern part of Siberia.

On the forth day Aleks became worse. He was coughing up more blood.

"I'm going up and see if we can get him to the infirmary or some kind of help," Sedecki said.

"Be very careful my friend," Viktor warned. "They have itchy trigger fingers and won't be pushed."

"Bastards," Sedecki spat when he returned. "Dirty bastards, no doctor and no medical help on the ship they said. They're lying. I know it. There has to be medicine and supplies aboard for the crew, the soldiers."

"Easy my friend, easy," Viktor said. "We'll do the best we can. One of us can stay with him while the other takes his toilet and gets the food and water."

"Yeah," Sedecki agreed and looked at Aleks.

After bringing bread and warm water at noon Viktor left Sedecki with Aleks and took his toilet break. He was gone so long that Sedecki began to wonder. But he couldn't leave Aleks.

When Viktor came back Sedecki left for his break.

Viktor helped Aleks to a *parasha* to pee and then steadied him coming back. Aleks crawled in his bunk, scrunched down and curled up.

"We got to keep him warm, covered up," Viktor told Sedecki when he returned. He pulled Aleks' coat up around his neck then he put his coat across Aleks' legs. "He must sweat it out. Give me your coat."

Sedecki agreed. He handed his coat and shirt to Viktor, who piled it on top of Aleks.

"We'll take turns watching him," Viktor said. "Keep him covered. Pile on whatever we're not wearing. Maybe we can break the fever."

They kept a close watch on Aleks that night, the next day, and the following night. They brought him food and water and helped him to a *parasha* for his toilets.

After the supper meal was brought down on the eighth day, Sedecki stayed with Aleks while Viktor went topside for his last toilet of the night.

"You're going to be okay," Sedecki kept telling his friend. "Just keep bundled up and sweat it out, you'll pull through."

Viktor finally came lumbering down the aisle.

Sedecki was cross, "Cripes, where in hell have you been, I'm about to bust a gut. I was almost ready to use the *parasha*."

"Sorry," he replied. "I sneaked through it a second time. I needed the air. This stench is getting to me."

"It's getting to me too, but I don't take that long," Sedecki said, looking sideways at the big Russian. "I just helped Aleks over to the *parasha*. He is weak in the knees but made it okay. I have to piss and I need air."

"Go, go," Viktor said. "The last toilet call is almost over."

Later that evening Aleks began shivering.

Viktor and Sedecki piled all the available clothing on their friend. Aleks continued to cough but finally seemed to drift off to sleep.

"You take the first watch," Viktor said. "Keep him covered."

"Okay," Sedecki said, watching Aleks.

"Keep him covered, stay with him as long as you can, but wake me if you need to."

"Okay, Viktor, okay, okay," Sedecki grimaced, "Cripes, I understand."

It became quiet in the hold. The only sounds were snoring, the constant hum and vibrations of the engine and the ice-flows grating against the hull.

Sedecki leaned his butt against the edge of Aleks' bunk and occasionally checked his forehead, which was sweaty. He did this every time Aleks coughed. The rags were full of blood.

Sedecki pursed his lips, closed his eyes and sadly shook his head. It pained him to see his friend suffering and there was nothing he could do.

Summer sunlight filtered weakly through the hatch opening all night. Sedecki had no idea what time it was. Twenty-four hours of daylight made time almost impossible. He guessed it must be two or three in the morning or later. He was sleepy. He took a pee then shook Viktor.

"Viktor, get up," he said quietly. "I can't keep my eyes open any longer."

Viktor crawled out of his bottom bunk

"All right, I'll take it from here. How is he doing?"

"About the same, got the sweats, still coughs and spits up blood."

"I'll keep him covered," Viktor said. "I've got the watch. You get some sleep my friend. When breakfast comes I'll get yours."

Sedecki got into his top bunk wearing his undershirt and shorts. He rolled up his shirt, stuck it under his head and dropped into a sound sleep.

There were four topside latrine calls a day. The first one began before breakfast at 5 AM, the second at 10:30 then 3 PM and the last at 8 P.M. The women were brought up first at 4:30AM. There were not many of them. Viktor heard them talking on the staircase.

Both groups of men were next and took their toilet turn at the same time. The minor rebels lined up on the port side of the ship. The hard-cores came out near the bow and lined up on the starboard side.

Aleks awoke. His lungs were burning intensely. He muffled a cough with a rag. Easing out of the bunk he was immediately dizzy. Sedecki was sleeping. Viktor was not there. He leaned against the bunks, holding on, suppressing another cough. After a few moments he slipped into pants, boots and a shirt then the outer coat. Fumbling around the bunk he started to cough and panicked. He grabbed a rag and crammed it into his mouth.

Viktor came quickly from the *parasha*, "Aleks."

Aleks stopped coughing and looked at Viktor. "I'm going up. Cap, cap, I have to have a cap."

"Here," Viktor put the cap on his head, took his arm and walked him to the stairway. "I was just checking. The women have finished. Some are now starting to line up for first call."

When Viktor started to go up with him, Aleks stopped.

"I can make it," Aleks said, coughing, "God willing, I can make it."

They talked for a moment longer then Viktor watched Aleks trudge up the stairs.

Other men were gathering on the stairwell as Aleks slowly trekked up the two flights. Some asked if he needed help. He would stop, cough, and refuse. He could hardly wait to get a breath of fresh air. The line was so slow he wasn't sure he would make it all the way.

Finally the air became fresher. He reached the last several steps as the line stopped. He began coughing and spitting so much that the men near him began talking. He held a rag to his mouth.

Shortly, Aleks was out on the open deck. He took a deep breath and that made him cough. He put his rag to his mouth and finally the coughing stopped. He gazed torpidly about. The cold sky was watery blue and hazy, as if it were covered with a thin curtain of gauze. A huge dull sun languished in the horizon miasma. The wind was calm and the deck was quiet, except an occasional bellow from the controller and the steady scraping of ice against the hull. The line in which he stood continued to move slowly. No one seemed to mind.

All of a sudden a prisoner broke away from the line and rushed across the port side of the deck for the gunwale. He wasn't particularly fast but it appeared he might make it.

A voice shattered the crystallized air. "Halt! Stop!"

The man did not stop. His cap fell off. He got his arms and one leg up on the gunwale when a volley of automatic fire tore through him and ricocheted off the steel. He slumped against the bulwark and slowly slid to the deck.

The sharp staccato resounded throughout the quiet ship.

Sedecki bolted upright like he was jabbed with a cattle prod. He looked down at Viktor then he jumped to the deck, grabbed his pants and froze, "What in—"

"Wait. Quiet," Viktor said, tears streaming down his face.

Both Viktor and Sedecki stood riveted in place.

"What the hell is going on?" Sedecki said.

Two soldiers jumped down from their platform and ran to the dead prisoner while others stood at the ready. The commanding officer, a major, quickly appeared on the raised platform.

"Everyone below ... NOW!" he shouted.

The controller turned the lines around, prodding the men off the latrine, hustling everyone back into the hatches.

"Check the number and bring his dossier," the major said, jumping to the deck.

A few minutes later another officer appeared with a dossier.

"Seven-nine-one," the officer said, opening the file, "Stanislaus Sedecki, twenty-five years, espionage."

They looked at the N-791 on the back of the man's coat.

The major stood next to the dead prisoner, "Roll him over."

A guard rolled N-791 on his back. The officer looked down at the numbers N-791 printed on the knees of his pants. Stepping over the blood that was pooling on the deck he stuck his toe under the cap and flipped it. The number was N-791.

He looked at the dossier photograph then bent down to study the face of N-791. "Stanislaus Sedecki," he muttered, "One and the same."

He handed his subordinate the file and said, "Verify the identification and make a formal report. When you are done, have the man stripped and toss the body overboard."

Sedecki was benumbed. The words formed, but he could not bring himself to speak. He watched the tears roll down Viktor's face. Then he turned, put his arms on the top bunk, leaned his head against it and also negan to weep.

Viktor placed an arm on the top bunk and the other over the shoulders of the only friend he had left in these ungodly Gulags.

"Sedecki," he said softly, "it was not just a severe cold. Aleks had tuberculosis. Worse, he had lung cancer. He was dying. There was nothing anyone could do. He's known this for some time, before he met you. It just got worse, unbearable. The Norilsk hospital confirmed it, but he didn't want to die in there. He talked the doctor into letting him out."

Sedecki stared past the bunk, shaking his head.

"He wanted it this way, Sedecki. He tried to find a way to switch places during the riot."

Viktor stopped talking and turned towards the hatchway.

Heavy boots were clambering down the stairs.

Victor began rearranging the clothing between the top and middle bunks.

Two soldiers carrying truncheons landed on the deck with resounding thuds and shouted, "Listen up! Where does number N 791, prisoner Sedecki, bunk? Speak up!"

"Here," Viktor said, wiping his eyes. Then he whispered to Sedecki, "You are Aleks, 799."

The soldiers clomped over to Sedecki and Viktor, "Names!"

"Viktor Stephanovich Zukovny, C two-one-four-four."

"Aleksandr Mikhailovich Leskov, N seven-nine … nine."

The first soldier looked at Viktor and his numbers then grabbed a coat off the top bunk, looked at the number 799 and turned to Sedecki, "This your coat?"

"Ya …Yes," Sedecki stammered.

"Seven-nine-one's bunk?" the soldier said.

"Middle one," Viktor quickly answered.

The soldier looked at the top bunk then looked at the middle bunk, picked up a short jacket and said, "Whose is this?"

Viktor was quick to answer. "Belongs to prisoner seven-nine-one, he has gone for his toilet call. What is wrong?"

The soldier looked at the two men and said, "Your friend, seven-nine-one is dead. He tried to escape."

The soldier looked at the 799 coat on the top bunk then at the 799 on the pants Sedecki wore. He failed to notice how tight the pants fit. Then he asked, "What belongs to prisoner seven-nine-one?"

Viktor quickly pointed to the jacket the guard held.

The soldier looked down at the jacket then squinted at both prisoners for an uneasy moment, nodded to his partner and they both left.

"Wheeew…." Viktor sighed, leaned against the bunks and looked at his friend. "You have to remember—your name is Aleksandr Mikhailovich Leskov. Repeat that to yourself over, and over, and over, and over. That's who you are now. Forget it and you are a dead man."

"I can't believe this," a bewildered Sedecki said, spinning away from Viktor. He looked to the ceiling and closed his eyes. *Aleks, my closest friend—dead.* Aleks, who has taught me the language, the scholar who guided me through St Petersburg, tutored me through the University like a Professor; my brother who taught me the ins and outs of these damned hell holes is dead. My God, my God.

In anguish, Sedecki ran a hand through his stubby hair, lost in misery. He laid his arms and head against the top bunk. Finally he turned to face Viktor.

"How did you manage it?"

"We had some rubles," Viktor replied. "That got me on the latrine platform next to Viskaya three days ago and again last night, wasn't easy. The *pakhan* still has unbelievable contacts. He sat on the latrine next to me last night and said it was all set."

"All set?"

"Yes, all set," Viktor replied, "Keep your voice low. The clerk, the free-man set it up."

"What free man?"

"A free-man, now listen," Viktor admonished. "This free-man clerk is a criminal, owes his existence the biggest *pakhans* in the Gulags, like Viskaya. He worked with the administrative files at Norilsk and now here in the NKVD cabin with the records of everyone on this ship. He's obligated to do the bidding of Boris Viskaya.

"Don't ask me how because I don't know, but Boris Viskaya has access to this clerk. Boris said he owed you for saving his life and it would give him great pleasure to repay you and Aleks. Switching the two dossiers was the least he could do. Yesterday I met with him on the toilet and he said the dossiers had been switched, pictures and all."

Sedecki slowly shook his head.

"Aleks was slipping fast," Viktor continued, "it was only a matter of days. It came down to just hours. I didn't think he'd even make it up the stairs. He said you were his brother and to tell you that you must live for him and the brother he lost long ago."

Viktor paused looking squarely at his friend and deliberately slowed his speech. "Maybe you don't know who you are or where you came from and maybe you never will. But one thing is certain. From this moment on you are Aleksandr Mikhailovich Leskov and in a few more years you might be able to get out of here."

The big man placed a hand on Sedecki's shoulder, "There was nothing I could do, nothing you could do. He knew you would try to stop him that's why he couldn't say goodbye to you. He hoped you would understand. You were his last wish. Now you must be brave my friend, you must live Aleks' life—for him and for you." Viktor paused. "If you don't I will personally be the one to break you in two."

Sedecki sat down on the edge of the bottom bunk with his head in his hands, tears in his eyes and Viktor's words ringing in his ears.

Three days later gunshots again crackled on deck. Two men were tossed overboard. The old ship plowed on through the ice and freezing temperatures without missing a beat.

Day after day the ice steadily scraped against the hull. Finally came the time when everyone could see areas of level shoreline rise gradually then precipitously up the majestic Kolyma Mountain Range.

During first latrine call Viktor said, "We're right where everybody predicted we would be—the Kolyma River, the coldest part of the damned Gulags."

"So, it's back to the mines?"

"That's all there is in Kolyma, my friend."

The ship was mooring to a pier when they returned to their bunks. Viktor glanced about then laid his arms on the edge of the top bunk and said, "Come close."

Sedecki moved shoulder to shoulder.

"I have some interesting news," Viktor whispered. "Remember the two that were tossed over the rail some days ago after we heard shots?"

Sedecki nodded.

"It happened on the latrine. A criminal killed the free-man, stuck a shiv in him three times. They dragged the criminal off the latrine and shot him on the spot."

"So?"

"Aleks, my friend, that free-man he killed was the records clerk."

Sedecki, not yet accustomed to being called Aleks, stared at him.

Viktor frowned, "The records clerk, Aleks, you hear me, the one who switched your dossier. Now no one knows about the switch except Boris Viskaya and he'll take it to his grave. The murder was his work. He has fully paid his debt to you."

Sedecki did not respond, he just nodded letting his mind wander off, lost in the meaning of it all. So, he mused, it is final. I am now Aleksandr Mikhailovich Leskov. Stanislaus Sedecki, if I really was that person, is gone forever. Cripes, I don't know who I am, where I came from, why I am here, or how I got in this damned country, and from this point on I can never go back. I must live the double lie. He closed his eyes and tilted his head back. I can't remember a damned thing except my life in these Gulags. I'll die never knowing who I am.

They offloaded by decks. Guards came to deck two with rosters.

When their names were called Aleks and Viktor went up the stairs, disembarked and stood another roll call on the shore. Afterwards they were in the first group of fifty that formed into fives.

They marched several hundred yards up a gradual incline, looked back at the ship and stood there shivering. Ambarchik is well into the far north, beyond where trees can grow.

From the slope Aleks watched the last group having roll call.

"This is not all of 'em," he said. "I count ten groups, maybe five hundred of us."

"Who cares," Viktor replied as they began marching. "Worry about ourselves, Aleksandr Mikhailovich."

They stopped marching at noon and were met by a small group of guards and a six by six truck. Bread, water and a piece of salted fish was doled out to the five hundred.

"Damn, this water's cold," Aleks said

"Better than being ice," Viktor replied.

The mobile eatery took off. The five hundred were given one more latrine break and the march resumed, becoming more strenuous and

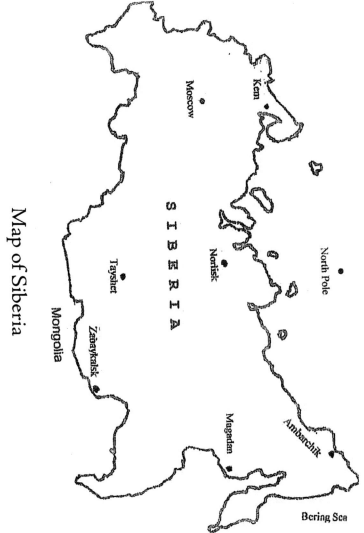

Map of Siberia

colder as they ascended the foothills.

Looking back at a commotion Aleks saw several men had collapsed. Guards stepped in with clubs raised high but others picked the men up and held them.

"Rest stop!" an officer yelled, "Rest where you are!"

Aleks sat down in the snow with Viktor and gazed at the panoramic scene. They could not determine the path the icebreaker and *zek* ship had made in the Kolyma delta. Some of the ice chunks were piled but the ice had all fused together again. The sea of solid white stretched to the horizon. The black muddy shoreline looked like a ribbon that tied the mountains to the sea.

"My God, that's ugly and yet so beautiful," Aleks said.

Viktor nodded, "There are beautiful things in the motherland."

"This is well traveled. The snow is packed with tire marks."

Viktor grabbed a hand full of snow and ate it. "I guess they're bringing stuff out of the mountains, loading it on the ship."

Aleks said, "There must be something else around the bend. While we were standing on shore I noticed a road of packed snow following the black coastline around the foothills to the north."

Viktor's reply was drowned out.

"Form fives!"

When they topped a foothill Aleks saw a wide valley with high mountains beyond. In the flat area of the basin were dark, weather beaten buildings. The area didn't look too big. He saw two rows of barracks facing each other with a group of buildings at the south and north ends. Outside the barbed wire were more buildings. Beyond them were huge mounds of fresh dirt and rocks and trails of packed, dirty snow.

At the main gate later that afternoon they entered the Ambarchik Gulag.

****

The weird, multi-colored striations of the aurora borealis blocked the sky like dancing ghosts when they walked from the mess hall to their barracks. Aleks was fascinated.

They joined the weary and gaunt men huddled around the barracks stove. The talk centered on Stalin's death in March and Levrenti Paviovich Beria, the NKVD Soviet Secret Police Chief, who, they said, was now under arrest.

"Things are changing," someone said gleefully.

"Well, at least we don't have to wear numbers here, like we did in Norilsk," Aleks said.

"Tell us about Norilsk," they all prodded. Viktor told them about the work stoppage, the riot and the killings.

"Maybe we could do that," a small, thin man said.

"No, won't work," Viktor replied. "Fifty-five days of riots and killings got us nothing. The committee men were tied to stakes and shot. We were shipped out, along with the hard core protesters."

"They're going down river," someone said.

"Who is?"

"The really bad ones, and the rest of your bunch," a tall skinny man replied.

"And the women too," another sadly added.

"I wish they'd brought them in here, if only for one night," skinny said.

"What's down-river?" Aleks asked.

"You don't want to go there."

Aleks glanced at Viktor, then at the man, who added, "If they survive the boat trip they aren't any better off. They'll wind up in the sick mines."

"What sick mines?" Viktor asked.

A man with a German accent answered, "Mines that are producing secret minerals." He appeared to be stronger, larger than the others.

"What secret minerals?" Aleks asked.

"Uranium and things like that." The German continued. "I was at K-2 before I came here. They were building a huge place inside a mountain, a city by itself. A railroad runs into it. They camouflage the track. I don't know why, no one is around to see it.

"The *zeks* that live in the minlag outside the mountain go daily into the mountain to work. No *zek* has ever left that camp, I was told. No one will ever will ... highly secret."

"How'd you get out?" Viktor asked.

"I never worked in the mountain. Word gets around. Nothing can be kept secret. They brought scientists and technicians to live permanently inside the mountain. It is said they are building Atomic Bombs in there. Someone heard the NKVD soldiers here talking about bombs being stored at Ambarchik."

Aleks looked at Viktor, then at the German. "Where's Ambarchik?"

"This is Ambarchik, but there's more maybe fifty-sixty miles north."

"That's where the gold that we mine goes to be flown," another man said.

"Flown out?"

"There's an airfield there," the German added.

Another joined the conversation. "Sometimes they pass overhead, you'll see."

"Don't interrupt," the German glared. "Some of our men have been there. They send a work detail up sometimes. There are quite a few airplanes there, big ones, little ones."

"Don't worry, you might not live to see one," a skinny man added. "This is a small camp. Last year we had over fourteen hundred men here. That's why we got five hundred of you. Every year is the same, three, four or five hundred die in the mines. In the summer more like you are shipped in—many are flown in."

Aleks looked at the skinny little man. "How long you been here?"

"This is my second summer. Hardly any of us have been here more than four years. The work is too hard, the hours too long. The camp hasn't been open very long."

When they were alone Viktor told Aleks about the two horrific bombs the United States dropped on Japan during the war, killing hundreds of thousands. "Now," he said, "maybe Russia has such a bomb, maybe an even bigger one, maybe several of them."

The Sunday after they had arrived was one of the days of rest allowed in the camp. Just before noon the camp guards came through the barracks rousting all of the five-hundred new arrivals—actually four-hundred and ninety-eight, two had died.

An NKVD major climbed up on an open six by six, raising his bullhorn.

"The following named men will step forward and form fives on my right."

The major called out twenty-two names. Aleks and Viktor were surprised to hear their names called.

When the men were formed the major again raised his bullhorn.

"These are the twenty-two men from the Norilsk camp who rebelled, refused to work, instigated the riot and committed crimes against the state." For ten minutes he harangued the prisoners that had been chosen as examples, knowing that all the others were listening.

Then he turned to the twenty-two men formed on his right and again he called all of their names. "These men whose names I have called are from barracks eleven of section two, compound one, and barracks five and six of section ten, compound number three, where most of our brave soldiers were murdered while carrying out the motherland's orders."

"I guess we did get a few didn't we," Aleks whispered.

"Silence!" the major roared trying to see who spoke.

"For treason against the motherland and the murdering of innocent soldiers the penalty is death. However, the motherland has waived the death sentence. Instead you are hereby sentenced to thirty years."

"Son of a bitch," Aleks blurted.

"Silence!" the major screamed. "The next man who speaks will be pulled out and shot."

In the heavy silence he peered intently at the newly convicted "murderers."

"This mass trial was held in absentia. Individual trials are not necessary. Let it be known that such crimes against the state will not be tolerated. These sentences will be entered into your dossiers in accordance with the directive I have just read."

"Only thirty years!" Aleks mocked the sentence when they were back in the barracks. "We are so lucky to have such a benevolent motherland."

"Not so loud," Viktor admonished, looking around. "There are ears."

"What more can they do Viktor? How old will you be in thirty years, plus the previous sentence? No, Viktor, it's a life sentence. It might as well be a death sentence and put us out of our misery."

"Aleks, quiet down, they still have solitary punishment cells. Think what Viskaya and the others who went south must have got."

"Probably executed," Aleks snapped.

"No, they wouldn't have transported them all that way to shoot them. They got life."

"I know, I know," Aleks said in resignation. "I am probably lucky. What would I have got for killing five State Security soldiers? I'd have been shot."

"Aleks this is foolish talk."

"I know, never mind, it doesn't matter."

Viktor looked to see who was within earshot. "Listen to me. Our friend gave you a new lease on life, such as it is. You need to honor that."

Aleks was staring towards the horizon, trying to control himself. "Shit, I know all of that, but thirty more years!" He pounded a fist on the bunk. "Aleks was"— he corrected himself—"I was, due for release in '63. But thirty more years Viktor, that's a death sentence."

Aleks closed his eyes, pursed his lips. "Whoa, I'm sorry Viktor, you're right. I apologize. It's just this system. Good God, I don't know who I really am and I do not understand how…." He stopped, shook his head and looked at the floor. "I will honor Aleks, I will, and I will be careful."

He decided he would stay as close as he could to his only friend. There were only two choices available to them—survive or die. "It's time for dinner, let's eat."

Aleks picked up his two bowls, the large can and the smaller tin. Two bowls, what luxury. The smaller tin had intrigued him since they first arrived. It was an odd rectangular shape and had colorful printing on the outside with a large word: SPAM.

"Why are there so many of these odd shaped tins here" Aleks asked as they walked in the cold sunshine.

"Ah, you haven't heard the story," Viktor laughed, partly because the subject had so quickly changed from death to levity.

"It happened here in Kolyma, but further south," Viktor said, "during World War Two. It's a big joke. We were allies back then, America and Russia. This American Vice President, what was his name … Wally, Walters, or something like that … no, it was Wallace, yes, Wallace. He came to Kolyma to coordinate American help for the war with Germany.

"They gave him a tour of one of the camps to show off how well our workers were organized and how good everything was going. They told him it was a 'production camp.'" Viktor laughed. "But first, they took down all of the fencing and birdcages. No one could escape anyway. They hid the barbed wire and gave all prisoners different clothing, had them shave. Some say they even painted the buildings, but I don't know if that part's true."

Viktor grinned. "Stalin really duped the Americans into thinking this was Soviet labor at its best. It was, but the Americans didn't know that it was *slave* labor. The only workers the Americans could talk to were actually NKVD, posing as workers."

Aleks smiled, "So they completely fooled the Americans eh, but why?"

"Stalin wanted help, supplies, food and materials to fight the war. And it worked. America gave us everything, food, clothing, ammunition, trucks, even airplanes. It was wonderful, everyone in the Gulags laughed about it. One of the things was the shiploads of canned Spam, when ships could get through, maybe some was flown in I'm not sure."

"What is Spam?"

"Canned ham," Viktor laughed. "Some used to joke that America ground up all of the pig leftovers including the guts, feet and hair, squeezed it into tins and shipped it to Russia." He gave Aleks a sideways smile. "The Americans may not have been complete fools after all."

Other than receiving an individual package from home, there is absolutely nothing in the Gulags to lift a man's spirits. But in late December there was news they could all cheer: Lavrenti Pavlovich Beria, head of the NKVD, Secret Police was dead.

He had been arrested and jailed, finally he was shot.

Shortly after his execution the struggle came to a head. Nikolay Bulganin became premier and Nikita Khrushchev became the Communist Party's all powerful First Secretary.

Aleks and Viktor made it through the winter.

The following June of 1954 the package arrived. Aleks was surprised. He had forgotten about packages from Aunt Zora.

"Look at the empty space," he said to Viktor. "It's been pilfered."

He emptied the contents onto his bunk and they began examining what was left.

"Viktor, what am I going to do," Aleks said, tilting his head back. "I have to answer this, write her a letter. She'll know the writing is not the same."

Viktor thought for a moment. "I know, maybe I'll pen the letter saying I'm your friend and you hurt your hand, temporarily. Or you can say that."

They endured the rest of the year and throughout 1955. The food remained the same, generally, but the scurvy that had been plaguing the camp decreased as new supplements were received that contained some vitamins.

"They finally woke up to the fact that scurvy is a problem," Aleks said.

Viktor snorted. "What they woke up to is they we're losing too many workers. They care about our health only when it affects production. They need money. They need the gold. They need to keep some of us alive. The work will kill us soon enough."

One-hundred and sixty-one of the small 1500-man camp perished that winter. In the spring shipments of lumber began arriving by air. More continued through summer and new barracks were built. The camp was expanding.

One hundred new replacements plus five hundred more arrived by ship and air during September.

Sitting on a top bunk Aleks and Viktor listened to the horror tales some of the new men were telling about General Derevenko, the "Czar" of all Kolyma, and his thugs who ran the camps.

"All of us on the plane came from the 754 area because much of the work there is about finished," one of them had said.

"Where's 754?"

"North of Magadan quite some distance. It's the uranium mines where they're making a new atomic plant. Most of us have been working on those dams for the last four years. They need lots of water. The dams are finished that's why they sent us up here."

"It will be better here," one of the two Korean men said in sing-song Russian. "Many men died every day working on the dams, any-place is better."

A lot of the men laughed. One said, "It won't be any better here, friend, maybe worse. We lose almost a third of all the men in this camp every year."

"What was your crime?" someone asked the newcomer.

The Korean, a middle aged man with a face that looked like someone smashed the bridge of his nose said, "No crime. When North Korea invaded in 1950 many became prisoners, me too. When we wouldn't swear to communism some of us were shot, others sent to Magadan."

"Were you a soldier?"

"No, construction worker," he nodded to his friend, "Pak was a soldier in the South Korean Army working with the Americans when he was captured. We have been together since Magadan. Pak doesn't speak too much Russian, doesn't want to learn, he is angry, he can't forget what happened. He speaks good English. He liked it better at 754 because many prisoners spoke Korean or English. Pak will speak only our native tongue and English."

"Where were those other prisoners from?" Viktor asked.

"All over, Rumania, Bulgaria, Germany and Korea, and America," the Korean replied. "A lot of American GIs that were captured when the North invaded us were sent to Magadan."

Aleks interrupted, "You can talk to me in English, Pak."

The quiet Korean, Pak, smiled.

Later, Aleks asked Viktor, "The war those two Koreans talked about, how did Koreans and Americans and others wind up here in

Kolyma? Was Russia in that war?"

"No, North Korea invaded the South. It is said that Stalin instigated it, got China to support the North Koreans and send troops, and they did. Americans and soldiers from other countries defended the South Koreans. Russia sent supplies, fighter planes, technicians and things to the North. It was a war of communism against freedom. Stalin got some of the human spoils—good slave labor."

"Stalin won?"

"No one won I guess." Viktor shrugged his big shoulders. "Like a game of chess, a stalemate. But it's always the little guys that lose."

In late February 1956 word was out that Nikita Khrushchev's speech at the party's closed Twentieth Congress was a bombshell (but kept from the Russian people for decades). He denounced Stalin for his "brutality, his intolerance, and his abuse of power. After that Poland and Hungary were released from "Stalinization" and allowed to reform their governments. At the same time he declared amnesty for millions of criminals in the Gulags.

I can't believe it," Viktor remarked. "They say millions of criminals are being released."

"You can't believe everything you hear."

"It's true Aleks. They're all talking about it—the KGB** people."

Aleks shook his head, "Released, impossible, and millions? Huh uh, that's crazy."

"There are only a few criminals here in Ambarchik," Viktor said, "and they are being released."

Aleks still shook his head. "But why would this Khrushchev release only criminals without some politicals also, maybe those with only minor offences?"

**   *KGB – Komitet GoSudarstvennoi Bezopasnost.* The soviet State Security Police was NKVD then MVD and morphed into the KGB under Nikita Khrushchev in 1954.

"Precisely because we are politicals—still a threat to the existing regime. They think we might overthrow it," Viktor laughed. "And by damned, we probably could."

His expression rapidly changed. "Stalin and Beria are long gone, but the regime still rules with an iron fist. Mark my words Aleks those criminals will be back—once a criminal, always a criminal."

In September 1956 the Hungarian Revolution, which lasted thirteen days, reached its peak and was defeated. The little country had tried to withdraw from the Warsaw Pact. However, Khrushchev and his Moscow cronies sent the Soviet Army in to crush the revolt. There were a number of Hungarians in the minlag working along side Viktor and Aleks. They were angry and sad upon learning what this man Khrushchev had done to their country.

In the ensuing years Nikita Sergeyevich Khrushchev survived to become Premier of the Union of Soviet Socialist Republics.

Aleks and Viktor also survived those turbulent years through sheer determination. Aleks worked his way into a trusted position of accounting for the minlag's gold. Viktor became a brigadier and years later would become a mine supervisor. Positions criminals once held.

Viktor had been right, the grapevine said tens of thousands of released criminals were coming back into the Gulags, but none were sent to the Ambarchik minlag.

In August 1964 two KGB men stopped Aleks and Viktor near the mess hall.

"Aleksandr Mikhailovich Leskov!" the Lieutenant blustered, "Come with us."

Aleks and Viktor both started to say something but the officer raised his hand. Aleks stepped forward and was marched off toward the administration building.

They put Aleks in a chair without saying a word. The Lieutenant stepped out of the room and closed the door.

Aleks checked it out. It was larger, but quite similar to the austere room in Tayshet where, as Stanislaus Sedecki, he had been convicted of espionage.

He concentrated on gathering his wits. *Have they discovered I killed those guards? No, I'd be dead by now. It's my identity, it has to be. They know I am not Aleksandr Leskov.* His mind was whirling.

The door swung open. A KGB major and two men in civilian clothes entered. The three of them sat down behind the table. The two in civilian clothes were dressed too neatly for this godforsaken area. *They must be high-ranking officers.*

The major laid a folder on the table.

The room was cool, but Aleks began to perspire.

The door swung open again. A KGB Colonel entered. The men behind the table stood. The major started to move but the colonel grabbed the chair near the wall and put it next to the major's.

The room was quiet as the major thumbed through the pages of the dossier.

"You are"—Aleks jerked—"Aleksandr Mikhailovich Leskov, yes?"

Aleks nodded.

"Well, speak up, the major snarled."

"Da."

Then the bombardment of questions began: age, date and place of birth, education, university, mother, father, uncle, and more. Aleks answered as fast as he could, boldly with conviction, but he was apprehensive. *What's this about?* The questions were personal, about his background, tender territory for him.

"You have been to England and America," the civilian on the left asked, in perfect English, "and you speak English, correct?"

Aleks was caught off guard, *England and America, Oh my god,* "Da."

"Da? When I ask you a question in English you will respond in English."

"Ya—yes, I understand!" Aleks stammered in English, trying to regain his composure. *Oh, my God, I can't remember anything Aleks told me about those countries.*

The questions came randomly from the two civilians and the major. The colonel said nothing. He just stared at Aleks with dark steely-eyes.

Aleks could play that game. *The colonel is the key* he was almost certain. He locked eyes with the colonel, glancing away only to acknowledge the inquisitor's question. Aleks was surprised when the other civilian began asking questions in German and in Polish, but he fielded the questions well.

Then it became dicey when they reverted to Russian, asking about his days at the university, his classmates and professors—ticklish inquiries. Rather than hesitate he responded smartly, even though some of his answers were completely bogus. He felt certain they were buying all that he said when suddenly the colonel cleared his throat.

Oh oh ... or were they?

The colonel's voice was harsh, the question more accusatory than inquisitive. "Your father, Mikhail Andreyevich Leskov, was a colonel killed in battle, yes?"

Aleks' eyes never wavered from the Colonel's. "He died gloriously, defending the motherland from the Germans when they crossed the Dnieper-Bug canal from Poland. My father was a hero and so was my Uncle Grigory."

The colonel's brow furrowed. His eyes narrowed slightly.

Aleks held the gaze, almost daring the man to contradict him, and continued. "My mother and my brother, Dmitri Grigorovich, died in St Petersburg. The war took all of my family, only me and Aunt Zora survived."

Aleks paused. *The best defense is offense.* His eyes had hardened, "But all of you know that, you have that in the dossier in front of you, do you not?"

"Insolent!" The major shot forth, "We will ask the questions."

Aleks sat stone-faced. He knew he had struck a nerve, but he also knew he had won a point. *If I am going down, damn it, I'll go down swinging. Screw the bastards.*

Later, in the barracks, Aleks explained the strange interrogation, or what ever it was, to Viktor.

"My friend," Viktor said, "After the KGB hauled you off I honestly didn't know if I would ever see you again. You are a very lucky man."

Am I? Aleks wondered. *I've been told that before.* He spent the remaining days of August constantly looking over his shoulder.

On 27 August 1964 in the same austere room the door behind Aleks opened, but he did not turn his head. The KGB major and a captain swept past him followed by one man in civilian clothes from the previous meeting.

Aleks expected the colonel but he did not come.

The major took his time fiddling with the dossier. Aleks began to sweat.

"Aleksandr Mikhailovich Leskov," the major blurted. "You were convicted of crimes against the state on three occasions, the last time thirty years for the Norilsk work stoppage...."

Aleks almost smiled at the words. *Work stoppage, my ass, it was a revolt, a complete riot.* But you people can't say that, can you, oh no, to you it has to be a work stoppage.

"... Bringing your combined sentences to a total of forty-five years," the major continued, "with a release date of 4 November 1993."

Aleks just stared at the man with a giddy grin, his mind beginning to float with whimsy, as if he was detatched from this charade. *Golly, major, I'm so glad you reminded me.*

The major stopped for a long moment, looking at the sardonic smirk on the face of this arrogant prisoner. His eyes narrowed. He returned his gaze to the paper in hand and continued.

"In accordance with the results of the investigative proceeding held earlier this month it is the decision of the presiding officer, that prisoner Aleksandr Mikhailovich Leskov's release date of 4 November 1993 be amended."

Aleks straightened up instantly.

The major paused and reached in the folder for another paper. "Therefore, it is the decision of Colonel Dimitri Fyodorov, presiding officer in the proceedings of 6 August 1964 that in accordance with Article 58, point 11, of the Ukaz of the Presidium of the Union of Soviet Socialist Republics, dated 7 June 1943, citizen Aleksandr Mikhailovich Leskov is to be temporarily released from the *Glavnoe Upravlenie Lagerei* effective 29 August 1964."

Then the major, who totally disagreed with this decision, closed the folder and stood up. "Officer Krylenko will attend to the details." He picked up the dossier and with a scowl left the room. The captain was close behind him.

Whoa … whoa-hoa, hold on a minute, what did he say? Aleks sat motionless with a blank stare—his world stopped. *Am I hearing right, did he actually say released?* His mind began to spin. *What in the hell is happening? Am I—*

"You are a very lucky man, citizen Leskov."

The words seemed to come from a hollow chamber, far away, but it was like a dash of cold water. He hesitated, blinked then focused on the man still sitting at the table.

"Let me introduce myself. I am Leonid Ivanovich Krylenko, a lieutenant in the *Komitet GoSudarstvennoi Bezopasnosti*. I will be working with you from this day forward."

Aleks just stared at the KGB man. He couldn't make his tongue work. The lieutenant was much younger than him, maybe mid twenties, fair complexion and blonde hair. He had soft blue eyes that reminded Aleks of several Latvian prisoners.

"Let me explain what will happen and how you will become a free man."

Leonid Krylenko went into lengthy detail. Aleks sat there nodding occasionally and now and then uttering a weak, "yes."

Sometime later, still in a state of complete shock, Aleks was returned to his barracks.

That evening, Viktor anxiously stormed into the barracks, "My friend, you are here! Tell me, tell me what—?"

Aleks pulled Viktor outside into the cold, where they could be alone.

"What a beautiful day, Viktor, a glorious day. The sunshine is magnificent, it is so warm," he rambled on and on, laughing. "I think I'm going crazy."

"Aleks, Aleks! My God, stop. Tell me what has happened."

"Viktor, Viktor" he grabbed Viktor's arms, "I'm being released!"

"What?"

"Released, Viktor, released tomorrow."

"Released? I don't believe that. What—"

"Let me tell you." Aleks walked slowly on, twirling around, dancing in an aura of cold sunshine, grinning and laughing like a circus clown. Then he explained, finishing with, "I am being temporarily released."

"That's incredible, unheard of, why? How can that happen? I do not understand."

"I don't know and don't care." Aleks finally stopped his circus antics placing his hands on Viktor's shoulders. "There's a catch, and I'm scared."

"Scared, a catch? Aleks are you playing with me?"

"They are sending me somewhere to a school where I am to teach English and German. Can you believe that?" His voice took on a more sobering tone and he squinted in the sunlight. "Viktor, I am not a teacher, I'm not even Russian, I barely know the language."

"You are Russian!" Viktor said gruffly, "And you speak the language well, better than I can."

"Com'on," Aleks made a face.

"No, it is true. I speak badly, the slang of these wretched camps. But you, Aleks, you speak the language like a scholar, polite Russian. You are well educated."

"I hope you're right, Viktor. I thought you had to graduate college to be a teacher, but this KGB lieutenant said even though I didn't— that is, Aleks didn't—finish at the university I could still be a teacher of foreign languages."

"You will do well, my friend, do not be afraid." Viktor grinned from ear to ear. "My God, my friend is getting out. I can't believe it. He's getting out."

Aleks gazed at the barbed wire and birdhouses with an excited grin. "I can't believe it either, but at work-call tomorrow I am to report to the administration building. It has to be true. I can't be dreaming."

"I'm sure they would not joke in such a manner," Viktor said in all seriousness.

"I'll miss you, Viktor, my dear old friend. I will never forget what you and Aleks have done for me. I will send you a package every chance I can."

Viktor looked down at Aleks with misty eyes. "I am very happy for you, Aleks. It is only right that you should get out of here."

Aleks' capricious smile disappeared. He realized Viktor had to stay here.

Neither man could sleep. All night Aleks floated half-in and half-out of sleep until the shrill gong made him almost levitate from his bunk. He jumped out of bed.

Immediately the barracks talk again centered on the unbelievable good fortune that had befallen Comrade Aleksandr Mikhailovich Leskov.

Aleks and Viktor finally broke away from the group and went for breakfast.

They ate in electrified silence, grinning at each other, smiling with their eyes, beaming like a couple of young kids—afraid to speak lest they break the intense spell. Time was standing still for Aleks and Viktor. Their life together was about to end and neither knew how to handle it. The atmosphere was both exciting and heartrending. They were sharing as best they could.

Once back in the barracks it was once more a euphoric time for everyone.

Then the gong split the air and the barracks emptied.

Aleks and Viktor, standing on opposite sides of their three-tiered bunk stared solemnly at each other for the longest moment. Viktor finally turned, strode down the barracks and went outside.

"Form fives!" He ordered his brigade.

"*Skorei, skorei,*" he added unnecessarily, the brigade was practically formed. He turned sideways, afraid the men could see his eyes.

"Stand fast!" He shouted in the most ill-tempered, commanding voice he could muster. Then he spun on his heel and reentered the barracks.

He stood solemnly before Aleks until a huge grin spread across his face. They embraced with out saying a word. At last Viktor stepped back and took one last look at his misty-eyed and dearest friend. He held out his hand and Aleks grasped it. Again they embraced.

"Good luck, my dear friend Aleks," Viktor managed. "Good luck from both of us, from all of us." Then he turned and headed for the door.

"Good luck to you, Viktor," Aleks called out. "Take care, my friend, please take care. I will never forget you."

Aleks watched Viktor pause at the door for a long moment without looking back. Then Viktor wiped his eyes several times and stepped smartly out into the Gulag yard.

Chapter 11

Lieutenant Krylenko led Aleks and three other released men to the bath house for what might be their last Gulag *sanobrabotka*. They were stripped, deloused and allowed to bathe. They were given razors and they shaved—beards only. They emerged into an adjoining room and were minutely inspected for any hidden gold.

"Open your mouth, wide. Now bend over and spread your cheeks."

They were issued clothes, real clothes, even a belt and a hat. The four men were put in the rear of a six by six. Two soldiers sat near the tail gate—Aleks chuckled to himself, as if we would now try to escape. Old habits never die.

After an hour of driving Aleks caught a glimpse of the shoreline and moved closer to the tailgate. The soldiers looked at him but said nothing. There were thick chunks of broken ice jammed together and piled along the shoreline. Snow had melted along the coastline and once again a black ribbon curved to the east out of sight.

They passed the dock and the big crane and continued north around the end of the mountains where the Kolyma range tapers down to the East Siberian Sea. When the truck stopped the canvas flap was lowered and tied.

"Now what?" one of the prisoners asked.

The man next to him whispered, "It's the airfield, dummy, secret stuff."

"Shut up," one soldier said.

So this is it, Aleks thought. The airfield, the place where they are storing atomic bombs, hydrogen bombs, and all that secret stuff that's not so secret. When they neared the airfield he heard the soft drone of engines. His eyes brightened.

He remembered being in an airplane long ago. In his mind he could see the wings, the propellers and he became excited. *Where, when was that? Yes* ... he was next to a little girl with blond curls. He was looking through the window beyond her. It appeared to him in a haze, the seat, upholstery, the window, the blonde curls, but when, where? My God, where?

The truck came to a stop. They offloaded between buildings and couldn't see much, were led inside and fed a dinner that was exceptional then placed in a room with no windows.

At two o'clock they were driven across the tarmac to an airplane. During the interval between leaving the windowless van and approaching the four-engine cargo jet Aleks got a glimpse of other planes. There were several large piston aircraft and jets like the one he was boarding. There were also a number of very small planes. They must be the jet fighters that the guys had talked about.

"*Skorei, skorei*—faster!" the soldier at the foot of the stairs yelled.

The three men in front of Aleks hurried up the rickety maintenance stand.

During the brief moments Aleks was standing behind the other men he looked under the belly of the plane towards the base of the mountain.

There were unusual carvings in the foothill. Doors? Yes, big doors partly opened. Caves, storage areas and hangers built into the foothill for airplanes and atomic bombs and all the other stuff that the *zeks* had talked about.

A guard gave him a shove and he scrambled up the stairs.

They sat on bucket-type seats facing low pallets of cargo covered with tarps and strapped netting.

"That's what we slaved our ass off for," the grouchy man whispered, nodding toward the pallets. "That's some of the gold we mined."

Aleks knew he was right.

The whine of the engines increased and after a long takeoff roll the plane was airborne. Aleks would have liked to view the area from the air but quilted padding covered both sides of the plane's interior.

They flew the great circle route over the North Pole from Ambarchik to a military airfield just outside of Moscow. The aircraft taxied to a large hanger and they deplaned.

"Come with me," Lt. Krylenko said and the four men followed him to a room inside the hanger. The flight crew members passed by into an adjoining room.

"As soon as the shipment is verified we will be on our way," Lt. Krylenko said.

Aleks smiled to himself, of course, the gold. The left hand does not trust the right hand. I don't blame them, I wouldn't either.

An hour later, a KGB officer entered the room, spoke to Lieutenant Krylenko then led the other three men from the room.

"They are going in a different direction," Krylenko said and motioned. "We are going to your quarters. It is not a jail, but it is guarded. In the morning we travel to our destination."

At 5 a.m. Aleks and Krylenko ate a meager breakfast—rated sumptuous by Aleks—and were driven to a train station. It was a warm sunny day, few clouds were overhead and there was a pleasant scent in the air. Aleks felt great, alive. But when you're not freezing your ass off in some Gulag up above the Arctic Circle everything feels like utopia.

Aleks watched Krylenko, wearing civilian clothes, show his ID at various points until they were finally seated alone in a first class compartment.

"So, comrade Leskov let me explain your situation and your future. Today, 29 August 1964, you are now a free man ... to a certain extent, that is. You will be watched, of course. But there is no reason to think that you would do something drastic. You would be apprehended within minutes.

"The relationship between you and I must be one of trust. I will be available for any questions or problems you may have. In private you may address me as comrade Krylenko or by my rank. I will address you as Aleksandr or Mikhailovich."

"Aleks, I would prefer Aleks."

"Very well then, Aleks," he said with a smile. "You see, we are trying to make your life as normal as possible."

Aleks didn't see, but didn't say anything. He was thinking of how in hell he was going to pull this off.

"The bag we gave you contains extra clothing that you will need."

As the train sped northeast from Moscow, Aleks let Krylenko do all of the talking.

"You were selected for temporary release for several reasons. A review of your initial crime, although serious, reveals your participation was somewhat minor. The second and third sentences were conducted under the old regime. I won't go into detail but things are changing Aleks. This is your opportunity to prove that we are correct in placing new faith and trust in you."

Somehow it just didn't sound right to Aleks to bounce from one extreme to the other. Faith and trust he says, what a pile of crap. It's like night and day.

He smiled at Krylenko. "Yes, I understand and I am very grateful."

"Fine," Krylenko said. "The school term begins September First.

You will be teaching three classes of English. High school classes which, as you know generally run from two to six every afternoon."

Aleks smiled, *I didn't know, but I do now.* "Do they know I was four months shy of graduating?" *Had they done their homework?*

"Ah, did I not tell you?" Krylenko raised his eyebrows. "I have your diploma in my files. The records have been amended. You have been issued a certificate in linguistics. A copy has been sent to the school at Navolya. You will be primarily teaching the upper four grades.

"You will be furnished quarters, a one room apartment, and you will take one meal a day at the school. You will be paid fifty rubles (US$13.26) a month—"

"Fifty rubles?" Aleks blurted. "That's nothing. We get fifty rubles in packages at the camp." As soon as he uttered the words he knew he shouldn't have.

Krylenko smarted, "Fifty rubles once a year in camp is different, Aleksandr Mikhailovich. Fifty rubles a month teaching is generous. You are given a place to sleep and a meal a day during the days you teach. Think about that. The average teacher's salary is slightly over one hundred rubles a month and they must find their own quarters and food."

"What if I want to find my own living quarters and food?" Aleks asked, nicely.

"That would be possible but only after this school year ends. By then you will understand that the other fifty rubles of pay you sacrifice is more than worth it, much more."

Aleks pondered that a moment. He turned and gazed out the window at a fleeting landscape that was flat then slightly rolling. So much greenery, he sighed, the trees, fields and occasional splash of flowers, my God it's great to be alive.

The sun was well past its apex, making a slow decent to the western horizon. Like the sun, Aleks' mind kept moving. One question—if it strikes a nerve what the hell.

"So, comrade Krylenko, I am a free man. But you say someone will be watching me. So, I am free, but I am not free, how is that?"

"It is quite simple, Aleks. You have been released twenty-nine years early," Krylenko smiled. "But you have not been pardoned. You must remember that.

"You will be free to come and go around the town of Navolya," he waved a hand. "But you shall not leave the town. It is a nice town, a population of about twelve thousand. You will make friends, of course."

"But I will stay in this town and go nowhere else."

"Correct," he smiled. "Any letters you wish to write you will give to me. Your mail address will remain as it has been. Mail you receive I will deliver to you. Also, do not attempt to circumvent these procedures and have someone else send a message for you. That would be disastrous, comrade. We would know," he raised his eyebrows, "oh yes, we would know. The new Union of Soviet Socialist Republics, under Premier Khrushchev wants to give you a chance to redeem yourself. You are an educated man and you can contribute a great deal to the motherland."

His patriotic speech rambled on.

They detrained in the late afternoon. A black sedan pulled up to the front of the station. Aleks smiled, remembering the Gulag phrase: KGB people deserve only the best.

Leaving town the scenery changed to verdant countryside so quickly it was like passing through a magic door. Aleks rolled down the window inhaled deeply, sighing as if visiting a place he had only dreamed about.

During all those years in the Gulags of the north everything was purely black and white, mixed with dreary, dull gray and cold, depressing weather. That was the total content of his mind, his entire life as he knew it, just black and white. His injured mind had known nothing outside of that monochrome existence. Now he found himself in a new world, a world of Technicolor, and he was beginning to feel alive.

Arriving in Navolya, they had a bite to eat at a small kiosk then went straight to Aleks' quarters, an old run down two-story building. The wood siding was as black and weather-beaten as those death-train boxcars that took him to Kem.

His room was on the second floor, near the middle. There were six rooms on each side of the hallway. Krylenko opened the door, pulled the chain on the ceiling light and handed Aleks the key.

"Toilet at end of the hall," he said. "You will be comfortable here." He reached in his coat pocket and handed Aleks fifty rubles. "The motherland is good to you, Aleks. This is a month's pay for which you did not work. You will be paid fifty rubles at the end of next month and every month thereafter."

The young KGB officer, seemingly pleased with himself, watched Aleks set his bag on the bed. He smiled and stepped to the door. "You should keep your door locked. I will come for you in the morning, about seven. Good night, Comrade Leskov."

Aleks locked the door and scrutinized the tiny room. The floor was worn linoleum. The walls and ceiling were plywood, covered with what once was a coat of tan paint. The lone window was a pane of pure grime. A metal daybed set by the wall with an old three-inch cotton mattress. A heavy blanket, enclosed on one side by a sheet, was folded on the bed. A thin little pillow set on top.

By the opposite wall were a tiny sink and a three-foot wide wood counter. On it set a hotplate. Above that were three small cabinets. Aleks opened the doors directly above the sink. Strange, there was no bottom shelf. Three wire racks stretched across the cabinet. A few dishes and utensils were setting in the racks. You wash dishes and let them drain on the rack? The other cabinets had shelves. Near the door was a small steam radiator.

An old wooden table and two straight-back chairs set in the middle of the room. Between the end of the bed and the door was a small closet with a tall door and several bottom shelves.

The following morning of 30 August Aleks was up and dressed, an ingrained ritual, before Krylenko began pounding on the door. When they stepped outside the air was damp. The sun was trying to burn off a misty haze.

Aleks and his KGB man walked the few blocks to school. Krylenko pointed out this and that and a bathhouse. On the wider street Aleks stopped in front of a kiosk.

"There was nothing in the room, how about tea?"

Krylenko hesitated, shrugged his shoulders. "All right, but let's not tarry."

The school was not at all what Aleks had envisioned. It was a huge three-story L shaped structure of dismal gray concrete and smudged windows. The yard was hardpan, making the entire school as stark as a prison. He smiled. The children probably think so too.

Anton Bukovsky, the school principal, was also a surprise. He expected to see an old curmudgeon headmaster ready for retirement. Instead he met a pleasant-faced, younger man who had a bright smile and was delighted to see him.

Aleks was given a complete tour of the school, including the classroom where he would teach English—quite small for the eighteen to twenty students he would have per class.

A janitor cleaning the windows turned and smiled. Aleks smiled back. He had noticed two other men cleaning. They went downstairs and Aleks heard female voices filtering down the hallway. He thought here must be a whole crew of cleaning people getting the school ready.

"Ah, it's almost eight," the principal said. "We must not be late for the meeting."

"What meeting?" Aleks asked.

"The first staff meeting of the new school year," Bukovsky replied, leading them down the hallway. "I have a staff meeting prior to the 'Day of Knowledge' and every Monday thereafter."

When the trio entered the lunchroom the drone of voices immediately stopped, and so did Aleks. He stared in disbelief at the mass of humanity rising from their chairs.

Women. The room was full of women and they all began clapping.

The principal went forward motioning Aleks along.

Krylenko stayed near the door.

"Come, come," the principal smiled, clapping and leading Aleks.

Bukovsky held up his hands. The women became quiet and sat down.

"Thank you," Bukovsky beamed. "Welcome to the 1964-65 school year. Before we get into schedules and other details let me take the pleasure of introducing our new English teacher. He just arrived in Navolya yesterday. Please welcome Aleksandr Mikhailovich Leskov."

Once again the women immediately rose and gave him a long, enthusiastic round of applause.

Embarrassed and bewildered, Aleks stared at the sea of smiling faces. He finally managed a smile and nod.

The principal held up his hands. The clapping ceased.

"Please take time to personally introduce yourselves after the meeting," the principal said and directed Aleks to an empty chair at the end of the first row of tables.

Aleks sat down rather ill at ease.

"Aleksandr Mikhailovich comes to us well qualified. He also speaks German and Polish; however, this year he will only be teaching English, in room 322."

The meeting ended at eleven. Aleks was thankful and ready to leave but found his route of escape was blocked by a horde of women, all beaming like he was the last man on the planet.

He felt like it.

Every one of them shook his hand and offered words of welcome. There were so many that the faces became a blur of gleaming teeth and rosy cheeks, except the one with the pearl-white skin, dark hair and penetrating eyes. She held his hand a bit too long as she smiled.

The last person leaving the lunchroom was Aleks. He joined Bukovsky and Krylenko in the hallway.

Aleks looked at Bukovsky, "There are no men teaching at this school?"

"No, there hasn't been a male teacher in years," Bukovsky answered. "Matter of fact, I am the first male here in a long time. I have been here four years now. Do not worry you will fit in just fine.

"You have your schedule. Your classes will not change much." Bukovsky made a clicking sound with his tongue, "Some of these women, all excellent teachers of course, but some do present challenges. Never mind, that's my problem. You will do well Aleksandr Mikhailovich. Seven-thirty the day after tomorrow, the Day of Knowledge"

He nodded to the KGB officer then went down the hall.

Krylenko paused when he and Aleks reached the street and said almost too eagerly, "I shall leave you here. I'll be in contact with you quite frequently, of course. Good luck, Aleks."

Aleks stood staring at Krylenko's back. He felt like it's some sort of dream, a scary dream. Something didn't seem right: Misery, torment and death one day, then happiness and freedom the next.

Dark eyes, pearl-white skin, and a beaming smile broke his thoughts. She appeared from nowhere, startling him. It was the teacher who didn't want to let go of his hand. Conversation with women was new to him. He spluttered something garbled.

"I am Tamara Mishinov," she said. "I know you don't remember my name, there were so many teachers at the meeting." Her smile grew wider as she squinted up at him. "Because you are new I thought you might need help in getting to know Navolya."

Aleks gently shook the hand she held out.

"I'm sorry if a bother, but I could show you around if you'd like."

"That's very kind of you, but...."

"It's all right, no need to be bashful," she said, turning to cross the street. "Come, I will show you where to eat."

Well, that would be helpful Aleks thought, why not?

As they walked she made small talk. Then she led him into a restaurant that had eight tables. The walls were painted white. It was neat, clean, and smelled of good food.

Taking off their coats Aleks noticed her full breasts. She appeared to be about his age, maybe a year or two younger. She wasn't fat, maybe a little chunky, no, plump, that was the word, plump. The description fit because she was short. Aleks wondered why he was so critical of this dark-eyed woman who was just trying to be nice. A stirring in his groin told him why. He could not take his eyes away from the strain of her breasts.

They both ordered a small lunch and Aleks found that she was quite nice to talk to. She would smile and express great interest as they sipped tea.

"Where did you teach last?" she asked.

Aleks hesitated, his brow furrowed. Decision time, how much do I tell?

"I haven't been teaching recently."

"I'm sorry," she apologized, "I didn't mean to be too personal."

"No, no, it's quite all right." He fingered with his spoon. Hell, what difference does it make? "I was in prison, in the Gulags."

He watched her dark eyes widen then slowly return to their soft glow. She offered a smile that was a bit disconcerting.

"That's quite all right," she said, "I can understand. I will not ask you why you were there, I don't want to know. There are many people in the work camps and I don't understand very much about them."

Work camps, *she thinks they are work camps?* They are slave labor camps, lady, don't you know that? Do any of you people out here know that? Don't you understand? Aleks wanted to pound the table and shout it out.

She must have read the anxiety in his face and sensed the anger in his troubled blue eyes. She reached out and put her hand on his.

"Are you all right? I'm sorry. I didn't mean to be inquisitive. Please forgive me."

"It's all right," he managed. "It's just ... just that I was there for so long."

"Come," she said, getting up and reaching for her coat. "Let me show you the rest of the town and talk about more pleasant things."

He paid and they walked into the sunshine.

"Navolya is a town of twelve-thousand five hundred, more or less, situated on the inside bend in the River, a mile long crescent. North, beyond the school and your dormitory, is the City Water Plant that supplies the town with drinking water, hot water, and steam heat."

"The whole town?"

"Yes, the whole town," she said then named the different main employers in town.

The sun was shining more brightly as Tamara pointed out the various stores, kiosks, restaurants and the lone theater.

They turned and walked westward toward the park and the river.

"It would be nice to walk through the park and along the river bank," Tamara said when they got close, "but it's getting late. It will be dark soon."

"Yes, I should get back to the dormitory."

"I almost forgot," she said, "I promised to help you buy a few things."

The sun was on the horizon behind them as they stopped at several kiosks then turned north.

"I was in your dormitory, many years ago," she said. "A new teacher came to Navolya. She stayed there temporarily. The second floor used to be just for women, but no women there now, only men."

"Where do you live?" He asked.

"I live with a widow lady, Klara, who has a house on the east side of town."

He hesitated, "You and your husband?"

"No, no," her eyes danced, "I was married. He died, many years ago."

"I'm sorry, I didn't mean to—"

"Not at all," she was quick to reply. "It was a normal thing to ask. Perhaps I can have you out to the house for dinner sometime. I can cook, but Klara, she is a jewel, and is better at it."

It was dark when they reached the dormitory. He stopped at the entrance and was about to take the small package she was carrying.

"It doesn't look like it has changed much," she said, "but then I haven't been here in quite some time. Are you on the second floor?"

"Yes," he answered, "near the middle." He wasn't sure of what to say, or what to do. He wasn't even sure if women were allowed in the building.

She broke the awkward silence, "I could help you straighten up the room if you would like," she smiled. "Men are not very good at such things."

"Ah … yes, sure," he stumbled, "if you think that, ah …."

"Of course, it's all right," she giggled. "There is nothing against it. Besides, a room always needs a woman's touch." She hesitated, "If you don't mind."

"No, no," Aleks grinned, opening the door. He led her up the steps, fumbled his key, got the door opened and pulled the light chain.

"Not much, is it?"

"A dormitory room is a dormitory room," she smiled, looking around. "It does need attention."

She laid the parcel on the table and took off her coat, got a cleaning cloth from the package, wet it and began wiping the table.

"Whoa, whoa, I can't let you do that."

"Why not?" she turned and looked at him. "First of all a place must be cleaned." Finishing the table she turned to the cabinets and sink. After wiping just about everything she began putting away the other items he had bought. She washed and dried her hands then stepped to the window.

"You will need some kind of covering for this window," she said.

Turning around she bumped into Aleks.

They stood there for a moment. She was smiling, looking up.

He started to put his arms around her and was surprised that she pressed to him so willingly.

He bent down and kissed her.

Then it was a wild, frenzied effort to get undressed. He was down to his pants and couldn't wait. He grabbed her in another wild embrace and began to explore.

"Wait, wait," she whispered, drawing back. She pulled the light chain and the room went dark. A dim glow from outside filtered through the window.

She slipped out of her undergarments.

Aleks was undressed as their eyes became accustomed to the semi-darkness.

He began caressing her and steering her to the bed. He flipped the blanket and she lay down.

There on an old metal daybed in the semi-darkness he entered into the most fantastic excitement he had ever known.

"Easy, slowly," she cooed.

But he was on fire and her words did not penetrate his sex-famished mind.

"Oh, my heaven!" she squealed with delight and wrapped her arms tightly around him.

Twice again they made love before she got up and began to dress.

"How long were you in the camps?" she laughed.

"Fourteen long years in those Siberian Gulags."

"In all my married years—all my life—I have never made love three times in one night," she laughed. "You are a tiger, a Siberian Tiger."

1 September 1964, the Day of Knowledge. Aleks was nervous but had decided to play it by ear.

Standing before the mirror rubbing his chin and the side of his face he grinned. It felt so good just to be able to shave and wash.

He dressed in his new shirt and pants but had trouble with his tie, he wasn't sure it was correct. He slipped into his jacket and donned his coat.

Emerging from the dormitory he stopped in his tracks.

From a few paces away Lieutenant Krylenko said, "Ah, good morning, Aleks, you look very business-like."

"Ga—good morning," Aleks managed, regaining his composure.

"I didn't mean to startle you."

"That's all right. I just didn't expect to see you here."

Krylenko smiled, "I was on my way to your room." He walked with Aleks to the corner and then turned obliquely away. "Good luck on your first day."

Aleks made a motion with his hand, frowned and kept walking.

There was a bite in the air as Aleks walked the short distance to school. The sun was bright but the buildings in the area still looked gloomy to him and the school was as stark as before. But no, something had changed. Of course, all of the windows were clean. What a difference sparkling windows can make.

Children from ages six to the high teens were standing in clusters. He had forgotten his dead friend had told him that children started school at age six or seven, finishing ten or eleven years later, and they attend the same school during those years.

This made him think of everything his friend had told him back in Norilsk. Things he had better remember. Each school is divided into three sub-schools: Four years of primary, five years of secondary, and two years of high school. The school year begins in September, ends the last of May and is divided into four semesters with a one week vacation between each term.

Bukovsky had said there are two sessions: 8 AM to 2 PM for grades 1 to 8 and from 2 to 6 PM for high school students.

He smiled as he passed by the youngsters. There were a lot of quizzical looks and a few smiles.

He went through the main entrance, down the hall and into the lunchroom.

"Ah, Aleksandr Mikhailovich," the principal called, waving his hand, "Come in, come in, we are about to begin."

Aleks moved rather slowly with so many grinning females staring. Tamara's face stood out from the throng and he felt like everyone in the room must know that they had had wild sex last night. He was ready to crawl under the table.

Bukovsky came to the end of the first table and placed papers by the empty chair.

"Here is your schedule," he said.

"Thank you," Aleks said as he sat down. "Sorry if I'm late."

"No, no, not at all, I was just passing out schedules."

The principal went on with his agenda. Aleks could feel the eyes staring at the back of his head. The meeting adjourned at quarter to eight and the teachers proceeded to their rooms.

Heading up to 322 Aleks was surprised by how clean and neat the hallways were and the rooms he glanced into. He found 322 to be quite different than yesterday. The windows sparkled, the linoleum floor, the tables and chairs, were all spotless. There were several posters on the walls and some archaic quotes in English. The blackboard was cleaned.

Staring at his small wooden desk with three drawers turned his thoughts to what his school days must have been like but he could visualize only the same fuzzy scenes as before.

He jumped at the sound of the bell. The chatter of young voices filled the hallways and suddenly children were in his room. They all mouthed a "Good morning" as they entered, some using English, others in Russian. The last one in closed the door. They all stood silently by their chairs.

The moment was awkward until Aleks finally said, "Please, sit down."

"I am Aleksandr Mikhailovich Leskov and I will be teaching English. Starting with this front row, would you please tell me your names?"

Those in the front row looked at each other and the student nearest the door stood and gave his name, adding in fair English, "Our class, two o'clock. Grade ten."

"Very good," Aleks said, scanning the tenth grade roster. One by one all eighteen boys and three girls introduced themselves.

He put his papers on the desk, turned and leaned his butt against the front edge.

"In my class we will speak English whenever possible." He said in English then he reverted to Russian. "We will speak Russian when necessary to explain a phrase, a sentence, or answer a difficult question."

While outlining other points he heard hallway chatter.

The first boy in the front row hesitantly stood up and said in English, "Please be excused?"

Aleks was surprised, thinking it was a boys-room request.

Then the boy said in Russian, "We must go to other classes."

Aleks faltered and said, "Yes, you may be excused."

The class rose in unison and filed out the door. Aleks followed them to the hallway. More students stood on each side of the doorway. Peering over their heads he saw Tamara.

To the students he said in English, "Please come in."

Tamara stopped. "Hello. This must be your second class."

"I think so."

"We should be out by ten, I believe. Shall we have tea?"

"I … I guess so." Aleks said, off guard again.

"I'll meet you out in front," she said and walked on.

The students were all standing when he came back in, such courtesy, how nice.

"Please be seated," he said in English, "Good morning," then he repeated what he told the first class.

Next was his three o'clock tenth grade class. Then to his surprise there was another, somewhat younger group gathered at the doorway. As they filed in he looked at the papers Bukovsky had given him. There it was—eleven o'clock, eighth grade class. That makes four.

Tamara was waiting at the corner. The sun was bright. It was considerably warmer and the air had that rural area freshness. He felt great, and standing there Tamara looked great.

She was obviously a country girl, tending to be a little bit stocky. She had a pretty face, and dark fascinating eyes. He would later find she was older than him, but so what, he considered her sexy. He was ready to take her to bed, to hell with tea.

"I have tea in my room," he said upon reaching the corner. "Why don't we buy some rolls or something and take it to the room?"

"I'd love to," her eyes danced and she looked around. "But I don't know if I should be seen going into the dormitory … daytime like this, and all."

"I'll tuck you under my coat and smuggle you in."

She laughed.

****

Small stalls lined each side of the main street. A canvas type of awning hung over the potpourri of shops selling a mixture of everything from tobacco to jewelry, clothes, soap and foodstuff.

"I love the Day of Knowledge," she said as they strolled. "We don't have to really do anything but match the faces with the names."

"I think the children love it more."

"Oh yes," she smiled, "they don't have to study, just meet their new teachers and then go out and play for the day."

"Sounds like a winner to me."

"You would, boys especially like anything that gets them out of school for a day."

"I found out today that I have four classes to teach, not three," Aleks said. "That is not getting out of something."

"You should complain, I have five classes, three in the morning and two afternoons."

They had soup and tea at a kiosk after she made a few purchases. Then she led him in a round about way towards his dormitory.

"You take the packages, go up and leave the door unlocked," she said. "I'll be there in a moment."

"Very well," Aleks said, and went on.

Their clandestine love affair continued into winter. Aleks skirted the subject of marriage the numerous times Tamara mentioned it.

Aleks heard that he was becoming the most popular teacher in the school, perhaps even in town. Many of the kids let it be known how impressive was this teacher who spoke three other languages and had traveled to England, America and—they stretched it—all over the world.

Word of his esteem filtered back to him through Tamara, Principal

Bukovsky and other teachers. Aleks was embarrassed but smiled, if they only knew. Even Lieutenant Krylenko mentioned it during the holidays.

That's when Aleks began to worry. If the KGB Lieutenant takes too much interest he may start double-checking a little more closely; he could even have someone who has been to England or America try some tricky questions. Aleks decided to keep his profile low.

It was a cold January night and the heavy pounding wouldn't stop.
Groggily Aleks rose up in bed, "Who is it?"
"Police, open the door."
In the dim light from the street his clock said 11:55. *Police?* What is going on?
The pounding was louder.
"All right, I'm coming."
He unlocked the door. Two officers rushed in and roughly grabbed him by both arms.
"What is wrong?" he protested, "What are you doing?"
"Shut up and get your clothes on. Hurry, we don't have all night."
Aleks dressed, was handcuffed and led away.

City jail was a drab two story concrete affair. Without explanation he was tossed in a cell and paced the bars until ten o'clock the next morning, Saturday, when the turnkey let the KGB officer in the cell.
Krylenko leaned against the bars. Aleks sat on the bare bunk and was quiet. It was not his turn to talk.
"My, my, what a bad boy you have been," Krylenko smiled, his arms folded on his chest. "Will we have to send you back to the Gulags, just when you were doing such good work?"
"Back to the Gulags," Aleks blurted, "what are you talking about? I haven't done anything. What in hell's going on?"
"They haven't told you?"
"Told me? Hell no, they haven't told me anything. I haven't

done anything."

"Haven't done anything?" Krylenko said. "What do you call rape?"

"Rape?" Aleks shouted. "Are you, are they crazy? I haven't raped anyone."

"Settle down, Aleksandr Mikhailovich, there is no need to shout."

Krylenko focused carefully on Aleks and decided to take his time. He had acquired a liking to this Aleks Mikhailovich, this strong, clean cut, educated man with the blue eyes and pleasant smile. He liked what he had been hearing about him. But as he had learned, Gulag men can zig and zag.

"You have been accused of rape and battery and that can send you back to the Gulags for an additional ten to fifteen years on top of what you still have to serve."

"Rape and battery, that is crazy." Aleks cried.

"Settle down, please be calm."

"How can I settle down or be calm, when you're telling me I raped someone. Who accuses me of raping them?"

"Tamara Mislinova."

"Tamara—rape?" Aleks was stunned. "That is the craziest thing I have ever heard."

Krylenko's hands went up. "I know you and Tamara have been having an affair. But rape is rape, my friend. So tell me what happened last night?" He watched Aleks for silent clues.

Aleks took a few deep breaths and reorganized before he answered. "Nothing happened, really." He ran a hand though his hair. "She came to my room about six. We had a bite to eat. Afterwards we had sex. Then she started again on marriage. She's been badgering me since November to get married. She kept telling me we could live at her place with Klara. Once married, Klara would approve."

"You have been to dinner at Klara Gorski's several times, correct?"

Aleks looked at him, "You know I have."

"Klara Gorski likes you, does she not? She likes to have you for dinner."

"Of course, she puts out a great meal."

"During your fight with Tamara, did you hit her?"

"Hit her? Hell no, I have never hit her."

"Then how do you explain the bruises on her arms and face and the cut?"

"Bruises, what bruises? She was fine when she left my room. She was mad as hell but she was fine."

"She has visible bruise marks on her arms, one on the side of her face and a small cut above her left eye."

"My God Lieutenant, she was fine when she left. She was really mad. I broke things off, told her I would not get married. She flew into a rage. I had to almost forcefully put her out of my room and close the door."

"You threw her out?"

"No, not in the way you say it. I took hold of her and firmly guided her out the door." Aleks paused for a moment. "I guess I could have put a bruise on her arm. I had to force her to the door and make her leave. But I didn't hit her or in any way harm her except to put her out of my room."

"Well, she is very convincing and she shows marks of abuse. She is crying rape."

"Lieutenant Krylenko, listen to me. We have been having sex four or five times a week since the day I got here. Why would I rape her? I don't have to rape her."

"Perhaps she said 'No' this time and you were in a fit of rage and did more than you thought. I talked to her in the hospital. She is very credible."

"She's in the hospital?"

"Yes, of course, they sent her there after they took her full statement. She has a bandage over the cut on her forehead and there are the bruises on her face and both arms."

Aleks put his face in his hands and leaned on his knees. "My God, what is happening to me? How can this be? I didn't rape that woman." After a few more questions Krylenko left.

Aleks lay on the wooden bunk with an arm over his eyes and envisioned the Troika to come. When a woman yells rape there seems to be nothing you can do. He thought of those convicted rapist he knew in the Gulags who said they didn't do it. Now he would be added to that infamous list and spend the rest of his life in another god-forsaken Gulag.

The day passed slowly. The night was worse. He was a nervous wreck.

Sunday morning they brought him tea and bread. He drank the tea but could not eat anything. He just sat and stared.

At noon he did eat a bit of bread with the tea. He told himself he'd better eat because he won't get this kind of food in the camps.

At suppertime he got tea, soup, bread and a decent meal. He ate everything. He no sooner finished when the key rattled in the iron door. He sat up. Krylenko was standing in the doorway.

"Come," Krylenko said, motioning.

Aleks got up and followed the KGB man. At the desk he was given his hat, coat and belongings. Krylenko opened the door. Stepping out into the cold night Aleks knew this wasn't right. Krylenko had not uttered a word. The frigid air hit him like a cold shower.

"Lieutenant, what is happening, where are we going?"

"To your dormitory."

"I don't understand. I thought—"

"It has all changed. I talked to the men in the rooms on either side of yours. I also paid Klara Gorski a visit. Fortunately, she has taken a liking to you. She knew about Tamara's little tryst with you most every evening. She also understands Tamara. Tamara has been her house guest for numerous years now."

"I can't—"

Krylenko cut him off as they walked. "Don't talk, listen. Tamara is desperate to find a husband and when you came to town she saw her chance. She told Klara about her plans to marry you. She left Klara's house Friday saying she'd marry you or you would be sorry."

"I can't believe…."

"The two men on either side of your room told me about the wild sex antics that have been going on for months. Those walls are thin. They heard you yelling at Tamara to get out of the room and the door slamming Friday night.

"But, Aleksandr Mikhailovich, you'll have to thank Klara Gorski. I don't think she would have ever come forward in your defense. People are like that, they don't get involved. However, because I called upon her in quest of the truth she reluctantly told me about Tamara. She is now packing Tamara's belongings and will have them ready for her when she returns."

"The bruises, the cuts…."

"The bruises on her arms were most likely caused when you manhandled her out the door. The bruise on her face and the cut could be self-inflicted, at least the doctor agrees to that. The charges have been dismissed and you are once again a free man."

Aleks sighed. "What about Tamara, what am I going to do about her?"

"I will talk to Principal Bukovsky in the morning. The police records are cleaned. No one will know what has happened this weekend, except Klara Gorski. I should not be surprised if Tamara isn't transferred immediately. We don't think it necessary to prosecute her."

"My God, what a nightmare, I was certain that I was going back to the Gulags."

"You almost did, Aleks … you almost did."

****

Winter passed and the month of May 1965 was almost gone. Thoughts of a warm summer were the main topic in Navolya after the brutal storms and cold. About to finish his first year of teaching, Aleks was a constant evening and weekend customer at the little eight-table restaurant that was always filled with warmth and the aroma of good food. There were four tables topped with multi-colored oilcloths on each side of the cheerful room. The walls had been repainted a warm cream color.

It was Saturday afternoon and Aleks sat at his favorite front table facing one of the big windows. All through winter and spring he would sit by the window, sipping tea, watching it snow and enjoying his own little world.

Mama Lyudmila was a chubby grandmother with rosy cheeks, sparkling eyes and short, curly brown hair flecked with gray. She loved to cook and took Aleks under her wing, feeding him every dish for which she was renowned. He loved it and it showed. He had regained the normal two-hundred pounds that his five foot eleven frame required.

The late spring sunshine had warmed the air. All of the tables in Mama's were occupied. Aleks finished lunch and the couple sitting with him had just left. The waitress cleared the dishes and wiped the table. Aleks gazed out the window, day dreaming.

"May I?"

Startled, he looked up to see a tall slender blonde with an armload of packages.

He scooted his chair back, "Ah, of course, of course." He stood up. "Please, sit down. Here, let me help you with those."

"That's quite all right," she smiled, placed her bags in a chair then sat down by the window, facing him.

The waitress came and the blonde ordered a biscuit and tea.

"I'm sorry. I didn't see you standing there."

"Think nothing of it. You looked like you were engrossed. I interrupted you."

"No, no, not at all, it's a pleasure to have company," he smiled. "I was just thinking of final exams and daydreaming."

"Ah, now I know," she smiled at those deep blue eyes. He was courteous, that impressed her. "You're the new teacher aren't you?"

"Yes," he answered somewhat embarrassed, "I teach English."

"Well, this is great. I have heard many good things about you. I have seen you once before here in Mama's, but didn't know who you were. I don't come too often."

"Ah, Mama Lyudmila," he smiled, "my adopted mother. A fellow couldn't ask for anyone better. I'm sure the whole town knows of me by now. I guess male teachers are a rare breed."

"In the lower grades, yes," she admitted. "Men can earn a much better salary doing other things even though they can teach."

Aleks' eyes were on the tabletop.

"Oh, I'm sorry," she immediately apologized. "I didn't mean it that way. Please don't take offense. That was stupid of me. Teaching English in a small town is highly commendable."

The arrival of tea and biscuit saved the awkward moment.

Her apology was genuine. "Thank you," he managed.

She took a sip of tea, feeling guilty for having put this man in an uncomfortable position.

"My name is Lidiya," she offered with a bright smile.

He looked into those childlike blue eyes set in a narrow, radiant face that was void of makeup. She had the look of fresh scrubbed innocence. Her shoulder-length, curly blonde hair was swept tightly past her temples and tumbled in the rear between two combs. He guessed her to be in her mid twenties. He liked her.

"Aleksandr," he replied, returning her infectious smile. "Aleksandr Mikhailovich Leskov. But please, call me Aleks."

"I am pleased to meet you Aleks. I understand that you are a very good teacher."

"Oh? Well thank you. Talk seems to get around."

"Yes, it is a small town."

Aleks liked her outgoing manner and pleasant smile. He decided to be up front. "Then you also know where I came from and why I'm teaching here."

"Yes, I know about that. It's of no great importance."

She saw surprise register on his face.

"Two teachers live in my house," she explained, "so there is not much about the school that escapes me."

She nipped her biscuit and took a sip of tea. "Don't feel guilty about being in the Gulags. Many innocent people have been sent there."

What a refreshing woman. Aleks looked into those sparkling eyes. They were softer, much lighter blue than his.

"Please, forgive me," she said, setting her tea down. "I understand the Gulags. My father died in the camps while I was at the university."

"True? You're not joking?"

"He was taken away eight years ago on false charges. It almost killed my mother. It was my first year at the university. Two years later we were told that he died of a heart attack. We didn't believe that, but what can you do."

"I'm sorry to hear that," Aleks said. What little tea was left in his cup was cold, but he sipped it anyway. "So you live and work here?"

"No ... well, yes. When I finished my studies I stayed in Moscow, coming back here only for short visits."

Aleks signaled the waitress and ordered more tea. "So you're just visiting."

"No, I came back for good six weeks ago." She paused. "My mother died."

"Oh ... I'm terrible sorry."

"Thank you." Lidiya looked away. "She wasn't well. She had cancer. So now the house is mine and it's too valuable. If I don't live in it I lose it to the government. Last month I secured a job at the city utility plant as an assistant engineer."

"Assistant engineer, you're an engineer?"

"Yes. My father was an engineer at the plant and it always intrigued me. He would take me there when I was little. So, I studied hard and obtained my engineering degree. I was the only woman in my class to graduate with such a degree."

"That's very admirable. Good for you."

"So, here I am back where I was born, living in my family's house, with a good job and two teachers to room and board with me."

The waitress poured tea.

Mama Lyudmila observed Aleks and Lidiya sipping tea. Mama was a jolly, no-nonsense woman with a warm heart and seemed to always have a twinkle in her eye. She loved to cook and watch those who enjoyed her food. Aleks once told her she should double the size of her restaurant because it was always full. She could make more money. Wise in her ways, she replied, "For what do I need so much money?"

Gazing at the twosome Mama thought if Aleks isn't brave enough to ask Lidiya to meet him again for tea Mama might have to take matters into her own hands.

Final exams were completed. During the next two months Mama Lyudmila watched the romance blossom right there in her restaurant. It was each Saturday during the first two weeks. Then it became lunch on Sundays and tea several evenings during the week. Finally, much to Mama's delight, she could tell that love was in full bloom.

"Do I need permission to get married?" Aleks asked Lieutenant Krylenko during the first week of August.

"We are not that rigid, Aleks. You do not need permission as long as you are certain that is what you want to do. Is she pregnant?"

"No," Aleks quickly answered, irritated by the suggestion. "We haven't been in bed."

"Ah," Krylenko said with a know-it-all smile, "true love, of course."

"Don't make light of me."

"Aleks, I am happy for you. A married man, a contented man, makes my job that much easier."

Aleks and Lidiya were married during the last week of August, 1965. Mama Lyudmila arranged a reception in a hall that a friend loaned her. Lt. Krylenko, Principal Bukovsky, Klara Groski, twenty-six teachers and a few others attended.

Through another friend, Mama Lyudmila also made arrangements for the newlyweds to spend a week at a hunting-fishing cabin on the river, ten miles north of town. She worked doggedly on Lt. Krylenko until he finally obtained authorization for Aleks to be ten miles from Navolya.

"My goodness," she had admonished Krylenko.

The rustic one-room log cabin was on a gradual rise where the river makes one of its numerous bends. Aleks kissed his bride as they entered the twelve by sixteen rustic cabin.

He gathered wood for the cook stove and fireplace as she tidied the table, chairs, and unrolled the bedding. A kerosene lamp set on the table and one on the mantle. Water came from a nearby spring.

"Isn't this just beautiful," Lidiya said, leaning back in his arms just outside the doorway and watching the sun create small diamonds on the river.

"As beautiful as you are," Aleks replied, "almost."

She turned around and kissed him. "I'm so glad I met you, so glad I married you."

"I love you, Lidiya. I can't believe I'm so lucky. I will do everything to make you happy."

She kissed him again, turned, snuggled in his arms and they watched the sun descend below the horizon.

"See those rapids up there?" Aleks said, pointing to that part of the river running north. "I will even catch a mess of fish for you"—he pulled her back through the doorway and turned her around—"tomorrow."

They spent the week drinking in the beauty of the land and each other. They laughed at silly jokes, strolled hand in hand, and loved. Like all newlyweds, they couldn't get enough of each other. At thirty-eight and twenty-seven they were in the prime of their years, starving for life like there may never be a tomorrow.

Aleks wondered if sometime in his past he could ever have been in love. If he had he knew it would not have been like this. Nothing could match what he felt for Lidiya. From the day he had met her everything had become different: Navolya, his KGB man, the school, his classes, even his dormitory. He had become a changed man and his whole world was now more beautiful than anything he could possibly imagine.

The week ended too soon. Returning to Navolya they went to Lidiya's house at the west end of town, where the river makes the mile long crescent. Aleks loved the house instantly. It set near the edge of the tree-lined park that embraced the river. The two bedroom cottage was of solid, old construction that had withstood years of heavy winters and could endure forever.

The kitchen, dining and living area was one large rectangular room. A huge sofa faced the fireplace and separated the living area from dining and kitchen. The two teachers shared the second bedroom.

"I told Vera and Raisa we would continue to honor the boarding agreement."

"Fine with me, sweetheart," Aleks replied. He would agree with anything. "Krylenko said his contacts with me would be accomplished in town." Aleks was beginning to think of the lieutenant as a friend, rather than a KGB officer. Strange, he thought, how things can change.

On the tenth day of May 1966, Lidiya gave birth to a seven pound ten ounce girl.

"My choice," Lidiya said, "so we'll name her Alisa, after my grandmother on my mother's side."

Aleks was content to name her whatever made Lidiya happy.

Mama Lyudmila gave them a small cradle her grandchildren had outgrown. She became Alisa's proud godmother and showed pictures to any and all that came into her restaurant.

Vera and Raisa were also thrilled with the baby girl and began helping Lidiya with more of the household chores.

As the years rolled by Aleks and Lidiya would take Alisa for walks in the park and along the river. Alisa would learn to fish before she was three. Lidiya would watch and sometimes drop a line. Eventually, Aleks would usually ask, "Are we walking, fishing or both?"

On Alisa's fifth birthday Raisa suddenly announced that she would marry a man she had met in Moscow and would be leaving when school was out.

Vera, the other teacher, said, "I do not mind sharing the room with Alisa, but if you want to board another teacher with me that is fine."

Lidiya was pleased to hear that and told Aleks, "Alisa needs her own room and we need our privacy."

"I certainly agree," Aleks said. "Forget about another boarder, Alisa and Vera can share."

During the summer of 1972 Vera spent two months visiting her Ukrainian relatives.

Aleks and Lidiya welcomed the opportunity to be alone in the house with only Alisa.

"We'll all go fishing," Lidiya announced one day during the middle of July when she had the day off. "I will pack a basket."

"Maybe I'll catch a big fish like I did with papa last week," Alisa squealed.

Lidiya smiled, turned to Aleks and asked, "How big was it?"

"Pretty big," Aleks grinned.

"This time I'll get a bigger one, papa." Her ponytail swished and she scampered off to fetch her pole.

They strolled hand in hand under the canopy of the huge umbrella-like trees. Alisa occasionally darted ahead chasing a bird or a squirrel then come back to take her papa's hand.

Choosing a spot by the river Lidiya spread the blanket. Aleks fixed Alisa's pole then stretched out on the coverlet with his hands behind his head and watched the leaves rustle and glisten in the sunlight.

It was great to be alive. He had become so content and in love with his wife and daughter that he rarely searched his mind anymore. I am Aleksandr Mikhailovich Leskov and married to the most wonderful woman and the father of a most beautiful daughter. I don't know what happened in my past but nothing, absolutely nothing could compare with this.

Lidiya dropped beside him and began drawing circles on his chest. She leaned over and kissed him. Aleks was about to melt. There was no one else around and if Alisa hadn't been with them he would have rolled Lidiya in the blanket and made love to her.

If Aleks had any idea of what tomorrow would bring he would surely have made love to her at that very moment.

CHAPTER 12

The following day brought gorgeous sunshine and warm balmy breezes to Navolya, a great day to be alive. It was Lidiya's second day off and the only thing on Aleks' mind was another afternoon of lounging in the park with his family.

He was surprised to see a black sedan stopping in front of the house. The driver got out, came around the car, opened the rear passenger door and Lieutenant Krylenko emerged.

Never before had the KGB man come to the house. Aleks turned around with his back to the window and had a strange feeling in the pit of his stomach.

"I'll get the door," Alisa said, drying her hands.

Aleks dropped down in the overstuffed chair that faced the bedroom. He told himself that something is wrong otherwise Krylenko would not be here, so let Krylenko come to me.

Lidiya opened the door, "Lieutenant, come in."

"Good afternoon, Lidiya," Krylenko beamed. "I have—"

She stepped past Krylenko, entered and ceremoniously announced, "I am Zofia Szorenia Stodenowski Leskov, Countess of Galicia and in the Kingdom of Poland and I have come to see my nephew, Aleksandr Mikhailovich."

Aleks couldn't see the stylishly dressed lady that Krylenko had brought to his house but her words propelled him out of his chair like a rocket and he stared ahead, afraid to turn. He wanted to run, flee the house, jump out the window, just run, run, run, until he could run no longer.

He was bewildered and he was caught. It's all over, the farce, the lies, the pretending and masquerading as someone you are not, even though you don't know who you really are. Now, here she is, the crux of his charade; the catalyst that could rip his life wide open; that could expose the warm, fuzzy cocoon in which he'd been hiding; the one person that could flush all he had learned to love right down the tubes and send him back to the Gulag hellholes.

He heard Alisa's voice in the bedroom and he looked at Lidiya. He couldn't run.

Standing in his house was a very aristocratic and elegantly dressed lady—Aunt Zora, more striking than he had imagined. She wore a fashionable soft gray tailored jacket. A matching skirt fell well below her knees and accentuated her tall slender frame. A lavender silk blouse was cropped around her neck with ruffles down the front. A small piece of purple silk with multi colored striations was gathered and fastened to one lapel with an exquisite gold arabesque pin.

She was magnificent. Her silver hair flowed almost to her shoulders and framed a classic face that, like Lidiya's, was narrow and expressive. Wrinkles at the corners of her eyes and the edges of her mouth enhanced her nobility. But it was the eyes, those deeply set eyes, so dark and incisive that held Aleks spellbound.

Countess Szorenia seized the moment, stepping forward she embraced her nephew, kissing both cheeks.

"Aleksandr Mikhailovich, my dearest Aleks," she said and took a step back to look at him.

"Aunt Zora," Aleks finally mustered and broke into a forced smile. "I, I am so surprised. I never expected...."

Alisa saved him. She came bouncing into the living room.

"Aunt Zora, my daughter Alisa," he said taking Alisa's hand and bending down. "Alisa say hello to your Great Aunt Zora. She has come a long way to see you."

"Ahem," Krylenko cleared his throat. "If it would please the Countess I shall send a car for you this evening at, shall we say, eight?"

He looked at Aleks. "I have made arrangements for the Countess to stay in town."

"Nine o'clock shall be fine thank you Lieutenant," Aunt Zora said with a graceful authority that was a dismissal as well as an answer.

Krylenko made his exit.

Aleks knew the charade was over. But Aunt Zora had not blurted out any denunciation, yet. Maybe it's been so long since she has seen Aleks … and we do look alike, same height and build, only a couple years difference in our age. It's been how long … twenty-four or five years? She's older now. Time changes things, even memories. Aleks decided to play it out. If she denounces me I'm a goner, but if she doesn't, well we'll see.

"Aunt Zora, I am sorry, let me introduce my wife, Lidiya," he turned, "Lidiya, my Aunt Zora, Uncle Gregory's wife."

"I am honored to meet you, Countess. Aleks has talked so much about you."

She looked Lidiya up and down, "Zora, you may call me Aunt Zora. I don't stand on pomp and circumstance with relatives."

"Please sit down Aunt Zora … here." Aleks patted a couple pillows on the sofa.

Lidiya was flustered, she had never met anyone of royalty, or titled. She didn't know whether or not to courtesy, and she had nothing appropriate for supper.

"If you will excuse me Aunt Zora, Alisa and I must go to market. It's almost two o'clock. We won't be too long. Alisa will help me shopping and with supper. You and Aleks can visit. You have a lot to talk about."

"Do not go to any bother because of me, young lady," the Countess said, as Lidiya left with Alisa in tow.

Aleks hadn't really heard what Lidiya or Aunt Zora said. His mind was in gear. He had no idea of what to do or say.

"Aunt Zora, would you like to go for a stroll with me, if you feel up to a walk."

The Countess rose from the sofa, "Do not be patronizing. I am old, but I do not yet have a cane."

Aleks stepped ahead and held the door.

Leisurely strolling, he said, "The river park is beautiful at this time of the year."

She was silent.

"Aunt Zora, you caught me by total surprise. I had no idea you were coming, even Krylenko did not tell me."

"He did not know until I was on my way from Moscow."

Aleks swallowed hard, "I don't understand. How did you even know I was here in Navolya, that I was out of the Gulags?"

"I am a Countess. The title does not mean much in some circles today, but I still have many friends and I know how to get things done."

She looked at him closely. "Let us continue this conversation in my native tongue."

Aleks was amazed. If she knew I was a free man, that I'm here in Navolya and she is able to come here, what else does she know? What is going on? The KGB forbids me contact with anyone to say I'm out of the Gulags, yet Aunt Zora seems to know everything and shows up. Even Krylenko didn't know. Now she is testing me, she wants to converse in Polish. Does she think I can't speak the language?

He faced her. "That will be fine. I don't speak Polish very often."

The park was cool under the high arbor-like branches, so dense in places they blocked the sun. They ambled through the park, along the river and stopped at the edge of a bank.

The Countess watched Aleks pick up a stone and skip it across the water. Then she turned, faced him and suddenly said, "All right young man, tell me—who are you?"

He knew it was coming, but it was still a shock—off guard again. His mind whirled through a hundred scenarios, but came back to just one. He focused. So, it's time to face the music. Game's over? Okay. He turned and looked into those fascinating dark eyes that were locked onto his.

She didn't flinch.

"I don't know." He spit it out as if he had rehearsed the words all his life—which he had.

"You do not know?" She said in disbelief.

"I don't know."

"Well, I know who you are not. You are not Aleksandr Mikhailovich. I do not know what kind of game you are playing, but I want a truthful explanation young man. *Where* is my nephew?"

He could not answer immediately. "Walk over here with me."

She refused his arm. There was fire in those deep, penetrating eyes.

Aleks led her a few yards away from the river bank to a large bench under the trees.

"Please sit down," he said.

She sat at one end. He took the other end to avoid being confrontational. He wasn't sure of how to begin but decided to be straight out.

"Aunt ... Countess, it is a long story and I shall tell you the complete truth. My dear and closest friend, Aleksandr Mikhailovich is dead. He died in 1953, right after the Norilsk revolt."

The Countess gave a short gasp and crossed herself.

Aleks told her the story, starting with his amnesia, meeting Aleks and Viktor, their deadly train trip, Multavo, then Norilsk and the uprising. He emphasized how Aleks befriended him, taught him Russian, told him about his family, his aunt, the trip to America, about St Petersburg, the university and the war.

"It began as one friend teaching another. I didn't realize it and maybe he didn't either at first, but then as his health deteriorated he was preparing me to take his place, to serve his shorter sentence. He knew he was going to die. I didn't know. Later on our friend Viktor also knew, but neither one would say a word to me." Aleks paused, gazing at the river.

"He died of lung cancer on the ship and was buried at sea." Aleks could not tell her about the faked escape and being shot. "He slipped into my clothes, my number, and a *pakhan* friend of ours had the dossiers switched. He died as Sedecki and I became Aleksandr Mikhailovich."

The Countess saw the misty eyes this young man tried to hide as he looked away.

"So you have been masquerading as my nephew since 1953?"

"Yes, ever since. I have no choice. I cannot remember who I am or where I came from."

"I see," she said rather coldly.

"As Aleks Leskov my sentence would have expired in 1963, but the added 30 years make it 1993. If I were Sedecki my term would longer—I'd never get out. Now they have released me temporarily to teach English, only because of your nephew's credentials."

Silently she was trying to recover from the fact that her nephew was dead and from her outrage and the shock of this man's impersonation. How could he? How should he atone? How should he be punished? Aleksandr Mikhailovich Leskov, her last living relative, is dead. She had not been quite ready for this.

Aleks stood up. With hands in his pockets he gazed around but his clouded mind saw nothing. Everything was beautiful, a wife, a daughter—life was fantastic. Now he is exposed for what he is and the world is spinning. He watched the current carry a small log down the river. Maybe I should just jump in and float down until the world finds me, or I drown. Lydia and my precious Alisa, my God, what have I done to them?

"Well," the word popped out like a firecracker when she finally broke the silence.

He turned from the river to face her.

"At least you have a fine Polish name, Stanislaus Sedecki, so you must be Polish. That is in your favor. You are out of the Gulags now and that is a good thing."

Aleks sat down and faced this very impressive lady. He remembered her nephew's words about her worldly experience and travels, how well educated, intuitive and very tough was this famous aunt. "I loved Aleks like a brother. We were brothers, the three of us and would die for each other. I had no idea Aleks would plan to die for me, but he did."

His eyes did not waver from hers.

"And yes, I am out now, but my sentence is not up. At first I thought the Gulag was doing me a benevolent favor. True, but not exactly. They badly need people to teach English, everyday English, and German. That's why I'm out, why I'm here."

They sat in silence for a long time. Aleks was thankful that she did not stand up and shout for someone to come and take this imposter away.

"That's the story, and it is the truth. I would give anything to know who I am and for Aleks to be here instead of me."

She remained quiet, staring into the distance.

He waited and waited, uneasily. What are you going to do Countess? Finally he could no longer stand the silence.

"Now it's your turn. What kind of god-awful influence do you have to get here?"

He watched her touch her cheek with those long slender fingers that wore many rings. Her hands were very graceful. Purple veins dignified their movement.

"What allows me to be here is the fact that I am the Countess of Galicia and in the Kingdom of Poland. Do you understand Polish nobility and titles?"

Aleks shook his head. "I speak Polish, English and German, and now Russian, but I know nothing about any of those countries. I don't know anything about titles."

"Then let me explain. I was the daughter of Feliks Wiecesław Stempowski, Count in the Kingdom of Poland. The title was bestowed upon his great grandfather by Emperor Josef II in August 1784. It then passed to father to father.

"I married Josef-Ignacy Stodenowski, Count of Galicia and in the Kingdom of Poland, the first of June 1915. I was twenty years old. His grandfather obtained the title from Emperor Franz the First in July 1807. It passed to his father and to him. His title of Count was confirmed again by Czar Nicholas II of Russia on 10 June 1897.

"Josef died in 1923. I maintain the title of Countess. I am listed in the records of 1924 as authorized to bear the title. When I die the title will become extinct.

"Although the reign of Czar Nicolas the Second and all Czars are over, Russian history is not. It took me a number of years but I prevailed and was told in confidence what my nephew's circumstances were. My demands to come here were at last granted and here I am. I must return tomorrow by the way I came. My plea for your clemency was denied," she waved a hand. "A Countess cannot do everything."

She pursed her lips and looked squarely at him. "But Russia could not deny this Countess a meeting with her nephew."

Her eyes were moist, her voice trembled ever so slightly, but she held his gaze. "I have traveled the world numerous times. I have lived through two horrible wars. I have married twice and lost both husbands. Now I am alone. I hope you are never alone."

She heaved a sigh and closed her eyes. Her shoulders seemed to have sagged a little and her striking face had taken a weary look.

She paused in that manner for a few minutes then continued.

"This Countess has grown old. I am seventy-nine. I am wearing out. My nephew Aleksandr Mikhailovich Leskov is my last living relative. I have been pestering the authorities, determined to find and see my nephew one more time before I die."

She looked off to the trees, shifted her position, straightened her posture and squared her shoulders. The change was dramatic. Her eyes were again bright and deep, the fiery glow returned. They were still misty and thus very sparkling as she looked at Aleks. She held out her hand.

"And I have finally found him."

Slowly they stood up and embraced like two lost souls, one in her twilight years, looking for the only person who might carry forth some part of her legacy or at least bear witness that she had existed; the other a man still lost and searching, hoping to someday find his true identity and purpose in life, but praying to just continue with the present.

She cradled her arm in his when they ambled slowly back to the house. It was later than they realized and Lidiya was ready to put supper on the table.

Aunt Zora said a blessing, crossed herself and they ate supper as a family.

The big black car came for the Countess at exactly nine o'clock. It would take her to her quarters in town. In the morning it would drive her to the train and by late evening she would be back in Warsaw.

She embraced her nephew, Aleksandr Mikhailovich, and kissed him on the cheek. She thanked Lidiya and bid her goodbye. When she bent down and hugged little Alisa she received a kiss that warmed her heart and put a proud smile on her old aristocratic face.

Then Aunt Zora, the grand Countess of Galicia and in the Kingdom of Poland, was gone.

As they lay in bed Aleks told Lidiya about his visit with Aunt Zora, leaving out the amnesia and Sedecki part. He had long anguished about telling Lidiya the truth and had decided the risk was too great. It would accomplish nothing but put her in jeopardy. *It's now confirmed that I am Aleksandr Mikhailovich Leskov and that is how I shall remain until I die.*

Seventeen months later, the third day of December 1974, Lieutenant Krylenko made another unusual visit to their house during a heavy snowfall. His distress was obvious.

"I am very sorry to inform you," he said, "that Countess Zofia Szorenia Stodenowski Leskov has died at her home in Warsaw."

Aleks turned and stared through the front window, "When?"

"It was six days ago. My superiors in Moscow wish to extend their regards and I offer my condolences. I have nothing further to report. Again, Aleks, Lidiya, I am sorry for your loss."

"Thank you," Aleks said. Then as Krylenko turned to leave he asked, "Lieutenant, did you know much about my aunt ... back then?"

Krylenko hesitated but said, "Yes, of course, it is in your dossier, and yes, I believe it did have some bearing on your release."

Aleks stared at the floor and nodded as Krylenko left.

Aleks was withdrawn the rest of that winter. Losing Aunt Zora was like losing his lifeline to the outside world. He would hold Lidiya and Alisa closer and more often now. It had been his primary quest to discover who he was, or even if Sedecki actually was his name. Now it no longer mattered.

The winters and summers came and went. Lidiya was promoted to first assistant at the City Water and Heating plant. That brought a few more rubles into the family till. Aleks began teaching one class of German in addition to his English classes. Alisa was growing like a shoot of early wheat.

On the third day of May, 1976, Aleks spent his lunch hour buying a fishing pole for Alisa's tenth birthday next week. That afternoon he was teaching his third English class of the day. "Nikolai, today you were going to tell the class about your weekend trip to Lake Rybinski. So if you—"

KA-BOOM!

The building shook. Windows shattered spreading glass on the desks and floor. Aleks ducked. Some students jumped up, others got on the floor. Chairs overturned. Girls screamed. Pandemonium broke out.

"All right, quiet down everyone. Quiet!" Aleks shouted. "Is anyone hurt?"

"My arm," one of the girls cried, clutching one wrist.

"Let me see," Aleks said. "It'll be okay, go down to the office. Anyone else hurt?"

No answers, just the whimpering.

He stuck his head out the window. No bomb crater, no hole in the building.

"All right, settle down. Move away from the windows. Stay on this side of the room. I'll find out what has happened. Everyone stay here. Nikolai, you are in charge until I return. Stay by the door. Understand? Everyone understand?"

They just nodded.

The hallways were becoming chaotic. Children were pouring out of the classrooms and running. When Aleks reached the office, Principal Bukovsky was in the hallway trying to restore order. Some teachers were hysterical and trying to get the students into the yard.

"What happened?" Aleks shouted over the squealing noise.

"I don't know," Bukovsky answered. "I'm trying to find out. Get all of the children into the yard. We will have to dismiss classes for today."

Aleks went back upstairs and instructed his class to proceed in an orderly manner to the schoolyard. He followed his class down the stairs then made his way to the principal's office.

One of the teachers came running up to Bukovsky, "Someone said it came from the north. It must be the utility plant."

She bit her lip when saw Aleks standing there.

His eyes went wide, "Oh God, Noooo."

He spun around, pushed his way to the door and began running towards the water plant.

Sprinting and panting a half a block from the plant, he saw an ambulance driving away. He was tempted to chase after it but continued on. He couldn't believe what he saw. It looked like a bomb had hit the southern part of the plant. The wall was blown away, water covered the entire area and was still running down the street.

Several people had gathered and more were trekking through the mud. Fire trucks were arriving.

The plant manager was in front of the building. Aleks caught him. "Lidiya, where is Lidiya?"

The manager turned, dazed, raising his arm, pointing, "Hospital," was all he said.

Aleks turned and ran towards the east side of town. It was more than a mile to the small two-story hospital.

A medical attendant confronted him as he burst in the main door. He didn't recognize her but she seemed to know him.

"Please, please," she said holding both hands against him, "wait right here. Sit down." She guided, forced him to a bench.

Finally a man in a white coat came down the hall. Aleks stood up. "My Lidiya, is she here?"

The doctor held up his hands.

"Tell me, damn it. Is my Lidiya here, is she all right?"

"Sit down, please ... sit down."

He made Aleks sit down, then said, "I am sorry, there was nothing we could do."

"That can't be!" Aleks yelled and jumped to his feet. "I want to see her."

The doctor blocked his way. "I can't let you do that. Please, you don't want to do that. Please Mr. Leskov, it was instantaneous. She must have been immediately in front of the blast."

Aleks collapsed. The doctor guided him to a chair. Elbows on his knees, head in his hands, Aleks sat there and sobbed his heart out.

Aleks, Alisa and the entire town buried Lidiya four days later. Aleks and Alisa consoled each other in utter grief.

Alisa's tenth birthday was the saddest day of her life. Aleks gave her the fishing pole knowing she would never use it.

Everyone at school offered condolences. He attended his classes a week after the funeral, but found it extremely difficult. His students offered a plan whereby one student would conduct the class while the teacher would stand in the rear and critique. They said it would give them needed experience and confidence. Aleks knew differently.

Mama Lyudmila brought dinner out to the house several evenings each week during the rest of May, arriving before anyone came from school. She told Vera that she would be personally on her case if Alisa or anyone tried to cook supper on the nights she would be bringing food.

When final exams ended Aleks found his blackboard completely filled with short chalk messages from all of his students. He was overwhelmed.

Alisa stayed close to her father all summer long. They would take extended strolls through the park, walking hand in hand along the river bank. They never baited a hook or talked about fishing that summer. On the third of each month they placed flowers on Lidiya's grave.

"Papa, I can take care of the house and you," his daughter said many times. "I know how to cook, I really do. Mama taught me. I do know how, papa."

"I know you do sweet one. We will take care of each other. We'll make that a big promise, all right?"

Take care of each other they did. Occasionally Vera would cook the meal but mostly she would help Alisa. The ten year old took command.

From that summer on the years came and went ever so slowly. Winters became longer and colder for Aleks. Recalling the brightest memories of Lidiya would bring warmth to his heart but then he'd slip into his melancholy loss.

He watched Alisa turn sixteen in May 1982. "Sweetheart, you look and act so much like your mother," he told her for the hundredth time. He marveled at how his daughter was blooming into young womanhood, growing tall like her mother.

Lt. Krylenko had been promoted to Captain. He met Aleks after school during the third week of May and walked him home.

"I am being transferred, Aleks. A new officer will be replacing me."

Aleks was taken back by this sudden announcement. He had come to respect the KGB man and treated him as a friend. "Why? Why, all of a sudden?"

"It's as much a surprise to me as it is to you. But it is done. I must leave."

"I am truly sorry to hear that," Aleks said. "Where will you be going, can I ask?"

"You can ask, but I can't tell you. I will miss you. It has been a pleasure to be in charge of a man like you. I have worked with criminals on parole or freed, and they were exactly that, criminals. Not that I consider you a criminal. You I consider a friend. All of my training said I should not have become involved. I shall sorely miss you, Aleks."

"And I will miss you. Who will be taking your place?"

"I do not yet know. But I will come by before I leave."

Friday, two days later, Aleks' last class was over. In his classroom he was pouring over the final paperwork. All day long he had expected

Captain Krylenko stop by and perhaps they could say their goodbyes over a cup of tea. There's still time.

He didn't see, but rather sensed someone's presence before he finally looked up and turned. A man dressed in a dark suit and tie was standing quietly in the doorway.

He was large in the middle, overweight, stood maybe five foot seven, which emphasized his tubbiness. A band of black hair stretched around his bald head, temple to temple. Not old, forties maybe. A thin black mustache made his face seem more round than it was. Aleks thought he could be described as almost comical, until he met the menacing black eyes and the smirk.

Aleks put down his pencil. "May I help you?"

The portly man kept his cat-bird smile, stepped in, closed the door, ambled in front of Aleks' desk and said, "I am Major Igor Andreyevich Varnova."

He pulled up a chair, turned it around, tilted it and perched his buttocks against the top. He looked down at Aleks. The grin pushed his puffy cheeks higher, made his beady eyes seem smaller.

"And you are Aleksandr Mikhailovich Leskov, the English teacher, the paroled convict."

Aleks replied, riled, "I was in the Gulags but I am not a convict, or a criminal."

"Ah, but you are," Igor said, grinning widely, "you are. Convict, criminal, prisoner, it is a minor distinction." His smile disappeared. "You are a convict serving a total of forty-five years for crimes against the state." He paused, "Most serious offences."

Being suddenly confronted was unnerving, now Aleks became enraged, a feeling he detested and hadn't had to contend with for many years. Obviously this man is my new KGB officer. So we're back to the typical KGB man. After all this time we're back to that. Great, that's just great.

"Where is Captain Krylenko?"

"Do not worry about the captain. He had to leave late last night. Your little picnic is over, Aleksandr Mikhailovich, and from this moment on we will play by the rules. We do not treat convicts with powder-puffs."

Powder puffs, what is it with this man? He wanted to take the idiotic grin off the little man's face. "What do you want of me, can't you see I am busy doing what your people want me to do."

"Ah, yes, the busy English teacher, I almost forgot," he said mockingly, then his smile disappeared. "It is best you understand that I will tolerate no nonsense. You will not step out of the limits of Navolya without my permission. You will teach your language classes without making capitalistic or other references detrimental to the motherland. Your picnic is over."

The irritating smile returned. He clasped his hands just below his rotund belly and leaned forward. "Do you understand, Aleksandr Mikhailovich?"

Aleks squinted. So, this is how we will play the game, you fat little bastard. Well, we'll see how long you last. "Yes, major, of course I understand. Is there some reason to make you think I have been violating anything?"

"Don't get smart with me," Igor replied.

He pushed off the chair, donned his little smile and left the room.

My God, Aleks thought as he heard the little man's footsteps travel down the hall, I've inherited an adversary, a stinking, egotistical KGB asshole. Now I'll have to watch everything I do and say. What in hell has brought this on?

The following week Alisa graduated with honors and was still trying to decide between Moscow and St. Petersburg universities. Aleks was the proudest father in Navolya.

It was several weeks after graduation when Aleks stopped by the school to retrieve a sweater. Principal Anton Bukovsky was in his office as Aleks passed by and he called.

"Aleks, my friend, come in, come in."

Bukovsky had just turned forty-five but had aged considerably during the seventeen years since they first met. His hair was turning gray at the temples. The lines in his face reflected the years and stress of his work. "Please, have a seat, Aleks. It has been a long time since we have had a talk. Has Alisa decided on the university?"

"Yes, she is filling out the papers for Moscow."

"Good. Bring them to me when she completes them. I will personally have them submitted with a recommendation. She is such a lovely young lady, extremely bright."

"Yes, more like her mother every day."

"Ahem," Bukovsky cleared his throat, avoiding talk of Lidiya. "Tell me Aleks, how have you been and what will you do when Alisa is gone?"

"I'm fine, I guess. You ask a good question. I don't know what I'll do with myself once Alisa leaves. And I don't know what to do about one or two women teachers living in the house alone with me. What do you think?"

"I don't believe it should be a problem, Aleks, but let me think about it." Bukovsky leaned back in his chair. "Close the door, Aleks."

Aleks frowned, got up and closed the door.

"I've been meaning to talk to you. I know things haven't been easy for you since Captain Krylenko left. How are you getting along with this new major?"

Aleks was somewhat surprised that the principal should even ask about a KGB officer. However, he knew where Bukovsky's sentiments lay, though they had never discussed such matters. But the principal broached the subject and Aleks momentarily recalled old thoughts of provocateurs.

"He's a tough little bird and goes strictly by the book," Aleks answered. "Have you talked to him?"

"Yes, the first day he was here he paid me a visit." Bukovsky looked around at the window behind him then at the glass between his and the outer office. He lowered his voice. "I don't like the man, Aleks. He is trouble and I don't like to openly say that about *those people*. But men like him are the problem with our country today. He's a throwback to the NKVD days of Beria and Stalin."

Aleks pursed his lips and raised his eyebrows.

"You are surprised I say such things?" Anton sat up and leaned on his desk. "You've been in the Gulags and you have dealt with these people, you know what I'm talking about. This man even wants me to confide in him of everything you do, like I should catch you doing a wrong, or I should make up something."

Aleks was shocked.

"Aleks, you and your family are my friends. I treasure your friendship. So I tell you this in the strictest of confidence."

Aleks was impressed, "I appreciate that very much."

The principal moved some papers, cleared the top of his desk and leaned closer towards Aleks, keeping his voice low.

"I have done some checking." He paused. "You are surprised I see. I have some friends in very good places. I have learned that this Igor Varnova has been kicked down the ladder."

Aleks pulled his chair closer to the desk.

"Yes, my friend, he has been passed over for promotion too many times. He has had a couple of screw-ups in the past ten years and serves only because some of his superiors are of the same old hard-line school. This job that he has been regulated to is almost as embarrassing as being given a basement desk until retirement. It's a lieutenant's position. He is forty-two and has a long way to go before retirement.

"He is out to prove himself, in one way or another. I think he will lie and cheat to reach his own selfish goals and climb back up the ladder. You are one of five men for which he is responsible. You must be very careful, Aleks. This man is dangerous. Do not give him an opportunity."

Aleks drew a deep breath and sighed.

"And as for Captain Krylenko, I have a feeling that he was sent off to that damned war."

Aleks sat straight up. "War, what war?"

"I wondered if you knew. The wounded have been returning. Families have been notified of too many soldiers being killed in 'training accidents'. The word is getting out. We have been at war in Afghanistan for some time now."

"My God, I didn't—"

"I didn't think you knew. Not very many people do. Many more men are being sent to that area and Krylenko may be one of them."

Aleks was shocked by this news and wanted to ask questions, but it was apparent that Bukovsky had ended the conversation. Aleks stood and offered his hand across the desk. Anton Bukovsky grasped it with a smile.

"Be careful."

"Thank you Anton, this has been a most interesting morning," Aleks turned to leave.

"Aleks," Bukovsky said with a very somber face, "we never had this conversation."

Aleks nodded and closed the door.

When Alisa departed for Moscow Igor took delight in jerking Aleks around, as he did every time he would come to Aleks' classroom or approach him on the street. He would not give Aleks permission to accompany his daughter. Aleks argued, fumed and voiced every protest he could. In the end there was nothing he could do. The major prevailed.

"I will be all right, papa," Alisa said when she boarded the bus that would take her to the train station.

Aleks found himself in a daily vacuum for weeks. The eagerness of beginning the school year now had an emptiness he couldn't fill. At times he felt totally adrift from his surroundings.

Before Alisa left Aleks had poured over the list of teachers that were looking for quarters to rent. He discussed the matter with his daughter and they decided Irina Chevyetsky would be the most suitable woman to share the spare bedroom with Vera.

Irina was older, forty-eight, a typical schoolmarm type and the least likely person to start tongues wagging. Also, Irina said she too would leave during the summer months, so Aleks and Alisa could have the house alone during summer college break. Additionally, Vera and Irina agreed to share some of the cooking and housework duties.

Except for the continued chain jerking by Igor the terrible, Aleks took solace in teaching his classes during the rest of the winter.

During the summer of 84 Alisa made it home for the second time.

"Oh, papa, I am so glad to see you," she exclaimed, jumping off the bus, throwing her arms around him. She gave him a kiss, stepped back and looked him over.

"You look great, they must be feeding you well," she giggled.

"Well, young lady, I do have two very good cooks at the house. Mama Lyudmila is jealous." Then he suddenly realized how she had grown. They were standing almost eye to eye. "My God, Alisa, you must have grown a foot this past year. You're taller than your mother."

"I know, papa, I've had growing pains all winter."

They laughed as Aleks picked up her suitcase. They began to walk home. It was a warm June day. The sun was high and bright. Somewhere not too far away a field had been cut and the sweet aroma filled the air.

"Is Vera and Irina still here?"

"Irina left last week and Vera is leaving tomorrow for the summer. So we will have the house to ourselves."

"Great!" she exclaimed. "We'll go fishing and for walks in the park. You can tell me everything that has happened. I'll tell you all about Moscow."

"I want to hear more about your medical studies, sweetheart.

Your letters were so interesting. It's hard to believe my little girl wants to be a doctor."

"Well, papa, I'm not so little any more, I am eighteen."

Aleks rolled his eyes.

"Papa!" She pulled his arm. "Becoming a doctor is a long way off yet. But I will have the whole summer to tell you all about it. You won't believe some of the things."

He was proud of his daughter. Her enthusiasm was infectious. A big smile spread across his face. It became even bigger when he said hello to all of the townspeople they passed.

With suitcase in one hand, hers clutched in the other, they strolled down the street with Alisa chirping like a magpie.

Near the end of summer Alisa returned to Moscow. Aleks walked her to the bus and they said their goodbyes. He stood watching her bus pull away.

Igor suddenly appeared beside him.

"A very beautiful young lady you have there, Aleks. You must be very proud."

Aleks jerked his head, surprised and irritated that the little bastard should even mention his daughter.

"So, she goes to the university in Moscow," Igor smiled. "That must be difficult for you to have such a pretty young thing like her in a big city like Moscow."

"Damn it," Aleks bristled, "what's with you?"

"It's just with all the crime in the big city," he smiled, "muggings, murder and things, and the rape, so much rape, and she's such a pretty girl."

Igor knew how to push the right buttons. Aleks was turning red, biting his lip. He stared at the insidious grin that dared him to go ahead and do it, just swing at me. He realized that Igor, as usual, was bating him.

All Aleks could manage was, "She's a big girl now, she can handle herself."

"Oh, I'm sure, I'm sure," the little man said, looking up at Aleks. He turned, walked away then stopped. "Oh, by the way, you need not bother to send any more packages to your Gulag friend."

"What? What are you saying?"

"Just thought I'd save you some money, my dear Aleks, you should thank me. Your friend is dead."

Dead? Aleks froze, speechless. He could picture Viktor exactly as he had left him in Ambarchik almost twenty years ago: a gentle giant of a man with big eyes, a huge smile, the gap between his teeth, and so easy going—a tender, enormous human being with a warm heart.

He looked off down the street and his eyes became misty. *My friend, my brother Viktor is dead.* How old, a few years beyond me, mid sixties or so? Poor Viktor, how sad, from his teens through his entire adult life, more than forty-some years in the Gulags, and die in that frozen hell-hole of Ambarchik. He never had the chance to walk in the sun as a free man; to eat a decent home-cooked meal; to smell the sweet aroma of new mown hay; to ... his thoughts stopped. A great dark sorrow squeezed his heart like those gloomy winter days without the sun, and from that dreariness he could see Viktor's calm face staring at him like a beacon.

Aleks wanted to roll into a little ball and die.

"When?"

"What does it matter, dead is dead." Igor replied, grinning, "Several months ago, or so. I was informed just last week," he lied. His grin became a big smile. "You know how slow the channels are."

He turned and walked away.

Viktor, my dearest friend, I am so very, very sorry ... may you rest in peace.

Tears rolled down his face all the way home. He wasn't aware if anyone noticed and he didn't care. All he could see was the image of Viktor, the giant of a man.

CHAPTER 13

The years passed slowly. Alisa spent every summer of the following years in Navolya. She received her medical degree in 1987 and began her internship at a Moscow hospital. She planned to stay on as a Doctor of Gynecology.

But in early June all of that was subject to change. She announced that she was getting married. Her letter said he is a doctor, a skilled surgeon. Stephen Eduardovich Kurakin is thirty-three years old, from a very good family, a major in the military and we're madly in love.

Aleks pleaded for permission to travel to Moscow for the wedding but was denied.

Time was growing short when Igor again came to his house in late June.

"Major Varnova, she is my only child and they even moved the wedding date up to mid July expecting me to come. There is no reason to deny my request. I'm her only parent and I have to be there."

"That my dear Aleks is not my concern," Igor replied with his deriding grin. "It is out of the question. The decision is made and that is final."

"The decision has been made," Aleks mocked him. His face became flush and he could feel the throbbing in his neck. "You mean, you have decided. You haven't even asked your superiors have you. This is your own personal decision."

Igor Varnova's little eyes narrowed and his fist slammed on the table. "You test me to the limits, Aleksandr Mikhailovich."

Aleks didn't flinch. He was about to reach across and grab the little man by the collar and … he took a deep breath.

"The doctor she is marrying is a major, like you and—"

"I don't care if he is a general!" Igor raised his voice. The smile had disappeared. "The difference between the army and the Committee of State Security is night and day. The decision has been made and that is final. Do you understand, Aleksandr Mikhailovich? Final!"

Three weeks later Aleks answered the knock on his door to find Anton Bukovsky standing there.

"Come in, Anton, come in."

"No Aleks, not now. You need to come to my house."

Aleks was puzzled, "Your house?"

"Your daughter called. You need to call her back. Use my telephone," Anton raised his hand as Aleks started to speak. "Aleks, her fiancée, the major, has been killed."

Aleks was stunned.

They hurried to Bukovsky's house. Anton dialed the number, handed the telephone to Aleks and left room.

"Papa," Alisa said crying,

"Alisa, sweetheart, I am so sorry. How ...."

Alisa couldn't stop sobbing.

"Alisa, easy honey, easy, tell me what happened."

She continued to sob hysterically. Aleks was finally able to settle her down.

"Tell me what happened."

"An officer from his garrison came and said Major Kurakin was killed on July 5th with eight others when their military plane crashed. That's all he said, papa, no details, wouldn't say anything else."

"I think you should come on home sweetheart."

She rambled on between sobs. Aleks tried to console her, but there was nothing anyone could say to a young bride-to-be who had just lost a part of her life. When the call came to an end he stood transfixed.

Bukovsky came back in the room and placed a hand on Aleks' shoulder. "I'm very sorry my friend. She is like a daughter to me too."

Two weeks later Alisa's letter was another surprise. She disclosed that she was pregnant and would be coming home.

She returned to Navolya in early August.

"I was so worried about you," Aleks said, when he met the bus.

"I'll be all right, papa and I'm going to have Stephen Eduardovich's baby."

"Of course, sweetheart, of course you are."

"And papa, the hospital here has accepted me even though I'm pregnant. They need doctors."

He put his arm around her, "Well, that's great, simply great sweetheart. We'll be fine. Irina and Vera weren't too happy about the short notice but finally found other quarters. They understand."

During a snowstorm on the afternoon of 18 February 1988, Stephen Aleksandrovich Leskov joined the world at eight pounds, six ounces, and Aleksandr Mikhailovich became a grandfather. Alisa and Aleks named Stephen after Viktor Stepanovich and Stephen Eduardovich.

Aleks couldn't stop smiling for months. He was so happy he no longer thought about his past. If he never discovered the truth about himself it might even be a godsend. He was a father and a grandfather, he was turning fifty-nine and life was great. Even Igor's constant haranguing took a back seat to his expanded family.

"We will insure that Stephen receives a good education," Aleks said one night at supper.

"But of course," Alisa replied.

"What I mean is we will tutor him in addition to his schooling and we will teach him English and later on maybe German, and Polish, just like your mother and I taught you."

"Papa, he's not five months old yet. There will be plenty of time."

Aleks ran his hand through his closely cropped gray hair, sighing, "I suppose." Then he laughed, "Sort of silly of me, isn't it."

"No papa, it's not silly," She said then laughed. "But first he has to be able to talk."

The seasons passed swiftly for Aleks. Shortly before Stephen turned four Alisa had agreed, at Aleks' insistence, to a routine of speaking only English three nights a week from supper until bedtime. It worked. His tow-haired, blue eyed grandson was a linguistic natural. Even on weekends Stephen would occasionally forego Russian and slip into English.

By the time Stephen was five he was delighting his grandfather and his mother with his English, which he spoke as well as Russian.

"I wish you two would make up your minds," Alisa would laugh.

"Well, watch out," Aleks warned, "we may to start Polish lessons next month."

The summer of '93 ended too quickly. Aleks was 63 and prepared for two more years of teaching before he would retire. (As Stanislaus Sedecki he was actually 64 years old).

Shortly after 1 September, the Day of Knowledge, the principal called Aleks to his office. It was an unusually cold day for early fall, but Anton's office was quite warm.

"Ah, Aleks, please sit down. I have some interesting news for you. There is a teacher's symposium this year that will be held not too far from here. I will take five teachers with me and I want you to be one of them. Would you like to go?"

Aleks was surprised. "Sure, I guess so. I've never been to one. Yes, I'd love to go. But isn't it a waste for me to fill someone's spot, I will retire shortly."

"Do not worry about academics this will be a holiday for you, you have earned it, but don't say anything. I have wanted you to attend one before you retire, so you will go."

"What about Igor?" Aleks asked. "He will not allow me to leave Navolya, even for a hike in the country."

"Leave our little friend to me," Anton Bukovsky smiled. "I will deal with Major Varnova. This is school business, teaching accreditation, friends, enjoying life—matters beyond him."

They laughed.

"The symposium is being held in Jaroslava for three days beginning the 27th of September. It is a beautiful city on the Volga with a large population, a half million or more. I will give you a copy of the agenda. We will leave here as a group and arrive by train on the 26th, a Sunday. It is a day's journey."

Aleks couldn't believe that he might be allowed to travel outside of Navolya and that Bukovsky really had the means to get around his antagonist.

The next day when his classes were over Aleks sat at his desk watching the little KGB man contort his face, spit fire and dress him down.

"You think you're smart, Aleksandr Mikhailovich. You and your principal think you have put one over on me," Igor's words were venomous. "Well, you'll attend your teacher's conference, but listen very carefully, this is the one and only time you'll ever go over my head and you'll rue the day you pulled this stunt." He ranted on and on.

After the major left, Aleks leaned back in his chair, drained. If I ever go back to the Gulags, he mused, it will be for throttling that fat little son of a bitch.

Traveling as a group the six teachers took an early morning bus from Navolya then they shared a compartment on the train and arrived at Jaroslava in the afternoon.

After checking into their quarters at a small inn all six took a stroll along the Volga and were delighted with the beauty and ambiance of the riverfront. Quaint shops in a mishmash of colors and awnings lined the avenue along the river. The women shopped as they strolled.

It was sunny, quite warm and the trees rustled in a soft breeze. They were enjoying the afternoon, but it had been a long day and the ladies were tiring.

"Principal Bukovsky," Inga Gonik, the eldest of the four, finally spoke up. "If you don't mind I would like to return to the inn. I am tired and it is near supper time."

Anton looked at the time. "But of course, Inga, of course."

The other three offered their respects also and the four of them departed.

"How rude of me," Anton said after they left, "to not realize they should be weary. It has been a long day. Are you hungry, Aleks?"

"Hmm, not terribly."

"What matter, come, let's find a place to rest, have a drink and a bite."

Turning away from the Volga they found a tavern.

Making their way to a table Aleks noticed another man enter. He was sure the man had been following them.

"Have you noticed him?" Aleks flashed his eyes when they got to a table.

"Of course, KGB, you can spot them. It upset Major Varnova terribly to learn that I have some influence. I knew he would have someone watching us. There was one on the train also."

Aleks made a face. "Well, Anton you are alert. I didn't notice anyone on the train."

After the waiter brought their vodka they ordered piroshki and decided to completely ignore the KGB tail.

Anton said, "I am sure there will be one of them watching us at all times."

The tavern was soon crowded with men and the profusion of voices became louder with the topic of the day—Communism and Democracy.

"They are much more vocal about politics here," Aleks said.

"Since Yeltsin dissolved the parliament last week the country is further divided," Anton responded. "A democratic form of government is crucial for the survival of mother Russia. But right now democracy has reached the litmus stage. Since parliament members have barricaded themselves inside the White House for more than a week now, and say they won't come out until Yeltsin steps down, it has been a standoff. But Aleks, something has to happen soon."

The loud voices built into a shouting match among a group near the middle of the room. Aleks looked at the boisterous bunch then turned to Anton.

"The way those guys are arguing the point I'd say you're right."

"My friend," Anton said, glancing at the rising tide of emotion, "I can understand that you have not taken sides in this issue. If I were in your boots I would not either, what with Igor standing in the curtains. But let me tell you something, putting glasnost and perestroika aside, if Yeltsin doesn't do something soon the hard-cores and far-out nationalists are going to take us into a civil war, another revolution. Mark my words."

The shouting had reached a feverish pitch. Suddenly a fist fight broke out. Tables and chairs scraped the floor amid sounds of breaking glass and screaming curses. Within seconds a full-blown melee swept the tavern like wildfire.

Bottles and glasses began to fly. The sound of wooden tables splintering and chairs crashing joined the cacophony of guttural shouting. Flesh pounded flesh.

"Let's get out of here!" Anton yelled.

Aleks and Anton found themselves being pushed and shoved as they stood up.

Hunching his shoulders Anton turned towards the door.

They were zigzagging and being jostled as they ducked through the fracas. But Anton kept going with Aleks right behind him.

They were but a few feet from the entrance when someone swung a broken table leg at another man and missed.

Aleks never saw it coming. It caught him with a smashing blow at the back of his head and he went down.

Anton Bukovsky stayed by his friend's side at the hospital until almost midnight, when he was told to leave. He returned early the next morning before going to the symposium. Aleks was still unconscious. At noon Anton called the hospital in Navolya and told Alisa about the tavern brawl and that Aleks was in the hospital unconscious.

Alisa packed a small bag and the next morning she and Stephen were on the train for Jaroslava. Arriving late Tuesday afternoon she saw Igor Varnova in the hallway. She ignored him and walked straight to Aleks' room.

Anton was sitting at Aleks' bedside. He shook his head, answering the silent question in her eyes. He stood up and gave her a hug.

She glanced over her shoulder, "What's he doing here?"

"They have been with us since we left home," Anton answered. "It is standard procedure. Do not let it worry you. Aleks is not in any trouble. We were not participating in the fight. We were trying to get out. I am sure the KGB man who followed us has vouched for that."

Stephen whimpered, "Mama, what is wrong with paw paw?"

"Papa is all right, Stephen. He has a little bump on the head. He is sleeping and will be fine. Here, hold his hand, he will like that."

Stephen sat in the chair and took his grandfather's hand.

Anton said, "I have made arrangements for you and Stephen where we are staying, but it's only one bed, so Stephen must sleep with you."

"Fine, thank you."

"When you are ready I will go back to the inn with you."

****

Wednesday evening 29 September, Anton stopped by the hospital before he had to catch the midnight train for home. Alisa was there.

Anton noticed that Aleks' head was now wrapped in gauze.

"Alisa what happened? I thought he only had a knot on the back of his head."

"The swelling and pressure increased," she replied. "They had to tap into the skull and make a drain otherwise the pressure would have killed him." Her eyes were misty. "That little 'knot' turned serious. The doctors here are very good. Now time is critical. He must pull out of this coma in the next day or two."

"I am so sorry, Alisa, it is my fault. I should have never—"

"It is not your fault. It's not anyone's fault. Please do not feel that way. Everything will be all right. You must go or you'll miss your train."

"Yes, yes, I know. If I can come back this weekend I will. When he is awake please call me."

Anton hurried from the hospital and caught his train.

On Saturday, 2 October, when Alisa left the hospital with Stephen she saw Major Varnova in the hallway obviously discussing Aleks' condition with the doctor.

"Nothing has changed," the doctor told the major. We have drained the fluid from his brain and all other signs are as normal as can be expected under these circumstances. This concussion is quite serious, perhaps more severe than before."

The doctor continued to talk when the words suddenly dawned on Igor. "Doctor, wait a minute. You said, more severe than *before?* What are you talking about, before what?"

"He has had a previous concussion that was quite severe. There's an old scar just in front of this present area."

"A scar?"

"An irregular slash, about three inches in length, looks quite old. It was not a clean laceration. X-Rays indicate he had to have suffered a bad concussion at that time also. I mention this because it may now have a compound bearing on his recovery. It is six days now and that, major, is not good."

Igor was doing mental gymnastics with Aleks' dossier. There were references to early lung problems, consumption, even cancer—which must have been wrong—but he could not recall any head injuries in the file.

"Thank you doctor, thank you very much." The KGB major spun on his heel and left the hospital.

He returned later accompanied by another man who carried a black satchel similar to a doctor's bag. Igor stood silently watching while his man took photographs of Aleks. He brought out an ink pad, a form and took Aleks' fingerprints.

"Wipe his fingers clean," Igor said.

Alisa ate supper and left Stephen at the inn. It was almost eight o'clock. Walking through the hospital entrance she saw the ill-tempered Igor and his underling walking out.

His surly expression and beady black eyes made her wince. She detested the little man as much as her father did. He'd do anything to put him back in the Gulags.

Alisa remained at her father's bedside, stroking his hand, his arm and talking to him. Her medical training and the doctors told her to continually talk to him and hold his hand, that a close family relative can sometimes do more than medicine to bring someone out of a coma.

Finally at 11:30 she left for the night and hurried to the inn to relieve the kind babushka lady who watched Stephen.

Shortly thereafter the nurse made her rounds and looked in on Aleks' inert form. Then she closed the door and smiled at the lethargic KGB guard in the hallway.

****

5:00 AM Sunday, 3 October 1993.

The ceiling was a very dim grayish white. The walls were also gray, marked with shadows. One shadow seemed to be a door. Off to the right was a dark window. Then he saw the IV apparatus and the tube in his arm.

His eyes opened with a jolt.

Where am I? What? He tried to rise, decided against it. A hospital, I'm in a hospital.

Suddenly his world exploded. A wild bolt of terror went surging through his mind, his heart, to his very soul. The hair on his arms rose. His bladder released into the catheter. His head began to spin and blood pounded his ears like a jungle drum. *Oh my God, my God!*

Aleksandr Mikhailovich finally discovered his true identity—and he was terrified.

CHAPTER 14

"Bloody Sunday" 3 October 1993. At 5:30 AM the ward nurse made the final round of her shift. When the door opened Aleks closed his eyes and remained perfectly still. She checked the monitor, examined his IV, tucked the blanket and sheet around his neck and left.

He saw clothes hanging on the wall. *If I could get out of this ...* but where would I go, what would I do? Where in the hell am I, Navolya, a prison hospital? No, this place is too clean. I have to get up and get out of here. If a doctor comes in he will know. Maybe I can fake it, just keep my eyes closed. Think, damn it—think. But he was lost. Uncontrollably, like a series of movie flashbacks his mind could not let go of the last forty-five years and he couldn't believe the magnitude of what had happened to him. My God, all of these years, all these damned years. He tried to calm himself and wondered how he could get out of here before being discovered. But then, I can't do that, I have a daughter and a grandson. His mind was swamped. Think!

The door opened again. He closed his eyes.

As the woman removed her coat Aleks sensed her and peeked. When she came next to the bed he opened his eyes and put a finger to his lips, "Shhh, do not talk."

"Papa you are—"

"Shhhhhh, quiet, I don't want them to know yet. I need to talk to you. Sit down."

Alisa sat down in shock and took her father's hand.

"We've been so worried. When—"

"Shussh, Alisa, listen to me. Don't talk. There are some things I need to know and I need to know quickly. We'll talk more in detail later. Trust me Alisa please trust me, all right?"

Alisa didn't understand but nodded, her eyes became misty.

"Where am I and how long have I been here?"

"A hospital in Jaroslava, papa, you've been here a week. When did you—?"

"A few hours ago and I haven't let anyone know yet. Keep your voice low. Where is Stephen?"

"He's at the inn with Anton. Anton journeyed in late last night. He will bring Stephen shortly."

"What time is it?"

"It's six fifteen. Papa, are you all right, why is everyone acting so strange? What is happening, have they done something to you?"

Aleks thought for a moment and wrinkled his brow. "What do you mean acting strange, what's strange?"

"The way you are talking papa, it's very strange and the nurse, she thinks you must be very important."

"Why?"

"Because of the pictures."

"What pictures?"

"When I came in she said they took pictures of you last night."

"What?" Aleks rose up. "Who took pictures?"

"She said the night nurse told her the KGB Major and another man took several pictures of you. I saw them leaving last night, but I didn't know."

Pushing the covers back Aleks sat up and grimaced with pain. His eyes passed over it once then backed up. There was a very small black smudge on the edge of the top sheet.

"Papa, what is wrong, why…." Her voice trailed off as Aleks again put a finger to his lips. He pulled the sheet up to him and sniffed. He pursed his lips in a puzzled expression. He sniffed his fingers, smelled the smudge again and then he knew.

"It is, its ink, it has to be ink." he said and fell back looking at his hands, "Son of a bitch."

"Papa!"

"I'm sorry, sweetheart," He paused, holding his daughter's arm. He now realized there would be no escape. They knew, the bastards knew. "Alisa, listen to me. There are some important things, *extremely* important things that we will talk about later. It involves Igor and the KGB. But please, right now you must trust me, understand ... you must."

"I do, papa, I do," but she didn't understand and she began to cry.

"Be brave, stop crying, everything will be all right. Just trust me and keep absolutely quiet, that's important, all right? It's time to tell them I'm awake. Now go, go tell them."

Very shortly Alisa returned with two nurses running ahead of her. Within minutes two doctors arrived. The examination and questioning began.

They talked and fussed and thoroughly checked him. Finally they removed the catheter and let him sit up in bed. Then they took the wrap-around bandage from his head and put a small patch over the drainage incision and continued to fuss.

When Anton Bukovsky and Stephen came in Aleks was sitting upright in bed.

"Paw-paw, paw-paw," Stephen cried and threw his arms across the bed.

It took a while to settle his grandson down.

He nodded to a smiling Anton.

The room was becoming crowded. At last the doctors and nurses left, leaving the man to his family.

Aleks kissed Stephen again then said, "Alisa, would you take

Stephen for a stroll. I need a moment with Anton, if you don't mind, please. A little man to man talk."

Reluctantly, Alisa and Stephen left. Anton sat down close to the bed.

"Anton, you are my closest friend and I may need your help. I place great trust in our friendship and confidence."

"Yes of course, you can certainly you trust me, just as I trust you." Anton said in a concerned voice. "Is this about the coup?"

"The coup?"

"The pro-communist coup that is coming to a head, today, now," Anton then realized Aleks had not heard. "The lawmakers barricaded inside the Parliament demanding that President Yeltsin resign, remember? We discussed it in the bar before you were hit."

Aleks nodded. Anton went on, "Well Vice President Rutskoi has been in there with them and has declared himself the 'Acting President.' He won't come out until Yeltsin steps down. Just before I got here there were military in Moscow's streets and fighting has broken out, actual gunfire Aleks. It's going on right now, on television."

Aleks frowned. "I know nothing about that."

Now Anton puckered his brow, "Oh, I'm sorry, I was rude. Then what is it my friend how can I be of help?"

Aleks hesitated and rubbed a hand over the bandage. He was going to tell Anton about his true identity so someone besides the KGB would know the truth after he is dead, but he changed his mind at the last moment and decided not to involve Anton. He regrouped his thinking and only said, "I am quite certain that Igor has something sinister planned for me."

Anton frowned, "Is that why there are now two guards in the hall?"

Aleks looked hard at Anton. *Two guards? That's it, it's over, they do know.* He was glad that he didn't reveal his true identity to Anton. It would be a death sentence for his friend.

"Let me just say this, Anton. *If* anything *should* happen to me I would want you to look after Alisa and Stephen if you possibly can."

"Not only I can," Anton said, "it would be my pleasure. But Aleks, do not worry nothing will happen to you."

"Thank you, Anton, thank you very much, I feel better. You are indeed a true friend."

After Anton left Alisa came in with scissors, clippers a razor and towel. She shaved his upper lip and trimmed his gray hair and scraggly beard to its usual half inch crop.

She asked all sorts of questions. She received no answers and she was infuriated.

He had decided not to tell Alisa anything. If she doesn't know then the KGB should not harm her or Stephen. When it's over she will know. That would be soon, too soon he was sure. There was no escape, no choice, nothing he could do. He readied his mind for the KGB visit.

9:30 AM, 3 October, Russia's "Bloody Sunday" was in full rebellion. Moscow, all of Russia and the world was witnessing a pro-communist coup d'état against President Boris Yeltsin. Newspapers had been completely shut down. All political parties, both neo-communist and far-out nationalist that had opposed the president had been banned. Lenin's tomb, the very essence of Soviet power, no longer had an honor guard.

Russia teetered on the brink of civil war.

Most key army commanders had shown their loyalty to Yeltsin. Tanks and armored personnel carriers were lined up on the banks of the Moscow River in front of the Russian Parliament—the 19-story, white marble building known as the "White House."

What the Parliament leader, Ruslan Khasbulatov, and Yeltsin's vice president, Aleksandr Rutskoi, and many other lawmakers had started was now a full blown coup coming to a climax.

A throng of more than ten thousand anti-Yeltsin demonstrators had broken past the police lines of Moscow's inner road. Before long they pounded their way through the security forces and now had massed in front of and around the Parliament building.

Seeing all of this support, the lawmakers holed up inside made a big mistake, they erroneously thought they had a victory in their hands. Rutskoi, the "acting president," appeared at a window and cried out for the combat-ready throngs of young men in the streets below him to capture the mayor's offices across the street and to storm the Ostankino television center.

They did exactly that.

At the distant Ostankino TV station several thousand revolutionaries crashed trucks into the front of the building and fired a rocket-propelled grenade at the entrance. The station was guarded by elite Spetsnaz commandos and a fierce battle ensued.

Pro-communist rebels, armed with assault rifles, clubs, metal bars and other weapons, stormed the mayor's high-rise and other buildings across the street from the parliament. From there they fired down on the army troops along the river.

At the same time, machinegun and serious small arms fire also exploded from the roof and the windows of the barricaded White House.

Troops in the armored personnel carriers on the bridge and along the river retaliated in both directions with deadly machinegun fire. But the lawmakers barricaded in the White House would not give up. Thousands of people in the streets took cover as the conflict escalated.

Suddenly at 9:55 AM a horrendous boom stunned the revolutionaries.

One of the T-72 tanks pounded a cannon shell into the upper middle floors of the White House.

A second tank hammered another shell into the Parliament's upper floors. Fire and smoke poured out of the shattered area.

At noon Yeltsin called a cease fire to allow everyone to surrender.
Seventy people, mostly women, came out with their hands up.

Yeltsin's defense minister issued an ultimatum to the hard-line
communists that remained in the building. But the rebel lawmakers in
the White House still would not give up. They responded with erratic
small arms fire.

At 2:30 PM on this Bloody Sunday, after another cannon bar-
rage, a small number of pro-communist rebels came out of the White
House waving a white flag.

Again, just before 5 PM, hundreds of lawmakers poured out of the
building. They, like the others before them, were arrested and taken
away in busloads.

It was almost 6 PM when "acting president" Ruskoi, and his cohort, Khasbulatov, the last two men to give up, came out of the White
House with their hands up. They were placed in handcuffs and taken
to the infamous Lefortovo prison to join the others, and the imprisoned KGB chief, Viktor Barannikov who, just a few months prior to
this Bloody Sunday, had been sacked by President Yeltsin.

The bloody coup had been crushed and Yeltsin remained the
strong democratic president of this "new" Russia.

The other unsuccessful coup attempt in August of 1991, against
then–President Mikhail Gorbachev, had been child's play compared
to today's fiasco.

© Peter Turnley/CORBIS Russian Parliament (White House) shortly after a tank fired the first cannon round 3 October 1993.

All day Sunday Aleks waited and waited. His mind ran back and forth like a pacing tiger knowing the hunters were coming for the kill. But the hunters didn't come and the waiting drove him up the wall. They let him out of bed to use the toilet and walk about the room.

Anton Bukovsky had left to catch his train back to Navolya. There were just the three of them alone in Aleks' room. Aleks played word games with Stephen and made small talk with his daughter to keep her inquiring mind off the sensitive subject.

"Papa, what is it?" Alisa had asked numerous times. "What is it all about? Does it have to do with the fighting going on at the parliament?"

"No," He replied and finally shrugged her off. "Please sweetheart, do not ask again."

In the afternoon Alisa went out and brought back the latest news. "I guess this fighting in Moscow is why Igor has not showed up today," Alisa said. "He has been here every day except today."

"Ah yes," Aleks cracked. "Igor loves me, can't stand being away from me."

"Papa, for the last time, what were those pictures all about? Please, tell me."

"Alisa, please, I told you not to ask, now please. We will know soon enough when Igor gets here. Do not worry your pretty little head. Okay? I love you, sweets."

When she and Stephen left at 8:30 Sunday evening Igor still had not shown up. Aleks had told her not to worry and persuaded her take Stephen back to the Inn and get some sleep.

The doctor came by again. After that Aleks tried to sleep but it was a restless night.

Monday 4 October. There was one lawmaker who had not been in the White House when the siege occurred yesterday. This man now secretively entered the new KGB Headquarters in Moscow central. He was immediately escorted to the top floor.

"General Dovyetsky," Colonel Balitsky said, "he is here."

The general grunted and the man entered the room.

"Dmitri Ivanovich, good to see you in these tragic times."

"True, true, very tragic, General," Dmitri responded, "but good to see you looking hearty." Dmitri was a balding, pasty faced politician, a hard-core communist who knew how to straddle the fence and play the new system during dangerous times.

"What can I do for you," the crusty general said as he offered tea. He did not like most politicians. He tolerated Dmitri because he was an old line communist in democratic clothing and he could be manipulated, which pleased the General.

Dmitri sat down, sipped his tea surveying this dangerous general with the swarthy face and heavy jowls, a large impressive man—an intimidating KGB General. Dmitri knew where the general's allegiance lay, but times had changed just yesterday. He had to be sure.

The general was impatient. His bushy eyebrows closed down over his dark eyes. "Did you come just for tea?"

Dmitri turned away from that intense gaze, took another sip of tea then set it down.

"General, my friends and I are devastated by the results of yesterday's outcome and are quite sure you share the same feelings."

"Yes, yes, Dmitri, don't play cat and mouse. The party took a beating, get on with it."

"Very well," the politician said, now reassured. "We think there is a way to topple that emperor of democracy." He paused. "Unclothe him and have him stand naked before everyone in the motherland and the entire world. It can be done my good friend, quickly—within days."

Dovyetsky set his tea down and leaned forward, "Exactly how do you and your lawmaking friends plan on doing that? Have you not just failed in the most embarrassing way with the majority of your ranks now sweating under my command in Lefortovo prison?"

"Yes, it was a disaster. But there are many of us left and when this plan is executed our comrades in prison will be released and given medals. This plan is so simple, so easy, but it must be set in motion fast, very, very fast."

Dmitri went on to explain the neo-communist thinking that would be a cinch to put in motion. When he finished he left the building as covertly as he entered.

The KGB General called Colonel Balitsky into the office and they finalized the mission. He issued an order for a certain prisoner to be immediately transported by air from a Kolyma Gulag to Moscow with the greatest of haste.

"At once Comrade General," the colonel said and left the office.

The colonel executed the order, ensuring that it would be carried out with extreme haste. In fact, he ordered two prisoners be flown to Moscow, in separate planes, to be certain that at least one got here safely.

He cradled the phone and sat puffing his cigarette. Suddenly he stood up, dubbed his cigarette, spun around, knocked on the general's door and entered.

"General, if I may, I have some information that will bear heavily on the matter at hand."

"Go on."

"Yesterday during all of that trouble at the Parliament building one of our officers absolutely insisted on reporting directly to me. He is a difficult man but extremely true to the party, so I met with him."

"His name?

"Major Igor Andreyevich Varnova. He is assigned as a Gulag controller up north and has just uncovered a most astounding case."

"So?"

Colonel Balitsky related the story of Major Varnova's incredible discovery.

"That is unbelievable," the general exclaimed. "Where is this major?"

"He is here in the building. I told him to stay as I wanted to inform you about the matter, but with yesterday's situation I forgot about him until now. I'll bring him."

"Good, this will change, even expedite everything. Colonel, do not mention anything about the other prisoners."

"Yes sir, of course not."

Major Igor Varnova couldn't believe that he was being escorted to the very top of this exalted Headquarters.

He told the general about his discovery as if he had actually suspected it all along.

General Dovyetsky was overwhelmed and showed genuine appreciation for Major Varnova's excellent work, saying he would be rewarded.

Then the general and the colonel went into detail with Major Varnova about his part in this daring assignment.

Igor Varnova left the headquarters with a catbird smile on his face and an unquestionable spring in his walk. He had just put a definite promotion on his shoulders and he had the personal attention of General Dovyetsky.

The general's warning made his smile a little less wide but there was still a spring in his step. He hurried along. Tomorrow would be a very big day. He had to be back in Colonel Balitsky's office at 6 AM.

After Igor was gone the General said to Colonel Balitsky, "I don't know why back in Beria's time they had a special mark in this man's dossier or what Beria had intended. But it couldn't have been better than this. I'm counting on you to monitor this mission. Later I will have additional instructions for you."

3:20 PM Tuesday 5 October. Alisa and Stephen were at the hospital with Aleks. They had nervously waited all day Sunday and Monday for Igor or any KBG to appear. Now Tuesday was almost gone and they were still waiting. Expecting to be yanked out at any minute, Aleks had not had any sleep and it showed.

The waiting came to an end when they heard boots coming down the hall.

Major Igor Varnova came strutting through the door. His men stood outside.

"Ah, Aleks," he said, smiling like an old friend, "you are looking so much better."

Aleks said nothing.

Igor turned to Alisa and very politely said, "Would you mind stepping into the hall with your son. I have some matters to discuss with your father."

Alisa looked nervously at her father.

He gave her a nod.

After they left Igor said, "Put your clothes on, Aleks."

Aleks hesitated.

"Come on, get dressed, you are being released."

Aleks retrieved his clothes from the wall hooks and began dressing, trying to second guess what was about to happen. Released? Huh uh. But it doesn't matter, I have no control. He thought of Alisa and Stephen then immediately tried not to think of them.

Igor opened the door and Aleks stared at the three men in the hall with weapons.

"Where's my daughter?" Aleks asked, walking down the hall with Igor and the three men trailing behind. Nurses and a couple doctors busied themselves, wanting nothing to do with KGB business.

"They have gone on in another car," Igor said. "Do not worry, they are fine."

They arrived at the outskirts of Moscow near midnight and stopped at a two story building that looked as old as the dormitory in

Navolya. They put Aleks in rear corner room on the second floor.

Looking at the bare walls, sink, little stove, day bed, table and chairs, reminded Aleks of his old Navolya dormitory.

Closing the door, Igor went to the window, turned around, stepped to the table, pulled out a chair and said, "Come, sit down, Aleks."

Aleks sat down in the opposite chair and they faced each other.

"I have great news for you Aleks," Igor smiled. "You are leaving Russia at daybreak."

"Don't joke with me. Leave Russia? That's impossible and you know it."

"I do not joke, my friend. It has been arranged. You will be allowed to leave and your destination may be ... England, Germany, perhaps America or Poland, who knows?" He pursed his lips, taking extra delight in pulling Aleks' chain. "If you'd stop being so uncooperative maybe your daughter and grandson *might* be able to leave too. But that's only a maybe."

Aleks stared impassively at the little creep. They're holding Alisa and Stephen over my head. Would they actually harm them? Aleks tried to brush the scenario from his mind, but his anxiety increased. Leave the country? What foolishness, such an event can never happen. He's playing with me. His mind was spinning again. But if they know who I am why am I still here? I should have been taken out and shot. So it's to come later, at their convenience, a public display?

Then Aleks thought of Alisa and Stephen. His eyes narrowed. "If you harm my family, Igor you bastard, I'll kill you."

Igor hesitated, his grin faded. The distrust and defiance on this old man's face irritated him. Leaving Moscow he swore he would not allow Aleks to crawl under his skin again. He would persevere in this bizarre undertaking. Nothing must go wrong. He controlled himself.

"Aleksandr Mikhailovich this is your great opportunity—what

you have waited for. We could wait until November fourth, your final release date, but the motherland is benevolent."

Aleks became incensed, *benevolent my ass.* He stared at Igor as the man rambled on and on. His mind began to wander. He saw the lips mouthing words but he really didn't hear. Igor's round face and beady eyes brought scenes from the Gulags to his mind, a mind that had been sick for so long. Flashes of Viktor and Aleks and all the gaunt faces and bodies; the bloody beatings and shootings; the Troika trials and the deaths, had to be millions of horrible deaths—all of this a kaleido-scope in his mind's eye. The world was whirling.

"Aleks?" Igor said, looking at the puffy, bloodshot eyes and the strange expression on his antagonistic face. "Aleks? Aleksandr Mikhailovich."

Aleks blinked and blinked again. Finally he brought Igor into fo-cus and stared at him for the longest time while his tormented mind tried to shift gears.

"Igor, do you really expect me to take this charade seriously?" His face contorted. His voice grew louder. "After the all the damned Gulags, after dealing with bastards like you for forty-some years do you really expect me to believe that Gorbachev, Yeltsin, the KGB or whoever the hell is in power, is going to allow me to leave the coun-try—just like that?"

Igor leaned back in his chair.

"What kind of crap are you trying to pull, Igor?" His voice reached a crescendo. "Soap me up then do it to me, huh you little sonovabitch." His fist smashed the table, "Screw you!"

Igor jumped back, his chair tumbled over.

The door flew open.

Aleks didn't flinch or turn around. He knew the barrel of a kalashnikov was pointing directly at his back.

Igor stood thunderstruck, arm extended, palm slightly up.

The silence was loud as all three men froze.

Igor motioned slightly with his hand.

The soldier backed out and closed the door quietly.

Igor's eyes were bulging. His face was crimson and he began to shake. "I should shoot you right now." His seething voice increased with each word, "Just take you out and shoot you myself this very goddamned instant!"

Aleks stood up and in a low voice said, "Then why in the hell don't you, you little bastard."

Minds raging, fists clenched and eyes locked, they stood ready to kill each other.

It was Major Varnova's adrenalin that ebbed first. He took deep breaths, opening and closing his hands. Sadistic, temperamental and irrational he was, but he was not a fool. He began to collect himself and finally spoke.

"Aleksandr Mikhailovich, sit down."

Aleks remained standing.

"Sit down Aleks, sit down."

Aleks slowly eased into his chair, trying to clear his mind.

"Listen to me and listen very carefully, I will tell you only once Aleks. You are not to leave this room. I have men in the hall and outside with orders to shoot." He kept his eyes on Aleks, picked up the chair with his foot and then sat down. He decided to play a trump card. "I have your daughter and grandson and if you value their safety you will do as you are told and not make trouble. I will come for you at five o'clock this morning. Do you understand me Aleksandr Mikhailovich? I will be here at five. "

Aleks said nothing.

"Aleks, listen," Igor said calmly, his hands on the table, assuming that Aleks had settled down, "you know what has been happening since Yeltsin took over. I'm sure your daughter has told you the latest." He lowered his voice as if the wall had an ear. "The winds of change—"

"Igor, cut the philosophical shit."

The throbbing in Igor's neck began again. His face flushed. He blinked away the dots, stood up and looked at his watch then at Aleks.

"Four hours from now I'll be back," he hissed. "This, Aleksandr Mikhailovich, is your final day."

CHAPTER 15

Four hours later it was first light. Aleks stared out the window. He had not slept last night or for three days. His face was pallid, drawn and his eyes were bloodshot. His mind was a raging fire, simply refusing to let go of the past forty-some years of anguish. Now the safety of Alisa and Stephen hung in the balance and he was a jittery, a nervous wreck.

A little whirlwind of debris tormented the barren courtyard. He watched the little dirt-devil hop and skip across the bare ground like a mischievous genie then, as if tired of the game, suddenly release the eddy and dash away to aggravate the trees. In a moment it would start all over again.

Hearing a key in the door, Aleks turned. The game begins.

Igor entered and placed some items on the table.

Immediately Aleks said, "Where's my daughter and Stephen?"

"Like I keep telling you Aleks, they are fine. You will see them soon as you do what you are told, now hurry put on these clothes."

Aleks stepped to the table, looked at the clothes then went to the sink and washed his face and hands. His frazzled mind was not functioning properly. He had no choice but to do what Igor demanded so he undressed and donned the clothes.

"Come on, Aleks, hurry up."

"Where is—?"

"How many times…." Igor grimaced. "I told you if you would cooperate they will be safe. Now get your coat and come."

Three black cars waited at the entrance. They put him in the middle car, the largest sedan.

"Paw-paw," Stephen yelled as Aleks got in the back seat. They hugged and the caravan took off.

"Here," Alisa said, handing her father a large paper container half full of tea. "It's not too warm, but it helps."

Aleks heaved a sigh, sipped the tea and gave it back to Alisa. His hands were shaking.

The sun was on the horizon as they drove into the city. Igor sat sideways smoking foul cigarettes.

"Where are we going?" Aleks asked, watching the blocks roll by.

"In due time Aleks, in due time."

The curfew in Moscow had lifted but Alisa motioned several times as they passed groups of soldiers at obvious check points. When they reached the green-belt area they stared at pockets of battle-scarred destruction.

Alisa let out a wail when they came to the Kalininsky Bridge.

Aleks stared in disbelief. Past the river on the left the beautiful nineteen-story white marble Parliament building resembled a Halloween ogre in the throes of death.

In the middle of the White House, from the fourteenth floor to the top, was a huge black cavity. Cannon bombardment had disemboweled the magnificent edifice. Small arms fire had shattered every single window. Drapes fluttered out of those jagged holes like black birds trying to escape and smoke had blackened the entire façade.

It was now 6:15 AM, but the enormous clock that rose majestically from the top of the building indicated 10:03—the time on October 3rd, three days ago, when it was knocked out in the heat of the tank shelling that brought an end to the Parliament siege and the neo-communist coup.

In front of the Parliament tanks and armored vehicles still lined both sides of the Moscow River. Aleks was astounded—a tank bombardment in the heart of Moscow. Even the Germans couldn't accomplish that.

Alisa was visibly shaking.

"The winds of change blow strongly in Russia today," Igor smiled. "About a thousand were wounded and hundreds killed Sunday. Quite a spectacle, isn't it?"

You little bastard, Aleks thought, you have brought us to the center of Moscow just to show us what happened to the White House, why Igor? Where are we going?

Army soldiers were everywhere when they entered Sheremetyevo Airport. They followed their escort car to an isolated area and stopped. The second escort pulled up behind them.

Igor got out of the car and stood by the fender.

Aleks watched him light another cigarette and look around. The man was acting strange, nervous, like he was afraid of someone. Is there something else going on?

Aleks tried to settle his thoughts. "Alisa, sweetheart," he said, with a tremble in his voice, "listen to me, carefully. I have no idea what they plan to do and I don't want to scare you. But I need you to be brave. If anything should happen to me you get in touch with Anton, do you understand?"

Tears began rolling down Alisa's cheeks.

"We have no time. You must be brave, Alisa, brave. Do you understand what I have just told you?"

She nodded but she didn't grasp any of this. She looked into her father's haggard eyes and at his fatigued expression. His hands were shaking. As a daughter and as a doctor she feared for her father. At the same time she too was tremulous and at her wits end.

Before he left, Anton Bukovsky had told her that Aleks seemed to think the KGB were going to kill him. He told her to be careful.

Also, Igor had made veiled threats about her safety and Stephen's. She could not understand what was happening and why everything was so mysterious, so filled with dreadful consequences. Her father would explain nothing. She thought she was going crazy.

Igor checked his watch one more time, tossed his cigarette and motioned to the men in front. He got in the car, turned to his charges and somberly said, "The time is near."

All three cars advanced.

They stopped directly behind the lead car at a workers entrance. The third car pulled behind them and those two men sprang out, held their weapons close to their sides and scanned the area.

The two men from the first car went in the terminal.

Then they waited.

Aleks was crippled with paranoia. This is an airport. It will be an international incident, kill me in front of foreigners, tourists, the world? Maybe I can make a break for it—end it. He wanted to bolt from the car right now but knew the doors were locked from the front.

Alisa had never seen her father in this condition. She was scared, couldn't find her voice.

Three minutes seemed an eternity.

Aleks was about to speak when one of the two men emerged from the terminal and hurried towards the car. Igor got out, talked to his man, turned and nodded to his driver. The doors unlocked with a click. Igor opened the rear door and smiled, "Aleks it is time to go. All of you come. No questions, no talking, lets go."

Alisa got out, bewildered and shaking. Stephen was next. She took his hand. Aleks came out with a strange expression on his face. Stephen grabbed his grandfather's hand.

They followed Igor and his man into the terminal and through a baggage passageway with the last two KGB men several yards behind. They walked some distance then climbed stairs and reached a cavernous area that had been cleared by several other men with weapons, which wasn't out of place in Moscow now, considering the recent parliament siege and coup attempt.

At 7:06 AM they came to a stop. The lead man took a position adjacent to the first KGB man who had been there waiting for them. The other two men stopped behind Aleks.

The man who had been waiting looked at Igor and nodded twice.

Igor understood, turned sideways, held out his arm and said, "Go, all of you, go."

Aleks and Alisa had never been in an airport terminal before. Both were confused, afraid.

They did not move.

The stress of the past week alone was overwhelming for Alisa, but now she was so frightened of the guns, the KGB and these bizarre proceedings that she was numb, helpless.

Aleks stared at the tunnel ahead of them like a deer caught in headlights. He began to shake and stammer. "Igor, I, I...."

"Go!" Igor shouted.

Aleks jerked, startled. Apprehensively he stepped forward and the threesome timidly started down the corridor.

They were trapped in an alien passageway, fear of the unknown ahead and KGB behind. Alisa glanced at her father. He was trance-like, quivering. She began to sob. Now more than ever she was certain he was about to have a nervous breakdown or a heart attack and she was panic stricken, powerless. Her crying became louder until it turned into uncontrollable wailing.

Then one man seemed to shift his weapon. Aleks' mind whirled—what were Igor's words, *"your final day?"* His brain swelled with terror like a balloon filling with water. He shuddered, let go of Stephen's hand and moved off to the side. He wobbled. He could not talk. Subconsciously he motioned Alisa forward then he began to list severely to his left. Several steps further on, with eyes glazed, one arm outstretched, he staggered. Suddenly his balloon burst wide open and his mind, swamped in a gigantic tsunami, became a vast ocean of silvery blue and he was plunging into its depths. Then it came from behind—

WHURR-RUMPH!

Aleksandr Mikhailovich went down.

CHAPTER 16

Alisa screamed, fell to her knees and cradled her father's head in her arms. "Help me!" She yelled. The closest person to her was the male flight attendant, securing the aircraft door.

Unconscious, Aleks was carried to a seat in first class. Alisa told them she was a doctor and she would handle it. She asked for a medical kit.

Aleks half-opened his eyes but immediately lapsed back into a lethargic state. Mentally overwhelmed and physically exhausted, he slept most of the way.

Alisa watched over him for eight hours before he awoke.

"Yes please," Alisa answered the flight attendant, "two coffees would be fine … black."

"How do you feel, papa?"

Aleks didn't answer. Still emotionally spent and confused he slumped down in his seat. Dully, he gazed at Alisa through half-closed eyes then looked away.

The flight attendant brought two cups of coffee.

Aleks stared dreamily through the window at the solid layer of clouds then he turned and saw the flight attendant's blue uniform, the silver wings and the airline logo. He straightened up, looked around and saw other passengers. His heart raced. Finally he realized where he was and he could not believe it. He leaned back, closed his eyes, sighed and watched the flight attendant place a coffee on his tray.

Alisa handed her father an envelope. "One of the attendants said they were holding the plane for us and this was given to her before we came on board. It's for you."

Aleks opened the envelope and saw their Russian passports. He examined them.

"Papa, this plane, what is this all—"

"Sussssh," Aleks cautioned. "Keep your voice down. Other people can hear. No questions. Let me clear my head for a moment then I will explain everything to you."

Sipping real coffee while his grandson still slept, Aleks quietly told his daughter who he really was and what had happened to him. Keeping his voice to a soft whisper he told of his amnesia, his years in the Gulags and his impersonation of Aleksandr Mikhailovich Leskov.

Flying across the top of the world for ten hours, Delta Flight 31 zoomed non-stop through the time zones like a Back-To-The-Future movie and touched down on New York's JFK runway 31L at 9:05 AM the same day, Wednesday, 6 October 1993.

Deplaning with no baggage, they approached the customs check-point. Aleks handed the passports to the INS officer. The officer studied the passports then asked the purpose of their visit.

"I would like to see your supervisor, please," Aleks said.

"Yes sir, but please tell—"

"I need to speak to the senior officer on duty, immediately please!"

She was watching and listening. He looked somewhat distinguished with the short gray hair and Hemmingway-style beard. It looked like it might be a political type matter because the gentleman was insistent. In any event, it was a confrontation.

She stepped over to the checkpoint. The agent on duty handed her the passports.

"He wants to see the senior officer on duty."

She glanced at Aleks' passport, started to speak ... but stopped, intently studying him.

"Please, come with me."

She escorted them to a big room with a number of desks. Three men glanced up as they entered. She led them back to a glass enclosed office. A large man in black trousers, a white shirt and black tie stood outside the office door. She handed him the passports.

"He wanted to see the officer in charge."

"Thank you." The man smiled, looked at the passports and at the three people standing in front of him.

"Are you the senior officer in charge?" Aleks asked.

The man pleasantly smiled, "Yes, I am Matthew Hawkins, Deputy Port Director. Won't you please have a seat?" He motioned to the vinyl couch and chairs alongside the wainscot and glass partition.

"We have been sitting," Aleks answered.

"Ah yes, yes of course," the deputy director smiled, "A long flight."

He began examining the passports with a furrowed brow.

"Aleksandr Leskov," He said looking at Aleks' passport, then Alisa's, "Alisa Leskov and Stephen Leskov."

Aleks waited a few moments then he said, "Those passports were recently issued to us. My daughter and my grandson's are correct, but mine is wrong."

"Wrong?"

"Yes, wrong. I am not a Russian."

Conversation among the other agents stopped.

Matthew Hawkins looked perplexed.

"Can you please explain that, Mister"—he looked again at the passport—"Leskov?"

"Aleksandr Mikhailovich Leskov has been my Russian name, but it is not my real name.

"Mr. Hawkins, my name is Stanislaus Sedecki. I am a First

Lieutenant in the United States Air Force," he said, bringing himself to a military posture.

Matthew Hawkins was flabbergasted, unprepared for this. He scrutinized this older man with the gray hair and gray beard. His eyes narrowed keenly. This gentleman must be at least in his sixties and he says he is a lieutenant in the United States Air Force? This has to be a joke. For a long moment he considered it as a joke—but the man's serious face told him it wasn't. "You, ah, you are a lieutenant," he paused, "a lieutenant in the United States Air Force?"

"Yes, exactly," Sedecki answered, "and this is my daughter and my grandson."

Sedecki saw the confusion on the deputy's face.

"I'm sorry. I know this may seem crazy to you, but I am a First Lieutenant in the Air Force. I flew an RB-47 Stratojet on reconnaissance missions over Russia and China. In December 1950 we were shot up and crashed landed in Manchuria. I was on a spying mission and judged a spy, but I should have been treated as a POW. I was taken from China to Russia, where I have been held in the Gulags and under KGB control for the past forty-three years."

"I'll be damned," one of the other men blurted then the room became quiet.

Matthew Hawkin's mouth hung open.

Finally, Sedecki broke the silence. "My serial number is—"

"No, no, that's, ah, okay," Hawkins interrupted, and tried to collect his sanity. "I'm just ah...."

At last a big smile spread across his face, "My God, I believe you, I do. This is really unbelievable, but I believe you."

In all of his INS years Deputy Director Hawkins had never encountered or heard of an incident like this.

"Agent Waverly," he bellowed, "Get Washington on the line immediately."

She darted into his office for the hot-line.

"Lieutenant, welcome home," Hawkins beamed and began pumping Aleks' hand. "This is fantastic." He looked at the other men in the room. "I remember now, a number of years ago some high Russian official, Gorbachev or Yeltsin—it doesn't matter—was quoted as saying it's possible there might be US Servicemen in Russia. No one would take it seriously, including me."

Hawkins waved his arm, "Please, please sit down. Miss, you and the youngster sit right down here. Wow." Then over his shoulder, "Waverly you got Washington yet?"

He looked at Sedecki, "Boy, are they going to love you in Washington. Yes siree, the boys on capital hill and those MIA and POW hawks, they're going to have a field day. What a windfall."

Aleks sat down between his daughter and grandson. He wondered what Russian wind had blown him home.

He put his arms around his two loved ones, hugged them close and smiled. Tomorrow, 7 October 1993 would be his sixty-fifth birthday, and he was home.

But there would be no celebration for Stanislaus Sedecki.

CHAPTER 17

The man was nervous, tired of waiting, fearing detection and worse, that the INS or FBI had screwed it up. Failure was not a word his people used. Life is cheap. He began to sweat.

As forecasted, October 6th was a lovely autumn morning in New York City. When he had first entered JFK airport at 6 AM the temperature had been 59 degrees. He wore a heavy shirt, no jacket and carried a small blue aircraft maintenance man's satchel. At 8:30 AM he entered a men's room stall, pulled blue coveralls from the satchel, slipped into them and clipped the security ID to his breast pocket.

He had just confirmed that the flight from Moscow was on final approach and would be at the Delta gate within fifteen minutes.

There was no way to gain access to the customs and INS area. He had been well aware of that. He only had a short notice for what was expected of him but he had scouted every ingress and egress of the customs and surrounding areas.

He also knew his mark would not be emerging from the normal customs clearance exit and would not be coming into the terminal. The INS or FBI would of course secretly usher the threesome out the INS exit that faced the tarmac and there was only one place he could get a view of that exit. Earlier he was almost discovered while checking it out.

Now, carrying the small satchel he made his way to the baggage area, slipped out onto the ramp and walked along the building to the last telescoping Jet-Bridge near the customs area. His superiors and his own reconnaissance had been right. This gateway was not being used.

When he was sure no one was looking he scampered up the metal steps to the enclosed platform at the end of the Jet-Bridge, eased in, closed the little door and squatted. Shortly he stood up, looked around and aimed at the INS door some two-hundred feet away. He adjusted his telescopic setting, leaned against the sidewall and waited, and he waited. At least thirty minutes had passed. He became more nervous by the second.

Finally, a black Chevy suburban pulled up to the INS exit. The door of the exit opened so quickly it caught him off guard.

"Shit," he muttered, missing his first clear shot. He aimed: whrrr-click, whrrr-click, whrrr-click, his camera snapped as agents hastily shoved a gray haired man into the mammouth vehicle. He only got the back of the man's head and a partial side of his face, an agent was in the way. When the suburban took off he stood there. *Shit, com'on, where's the woman and kid?* He waited a moment, but no woman, no kid. *I've got the main subject I'd better get out of here.*

He hurried down the metal steps to the ramp area and abruptly stopped. A tug was passing by. He said, "Hi," waved at the operator then hurried into the baggage cart passageway. He made his way into the main terminal to a men's room, removed his coveralls and stuffed them into the blue satchel with his camera. Leaving the men's room he walked across the terminal, stepped briskly through an exit and crossed the traffic lanes to the far curb of the median. Almost immediately a black Mercedes picked him up.

The government suburban drove to the military parking area of JFK and stopped by a small Jet belonging to MAAG, the Military Assistance & Advisory Group. Sedecki and four FBI agents boarded the sleek jet and the door closed.

"Hey," Sedecki protested, "where's my daughter and grandson?"

"Do not be alarmed," the agent in charge said, "for security purposes you are traveling separately till we get to Washington, separate

cars, separate planes."
Sedecki didn't like the idea.

The MAAG jet landed at Andrews Air Force Base thirty-six minutes after takeoff and was met by another suburban with shaded windows.

1:12 PM, Wednesday 6 October, White House Situation Room. The talking stopped when the general entered.
"Well, do we have it?"
"Yes Mr. President, let me summarize," General Martin said, "Stanislaus Sedecki, born 7 October 1928 in Hamtramck, a suburb of Detroit. A licensed pilot at age 17. Graduated high school 1945, University of Michigan, summa cum laude and R.O.T.C. in 1949. Was accepted for Air Cadets, came out a Second Lieutenant with his wings in December 1949."
"Parents, relatives?"
"All deceased, sir. Father: Felix Sedecki, World War One army captain then worked for the State Department. Had various European postings, Berlin, 1930 to 36 and Warsaw, 1936 to 39. He, his wife and two children were evacuated from Poland when Germany invaded in 39. Retired from State in 1956, died of a heart attack in December 1971.
"Mother, Mary Beth Taylor-Sedecki, homemaker, died of cancer, 1958. The lieutenant had a sister, Florence, killed in an auto accident in 1947 at age 16. No other siblings. No other relatives that we know of."
"What else?"
"He was an exception at mathematics, electronics, cryptography, and a hell of a pilot. That landed him in PARPRO***, the Peacetime Air Reconnaissance Program. He had checked out in the new B-47. In February of 1950 he was sent to Eielson Air Force Base in Alaska and flew numerous covert spy missions beyond the Bering Sea and Artic Ocean, over northern Russia and China. On a 23 December 1950 spy

***   (see addendum)

mission he was the co-pilot and electronics officer. Their RB-47 was badly shot up and they crashed landed in Manchuria. He sent a coded Zip signal that cited the crash coordinates, all three crewmembers were alive and they were destroying the aircraft, film and equipment. That was the last we heard of them.

"Russia and China knew of the transgression but of course said nothing. They wanted what was left of the aircraft, what classified equipment they could recover, and any details they could extract from the three officers.

"Our official position was they crashed in the East China Sea. We listed them as MIA in the Korean War records and later changed that to KIA on 1 July 1953 when North Korea, China and Russia continually denied they were POW. "

A soft buzzer sounded as the door opened and FBI Director Mathews entered the room. Before he could sit down the president asked, "Is he legitimate?"

"Yes Mr. President, he is Stanislaus Sedecki, a USAF Lieutenant. We now have his complete file. The fingerprints match. Details of his military duty, the RB-47 zip message and mission details coincide with what he has been telling the debriefing team. Medical and dental records coinside, there is no doubt. The man is Stanislaus Sedecki.

"Also I have something interesting, sir. Sedecki's records have not been touched for more than forty years, but yesterday a DOD employee tried to gain access to them. He's in custody."

Mathews paused as the president slumped back in his chair.

"And Mr. President," Mathews added, "Sedecki states they were tortured in China and sent to Russia in a prisoner swap. He suffered amnesia for forty-three years from a blow to his head, which our doctors say is verifiable. He presently has a bandaged drain in his head from a blow that evidently ended his amnesia. He said the other two pilots were killed while escaping a month after their capture. He is supplying CIA with a wealth of information.

"Mr. President, he also swears there are American GIs being held in the Kolyma region of Russia and maybe in other areas, although he admits he has not personally seen any."

The president gazed past the end of the table, "Forty-three years as a prisoner of war and held in Russia all this time … my God, him and how many others?"

"Mr. President this has to stop right here, at this table," his chief of staff, Jerry Barnes said. "If this cat comes out of the bag, well I think everyone in the room knows what that would mean."

"Mr. President," the deputy director of the Defense Intelligence Agency injected, "This is not only about this man Sedecki and the Cold War and Korea, this would include Vietnam and even go back to World War Two. It could tear this country apart. And it would certainly topple the present Russian administration."

"Yes, yes I know," the president said, running a hand along his chin, "that issue should have been dealt with back during the transition, not now when a crisis evolves."

"It *was* dealt with back then Mr. President," Barnes said, "but you had too many other things on you plate at that time, sir—just as all of your predecessors did."

The DIA deputy filled the brief pause, "He and his family will be placed in the protection program, given a monthly pension as a retired colonel with thirty years service, plus all back pay from 1950. They will be well taken care of Mr. President."

The cell phone in Jerry Barnes' pocket vibrated. He answered and left the room. He quickly returned. "It has just hit the fan. The story is breaking. Damn it, they got pictures! How in hell did that happen? I just took calls from the editors of the Post and Times. They have pictures along with a POW story. TV has it and is ready to roll. They're going to hold off till I get back to them. We have no more than thirty minutes. Other calls are coming in."

In the Oval Office moments later the president put the telephone to his ear and with translators held a conversation with the Russian President that lasted twenty-three minutes.

Immediately after that Jerry Barnes put the word out to the Post, NY Times and all other media asking them to hold their stories, that the POW claim was bogus and a press conference regarding the issue has been set for three o'clock.

Aleks (Sedecki) and Alisa were alone in a safe holding room at Andrews AFB Maryland. Stephen played on the floor with a toy. Aleks sat close to his daughter and talked quietly. "I want you to listen very carefully Alisa, this is extremely important. I know you're bewildered by all they have just explained and I know what they want us to do sounds pretty crazy, but you must trust me, okay?"

"Yes papa, I do, it's just so confusing."

"I know Alisa, I know. I can understand the international and patriotic crap they are giving us and the ramifications for the US and Russia, and all the rest of their rhetorical hodgepodge about MIA and POWs. But something is strangely out of whack here. How could it get this way over the years? There must something they're not telling me. I just don't know all of the facts, not yet.

"However, I do know this: The immediate concern about our lives being in serious danger is true. Some Russians or Russian Americans, mafia, or crazy people in the street, will want us dead, or in some way want to harm us, and there's no place to hide if we're in the open. No one could prevent it.

"This is a bad situation, but it's temporary. I feel we have no choice but to go with this new identity and say nothing for the time being, only for the time being. Once this political *purga* ends and things settle down I'm sure...." He paused. "Well, we'll see. For now we'll do things this way, okay? And sweetheart, I don't want you to ever mention it or discuss it—not with anyone."

"Yes papa."

"Be brave, Alisa. Just be brave and we'll pull through this."

"I'll be brave, papa. I'm just so glad you're all right."

3:05 PM 6 October. White House Press Secretary Bob Langford stood at the podium to read one of the biggest official disinformation statements ever produced.

"A bizarre plot to discredit the sovereign government of Russia and create turmoil here in America, and internationally, has been exposed and the perpetrators placed in custody.

"This morning a Russian citizen, his wife and child, arrived at JFK on a flight from Moscow claiming he was US Air Force Lieutenant Stanislaus Sedecki, a Korean War POW and that he had been held in the Russian Gulags for forty years before he escaped. He claimed he married a Russian woman with a child and took her name while in hiding for three years in Russia. Then with forged passports they fled Russia on today's Delta flight.

"This is another neo-communist endeavor to topple the current administration in Russia after the coup attempt at the Russian Parliament three days ago was completely crushed.

"This man's co-conspirators thought he could pass our INS authorities on his bogus visa and passport and ultimately make his way to the national media to make his fictitious claim. Our INS people were alert. The imposter and his family were caught and arrested. His communist cohort did snap pictures of this man leaving JFK airport while under FBI arrest. These pictures and the counterfeit story were sent to numerous news media here in America and Europe in hopes that they would spread the bogus story.

"This imposter had been told by the ringleaders that all of

Lieutenant Sedecki's files would be missing from our military archives and because he was of similar age, height and stature, and spoke perfect English, he would pass our inspection. However, his comrades had failed to obtain such military records. When confronted with these files and other evidence, the imposter and his wife both confessed and they named their co-conspirators in Russia.

"This imposter has asked for political asylum for himself and his family, claiming if he returned to Russia it would be an obvious death sentence. That matter is currently under consideration.

"Lieutenant Stanislaus Sedecki was a Korean War Hero who crashed in the East China Sea on 23 December 1950 after flying a reconnaissance mission over North Korea.

"This insidious plot to discredit the governments of Russia and the United States has failed. Once again it is reiterated that there are no American Prisoners of War or any other Americans being held against their will in Russia.

"I am sorry, I cannot take any questions. Thank you."

The press secretary stepped off the podium and left the room in a complete uproar.

Minutes later on the same day, 11:40 PM Moscow time, the Russian Government repeated the same official pack of lies and disinformation on Russian Television and to all other media, denouncing the neo-communist plot and further stating that the perpetrators—numerous politicians and KGB personnel in Moscow—had been arrested [which was true] with more arrests to be expected.

Thus, the lowly foreign pawn that could have toppled a sitting president and a superpower was knocked off the world's chessboard like an expendable game piece.

EPILOGUE

Sedecki and Alisa died their hair. He shaved his beard and they were placed in protection near Carlsbad, California, which gave him access to Camp Pendleton, Miramar, and the San Diego Naval Base as a military retiree.

On 22 October 1993, fifteen days after Sedecki's sixty-fifth birthday, Alisa, with escorts, was shopping when her escorts received a call and they rushed her and Stephen to the military hospital at Camp Pendleton.

Agents who had been at the house said her father suddenly collapsed with a heart attack and they applied CPR as they rushed him to the hospital but he was pronounced dead on arrival.

Aware of the tremendous stress her father was under Alisa did not doubt the heart attack or that the agents did all they could to save him. After talking to the doctor and seeing the autopsy report she accepted the cause of death to be an acute and massive coronary thrombosis.

Although she herself was a doctor, she had no cause and was not aware—nor was she advised—that she could have requested an independent autopsy. Anyway, America is not like Russia, there was no reason to distrust such matters.

Sedecki was buried at Arlington National Cemetery under his newly established name. After a period of morning Alisa requested that she and Stephen be moved to a cold weather climate. They were relocated to the upper Midwest where they reside to this day.

***Addendum:

PARPRO—*Peacetime Airborne Reconnaissance Program.* An aerial reconnaissance program established by the US during the Cold War to gather intelligence on the Soviet Union's growing military, the development and locations of their nuclear bombs and the capability of their Air Force to drop such bombs on the United States.

Go to: http://www.afa.org/magazine/June2001/0601overfly.asp

While he was in the Ambarchik Gulag and suffering amnesia, Sedecki was unaware he had flown an RB-47 with two other airmen over Ambarchik in 1950. Upon his Gulag release in 1964 what he saw when boarding the plane were Tu-4 bombers (copied from US B-29s that crashed in Russia during WW-II and shot down during 1946-1960 spy missions). Tu-4s were capable of dropping a nuclear bomb on the United States. The small planes were Mig fighters that challenged US spy planes. Mig fighters from southern bases in Siberia would also challenge US B-29s from Okinawa and Yakota Air Base, Japan that were flown under the guise of training missions. Several of those B-29s were caught flatfooted over Russian territory by Mig fighters during the 1940s and 50s. Unable to make it home they crashed or ditched in the Yellow Sea and the Sea of Japan with "mechanical failure." Some later PARPRO missions also involved flights from England. Neither side would admit to any complicity. American spy missions were later handled by the SR-71 Blackbird and the U-2, one of which was also shot down on 1 May 1960.

During the Korean War when American pilots flying F-86 Saber Jets were shooting down Mig Fighters at a ratio of 10 to 1 in the northwestern part of North Korea called MIG ALLEY, the farce was steadfastly maintained. The Russian Migs had North Korean Air Force markings; however, the world did not know that those planes were piloted by Russian Air Force pilots, not North Koreans. Neither the

United States nor the Soviet Union would admit it at that time. For either of them to have acknowledged that Russian pilots were fighting in Korea would have been tantamount to an act of war between the two superpowers.

Such was the state of affairs between the Soviet Union and the United States and the price paid by the US during the Cold War and arms race, especially after the hot war in Korea. That status quo was carried into the Vietnam War, and to a great extent still continues.

The rooster crowed: in World War Two
the Korean War and
the Vietnam War, and

for every president and his administration since the end of World War Two. Many of the men placed in harm's way in the name of the United States of America have been continually denied.

78,000 Americans still missing from World War II
8,000 Americans still missing from the Korean War
1,800 Americans still missing from the Vietnam War
120 Americans still missing from the Cold War

2004 Source: Joint POW/MIA Accounting Command,
U.S. Army Central Identification Laboratory, Hawaii

Additional information about American MIAs and POWs possibly being held in Russia, China, Vietnam, Laos or Cambodia can be found at numerous websites and in the following Non Fiction books available in most public libraries and/or purchased at book and online stores:

SOLDIERS of MISFORTUNE
By James D. Sanders,
Mark A. Sauter and R. Cort Kirkwood
Published in 1992 ISBN: 0-380-72144-9

******

THE BAMBOO CAGE
By Nigel Cawthorne
Published in 1991 ISBN: 0-85052-1483

******

KISS THE BOYS GOODBYE
By Monika Jensen-Stevenson and William Stevenson
Published in 1990 ISBN: 0-525-24934-6

About the Author

LEE YAGEL was born in Missouri, raised in Detroit, Michigan and on the Lake Erie shores of Western New York State. He has traveled extensively throughout Europe, South America the Pacific and the Asian Rim, and all fifty states in the U.S.

From March 1943 to November 1967 he served twenty-four years in the US Army Air Force in World War Two and the USAF in the Korean War and in the Vietnam War. His military career took him through the South Pacific, Philippines, Guam, Japan, Korea, Vietnam, Thailand, South America and Europe.

After his military career Lee became a licensed real estate broker. He owned and operated two real estate offices for twenty years. He and his wife now live in the Luke AFB area of west Phoenix. He is working on another novel and they continue to travel extensively worldwide.

Printed in the United States
83029LV00003B/2/A